About t

The skills, education, experiences and the spiritual gifts of an Indigenous woman and her family and friends in North America contribute to the basis of *Dream Visitors*. Informal education comes from her work and life experiences being raised in an Indigenous community and living for a short time in the United States. Formal education comes from two Bachelor of Arts degrees in Public Administration and Governance, First Nations Technical Institute/Ryerson University, and in Aboriginal Adult Education through Brock University. Taking Creative Writing, Short Stories and Romance Writing courses through Mohawk College became her hobby in the last ten years.

DREAM VISITORS

B. G. Miller

DREAM VISITORS

Vanguard Press

*Vanguard Press is an imprint of
Pegasus Elliot Mackenzie Publishers Ltd.*
www.pegasuspublishers.com

First Published in 2024

**Vanguard Press
Sheraton House Castle Park
Cambridge England**

Printed & Bound in Great Britain

This book is dedicated to the children of the world because Every Child Matters.

Acknowledgements

My deepest gratitude is felt for my family, friends and colleagues for their support and encouragement to write this book, and a thank you is extended to my sister who reviewed the story and to my niece for the cover art and to Pegasus Publishers for their patience and guidance in the production of this book.

CHAPTER ONE – VISITING THE SEVENTH GENERATION

A tired female in her mid-teens ascends the hill to the centre of the camps. Above the valley, the sound of laughter of children and adults is mixed with rumblings of deep voices that easily carry across the camp. Behind the scattered shelters a silhouette of the hills and golden orange and yellow trees can be seen on a greyish-blue horizon. The sunset, a soft golden glow, is barely seen through huge protective trees. She can smell the smoke from the eight fires flickering into the twilight. The bouncing flames produce sparks into the sky that flutter to the earth in the warm air like the summer fireflies that are native to this area. Beyond the din of the groups, a trained ear can hear the heavy splash of a fish.

She searches the fires for her family or a good spot to rest after a day of work, feasting and dancing. She greets an elder watching his young grandsons as they wear off their meal wrestling near the mothers' fire. One of the girls is combing her sister's long, dark mane, releasing twisted strands of hair from a thick braid. A young boy lays on his sister's lap, yawning as she runs her fingers through his hair. Around each of the fires, eight to ten people sit or lay comfortably on soft grass or propped up against fallen trees. At the fires, people are updating each other on events that had happened in their territories because every other year representatives of the Hodinǫhsyǫ́:niˀ (Ho dino sehownee) and other nations meet at this same river at this same camp to hunt together, and trade food, articles, tools, and many, many stories.

There is a serious discussion or story being told at one of the fires. The speaker stands bent facing his audience. All eyes are staring at a strong, stocky speaker who appears to be in his early twenties. She is surprised to see the speaker is her brother, Hasegá:dǫ:.

Her older sister, Onráhdagǫ: looks up from her reed mat. Smiling, she says, "Desah, come sit with us."

Desasǫ́dręh decides to accept the shortened version of her name and sits with her sister and her friends. She loves her sister's company, but the real reason she accepts the offer is because they are sitting close to her brother's fire. She will be able to hear him speak.

While Hasegá:dǫ: explains how he fell asleep early on his last night of fasting, he begins, "I have heard the elders say that if the dreamer is steering a canoe in a dream, it means that the dreamer is in control of their life. If another person is steering it, then that person is in control of the dreamer's life. It was this message that interested me to pay attention to my dreams."

After a short pause and four steps around the fire, the speaker uses this motion for a chance to organise his thoughts before interpreting his dream.

He continues, "I can see myself paddling my canoe down a wide river."

He shows the motions of rowing on his right side as he says, "I watch myself paddling on the same side of the canoe, but the canoe does not turn. This keeps my interest. The canoe keeps moving straight down the river where tall green trees grow on the banks. While I canoe, my spirit flies ahead to see where I am going."

Their older brother, Haihǫnyánih, gives a grunt and smirks at the details of this dream.

He asks jokingly, "When did you learn to fly, little brother?"

The others laugh in response.

One of the elders at the fire points his hand at the men who are making fun of the story and holds up his hand as if to tell them to listen. He nods in the direction of Hasegá:dǫ: to continue.

Not waiting for more reactions from his audience, he says, "This story comes from four nights of fasting. I am about to describe our future Hodinǫhsyǫ́:niʔ. Remember, the sights I describe may not be true about the whole generation, or of all nations or of all

13

the 'new people'. This story is about a few Hodinǫhsyǫ:niʔ families to show me what they want me to know. It was very hard for me to understand some things at times. There are many things that are different from our way of life. Some things we do not have words to describe. I will try my best and tell you their purpose."

His voice rises in volume as he says, "Not all, but some of the children, elders and parents have little respect for each other or themselves. Some of the people are unorganised, lost, separated, and angry, and rageful to their core. In many ways, the Ǫgwehǫ:weh have copied the 'new people', disconnecting from their old ways, beliefs, ceremonies, languages and their families. This transformation happened slowly over time. They have changed in good and bad ways. Some people have adjusted to survive in two worlds."

A slight male whose voice is changing asks, "Why are the Ǫgwehǫ:weh angry?"

The speaker continues, "It is hard to understand why they are mad at everyone. They do not realise that they are mad at themselves, or they do not feel well. Some people that are able to work, work too hard, and others do not work for their own reasons. Some do not work to hide from their world. Few people share with their clans, and some have more than they need. Some Ǫgwehǫ:weh can starve while others eat well. Both do not understand the other's way."

There is a silence among the men; only the crackling of the fire and the frogs croaking in the distance can be heard.

Then a member of his fire asks, "Who are these 'new people' you talk about?"

"The 'new people' travelled across the magnificent waters."

He points east of Turtle Island. "The Mohawks have mentioned these magnificent waters many times in their stories."

"Are the new people similar to the Ǫgwehǫ́:weh?"

"Yes, in some ways. The 'new people' have light hair, skin, and eyes, and some are darker than us, wearing coverings unknown to me. It seems that when the new people first came to our lands, our people tried to teach them the Great Law, our way to live in harmony. This new life was strange to the new people at first. They learned to enjoy it. They admired the peace of sharing and our way of being equal, comparing their life from across the magnificent waters to their new life here. Eventually, more 'new people' came, causing conflict among the Ǫgwehǫ́:weh and their own people. They did not understand our languages or our ways."

"Did they have wars?"

"At one time, the Ǫgwehǫ́:weh fought against each other, competing for hunting territories. We know that the system of neutral grounds agreement was developed and exchanged among our people and the Anishnaabe. The new people did not understand our system and began hunting and living where they wanted. After some time, our people began trading skins with the new people to survive in a new world. Our people became greedy, causing small battles among themselves and the new people.

"Soon, there was a great war over land and their beliefs between the nations of the 'new people'. Some of our people picked a side and fought alongside the new people. Some of the Hodiṇǫhsyǫ́:niˀ nations moved away from the troubled territory in all directions of the great waters where we live now."

Pointing to the river, he says, "Five nations followed a young leader of the Mohawk nation and made an agreement to become allies with the British new people to protect their people, our people, and the land. Our nations settled along the water borders. The war ended. Our people moved away from the territories that we enjoy now and moved north, west, south, and east. For their support in the war, they were given coins, and land from mouth to source was set aside for the Mohawks and the nations that follow."

"Was there peace again among nations?"

""Yes, over time, peace was restored and the Hodiṇǫhsyǫ́:niˀ's protection was not needed along the shores and borders between the great waters. The new people slowly began settling along the River Ouse, with no regard for the treaty between the Hodinǫhsyǫ́:niˀ and the British. In time, the land agreement along the river was ignored and they pushed our people out of their homes and villages, killing some of our people. Our leaders beseeched their leader across the magnificent waters to quit tormenting our people and continue to protect the land as promised. It had seemed no one would listen."

Hasegá:dǫ: takes a deep breath and continues, "The new people thought they knew what was best for the Ǫgwehǫ́:weh . They began to use their laws to control our people to be like them. When that strategy did not work, they made new laws to take our children away from our families and communities to teach them their languages and their beliefs. They are proud people as well, and some do not want to admit the errors committed against our people through their laws. Instead, they cover their mistakes with fast-spoken words. Our people were tricked because they did not understand their words, their language, or their ways about owning the land that belongs to the Creator."

"Their words must be the bad medicine of the new people," says an older man.

The men around the fire nod in agreement, not wanting to interrupt, and trying to imagine the world the speaker describes.

"Some Ǫgwehǫ́:weh have moved away from the circles of their families and their communities to the

17

villages of the new people. The further away they moved into those areas, the more confused they, and their children, became. They try to learn and carry on their own culture, especially when they live among the new people."

The elder asks, "You said they do not know they are mad at themselves."

Hasegá:dǫ: encircles himself, slaps his chest, then his head. Describing his experience, he says, "Yes. Conflict is caused between what their spirit knows and what they have learned in the new world. There is confusion, making them angry."

He says, "I have seen those people that live in the camps of tall structures and no fires." Mimicking the staggering walk of the people he has seen, he says, "They can share the same shelter, yet they do not acknowledge or talk to the others that sleep there. Some live in temporary shelters in their villages. I have felt their loneliness and witnessed the death of their spirits as they pierce their arms with tiny spear-like objects. Some wander the well-packed trails as lifeless thin bodies, moving their arms and muttering to the spirits. They are aged from hardship."

The speaker's shoulders soften, and he lowers his eyes to the base of the fire, pausing before he takes a deep, forlorn breath. Desasǫ́dręh watches her brother and feels sorry for his spirit.

"There must have been good things you witnessed. Do they talk like us? Do they speak our languages?" asks a curious elder.

Straightening up, he says, "Yes. There are some good things that make their lives easier. Some have lives that are too easy."

He looks happy to change the subject. Showing the size of fruit, he says, "The strawberries, raspberries and grapes are bigger than the ones we pick. Some of our future people's bodies are heavier and shorter than our people. Some have light eyes and the skin of mixed blood. The coverings they wear are something they squeeze into what they call 'clothes' that are not made from animals. Their coverings are bright as flowers, berries, and the trees at the end of summer.

"Most of them speak the language of the new people. Some Ǫgwehǫ:weh speak our languages, and teach the little ones. The only way I could understand the future Ǫgwehǫ:weh without our language was through their dreams and spirits. They had no words to explain to me how they felt. I could feel their happiness and their agony through their spirits."

Desasǫ́dręh understands what he means. She remembers a dream she had on her first fast about a little girl on a raft. She could feel the sadness and the low spirit of that little girl.

A boy squirms from the tension, and looks at his father, the disbeliever, as if to get permission to ask a question. Haihǫnyánih smiles and points his chin to his son across the fire to encourage him to speak.

19

Hasegá:dǫ: notices and says, "Speak your mind, nephew."

The boy asks, "You said their bodies ache. What makes them sore?"

Hasegá:dǫ: was afraid someone would go back to the sorrows of the people. After a very long silence, Hasegá:dǫ: says, "Their bodies ache from sickness, and their hearts ache from sorrow and anger."

His body trembles slightly and his chin becomes tense with emotion from the sights that overwhelm him, "For a long time they have lived in sadness and cry without tears."

Tears came to Hasegá:dǫ:'s eyes and his voice thickened as he tried to sort out his feelings and the scenes of his mind. After a few moments, he manages to control his emotions enough to go on with his story.

"The elders, children, women, as well as their men, have been violated in many disrespectful ways. They have been ruined spiritually, hunted, and captured or killed, some eaten."

Another elder interrupts his story. "Eaten?"

"Yes. Eaten. There are reports from their ancestors that suggest they have eaten our people. They say the meat of the Ǫgwehǫ́:weh has a nutty flavour."

Haihǫnyánih is astonished at this report. "Like nuts! Do you mean we taste like acorns or other seeds from trees?"

Hasegá:dǫ: looks around the fire. "They are not

treated with respect as a child. When they grow into an adult, they treat their families in the same way, without respect. It disturbs me too much to talk about it this night. Let me tell you that there will come a people that will not honour the ones with whom they share Mother Earth. Our people became afraid of the 'new people' that steal their children and take them away, killing their weak little bodies with sickness, or their spirit by depriving the children of love and belonging."

After hearing this, Desasǫ́dręh notices the men sit up defensively as they listen to her brother's story.

An anxious fellow says, "Where do they live? What do they eat?"

The speaker takes a deep breath before deciding how he is going to explain what he has learned about their shelters and their food.

He looks into the eyes of the young fellow, and says, "They eat more than they need and drink water that boils like a sour spring. They live in homes like our longhouses made of trees, but only parents and their children live there; not as we do with many clan members. Inside and outside of their homes are the colours of berries and flowers. Their shelters are strong, and sun can shine through the sides in some places."

Haihǫnyánih, his older brother and still not a believer, asks with furrowed eyebrows, "How can the sun shine through the sides? Are there spaces between the logs to allow the smoke to leave? What do you mean?"

Hasegá:dǫ: is afraid he will lose his audience.

He hurriedly explains the best way he can, and says, "The sides have holes covered with something that looks like hard water like the clear ponds in the winter. This hard water substance does not melt in the sun."

Looking around the fire to see if anyone else sees the humour in this theory, Haihǫnyánih laughingly retorts, "The sides stay hard water in the sun? Where do they find this hard water?"

A grandfather spoke in his defence. Pointing north, he says, "Ǫgwehǫ:weh tell stories of these fields of hard water that never turn to water. Hasegá:dǫ: says the sides look like hard water. Continue, Hasegá:dǫ:, tell us, where did they get the sides of their homes?"

The speaker looks at the fire, still carrying the memories fresh in his mind, and he says, "I do not know. But this hard water keeps the wind out and allows the sun to shine into their homes."

Hasegá:dǫ: had learned they made it from ground rocks that they cook until they can shape it, but he knows his audience is already in disbelief, so he leaves the thought in the air.

He says, "Our people are confined to a small hunting territory because the trees and the creeks that the Creator and Mother Earth provide are almost gone outside of their territory. The people seem to have forgotten that the trees give Mother Earth and all beings breath. She could choke, they and their children could choke."

An elder at the fire says, "They cannot have clear heads and minds if they cannot breathe fresh air."

He looks at the man. "Some elders are very sick from life and are set up in their own shelters, away from their families. At this place, some elders walk and mutter to their spirits. Some sit and stare because their thoughts leave them. Their spirits are low until they give up."

The grandson of the elder asks, "If the elders share a shelter together, who helps them? Who teaches the children? Do their uncles teach them to fish?"

"No. Their ways are different from our ways; most people do not fish, or hunt to survive. Trout cannot live in the waterways because you cannot see to the bottom of the waters. Very few members gather and grow their own food, but many of them trade."

"What do they use to trade?"

Shaping out a little rectangle, he says, "They use something they call 'money' to trade for food. Some call it ohwíhsda²."

"They must hunt to live. Where are the animals? Where do they catch ohwíhsda²? What does ohwíhsda² taste like?" asks a disgruntled listener.

"They cannot and do not eat ohwíhsda². The

animals live just out of sight of the people, where there are many trees. It is rare to see buffalo, beaver, deer, and pheasants in their territories. The future Ǫgwehǫ́:weh are deaf and blind to the animals that live so near their shelters."

A man sitting closest to the speaker looks disturbed to hear about the future sons and daughters and Mother Earth.

Grumpily, he asks, "Where do they get their food?"

Hasegá:dǫ: motions with his hands to describe the things that he had seen, because he has no words to help his audience understand.

Shaping the four-dimensional object with his arms, he attempts, "They reach inside this thing that is this tall and this wide. The sides are hard like thin flat stone. We have nothing like it. The inside of the object is as cold as the inside of the deep caves where we hold our food in the summer."

"What is in this cold object? Are there berries, greens, rabbits, or nuts in them? How do they get in there?" asks another person.

"I do not recognise their sustenance. Some of the food and nuts look like they are from another land. The meat is of animals that we have never hunted. It looks like a fat deer or a small buffalo with short fur and big eyes."

This statement sparks a lot of questions in the men's minds. Desah can see them trying to imagine the type of animals that her brother mentions. The audience knows that this story is ending for now, but will stretch over a few evenings. They will save their hunting questions for another night.

A boy, whose voice is changing, asks, "Do they participate in the activities of men to test their skills and strength?"

"Yes, they do," answers the speaker, glad to stick to a happier subject.

"They participate in activities that are like our games of tests. They call the games 'lacrosse' on the ground and 'hockey' on the hard water. Few men or children participate in a contest in a small area; not as we do, where many clans come together in a clearing or on the hard water. Their space is smaller, with no grass or trees. They shield their heads and bodies with something as hard as a turtle's back. Many more people enjoy watching than competing against each other. The nets on the sticks are bigger than ours, and their sticks are not alive with wood."

Making the shape of a ball, he says, "I do not know what the game ball is filled with."

One of the men says, "They must not be as skilled as our people if their nets are bigger."

The men at the fire acknowledge the comment; some smile, and some laugh.

The elder at the fire says loudly, "I worry about the problems of the future people. Do their Chiefs provide wisdom to guide the ones that are carrying problems? Do they come to the Chiefs with their issues?"

"No. They talk about their issues to other people who have skills of listening.

They have two types of systems in most Ǫgwehǫ:weh territories. One system has only one Chief, and the other has fifty Chiefs. The new leaders in these two systems are working towards the same things separately, causing conflict and disagreements on important things that could affect the future of the people of their territory.

"One system is called the 'elected'. The law for their people is that one person from the community is chosen by some members as their Chief. There is no ceremony with the Clan Mothers, and this naming is not celebrated with the whole territory.

"The other system is the hereditary Chiefs, where their titles are handed down and men are stood up by the Clan Mothers, and this naming is not celebrated by the whole territory."

"Only one Chief speaks to a decision?" the elder asks in astonishment.

He continues with disdain obvious in his tone and on his face, "What happened to all the Clan Mothers? 'Standing up' the Chief is their responsibility. With whom does the Chief discuss the issues of the people if there are no other Chiefs, or Clan Mothers? Do they have clans? How do they make a decision that is good for all their people without discussion? What has happened to the Great Law that the Creator has set down for us to follow?"

Hasegá:dǫ: tries to appease the elder. "There are many events that altered and added another way of making decisions on behalf of the people. It could have been the Great War, when they moved away from our territories, disconnecting the people from their homelands, their way of life and each other. Hodinǫhsyǫ́:niˀ numbers became fewer from starvation and much sickness, and dying from contact with the new people, leaving too many empty seats in the hereditary system. Decisions according to the Great Law of Peace took too long for the restless new people. They posed a new way of making decisions. The Mohawk Chiefs and our Chiefs, the Cayugas, did attend this discussion to sanction the new way." The speaker's forehead is creased and his face taut with emotion as he leaves this part of his dream for now.

"There is more to this story that cannot be told this night."

Deep in their thoughts, the group sits and stares blankly at the slowly fading flames, each interpreting the speaker's dream in their own way.

An older fellow asks, "Tell me, Hasegá:dǫ:, what was the most unusual sight?"

Smiling, he says, "Everything is unusual. They have a 'dream thing' that has moving images in it where many of the new people talk and talk or sing and laugh or cry."

Motioning with his arms, he shapes the television and says, "They do not have to leave their homes to see other new people or the lands beyond their territory."

"What does it say?" asks a young fellow that has recently joined the group.

Remembering the movement of the images on the front of it, Hasegá:dǫ: says shortly, "The 'dream thing' says everything and nothing useful to us. I think it tells people and children what to think. People do not have to think for themselves."

A fellow listening in sorrow for the future Hodinǫhsyǫ́:niˀ asks, "This future you have visited, can it be changed? How can we help our future sons and daughters?"

Sitting down, Hasegá:dǫ: says, "I do not know. I felt and saw too much to tell you about everything this night. After my visit, I got into the canoe and returned to where I started upriver."

After a bit, an elder says, more to himself than to the others, "There can be many generations between the people he speaks of and our people. The future people must travel their own way to survive this new way of life, good and bad."

Pointing south, he continues, "As our ancestors have adjusted to travelling from the hot lands to our lands that we now enjoy, the future people will adjust to their new lands and their new ways."

The men at the fire sit in silence. In the distance,

there is the familiar sound of water rushing down the river, splashing against its rocky sides. A hungry salmon or trout makes the sound of a splash as it catches its supper flying above the water. The fires turn to glowing embers under a heavy covering of grey ash.

The elder, who has witnessed many generations, catches the eyes of each person, and he motions his hand to draw the line of generations, then points to the fire. "Remember, our people carry the blood of our ancestors. We must trust there will be children born that will add the Hodinǫhsyǫ́:niˀ teachings to their way of life to become truly happy and at peace with their spirit."

The elder nods and points with his chin towards the red coals. "If we throw another log on that fire, it will start to burn hot again, like our blood… in the bodies… of the faces that come, our future sons and daughters."

As the fire dies down, everyone slowly leaves and moves towards their own camps. Desasǫ́dręh, along with the rest of the women and young ones, gather the coverings on the ground and head to their temporary shelters. Many questions come to her mind as she crawls in next to her sleeping sister, Onráhdagǫ:, making sure she is fully covered. Then she lays still with the thoughts of Hasegá:dǫ:'s story whirling around in her head with the many questions that were not asked this night. The night is restless with the questions coming to Desasǫ́dręh's mind. She does not want to forget them. 'How does he know who to visit? Over the nights of fasting, does he visit the same generation?' Desasǫ́dręh decides to approach her brother about his dreams. She's curious about visiting the next generation and would love to visit there. To the night air she whispers, "Tomorrow I am going to approach brother to find out more about that time."

The next day, the smell of wood burning wakes her up. Her first thought is 'the girls in my village that are coming into their time have already committed one night fast'. She is one of them. The trip was over night. She was not sure what the trip was about at the time. Now she looks forward to another one. She will announce her intention to her grandmother, and mother, that she wants to commit to a two-night fast. They will tell the other women to gain approval before she begins preparing.

Desah peeks out of her shelter; Onráhdagǫ:, the youth and the adults are already at the river cleaning up before the morning chores. She rushes to the river. She throws off her outer coverings and jumps into the cold water. Usually, she takes her time to get used to the cold, but today there is no time. Quickly, she scrambles onto the shore. Still wet, she wiggles into her outer coverings.

Desah's focus is to catch her brother before he leaves. She rushes up the bank, her hair still wet and her feet slipping around in her moccasins.

Her sister reaches out to her arm. "Watch now. Where are you going, Desah?"

"I am going to find Hasegá:dǫ: before he leaves for hunting or fishing."

"Slow down. He will not leave before he eats something."

As she approaches the camp, Desah spots her brother. Smiling, she thinks, 'Yes, Onráhdagǫ: was right. There he sits on a stump, gnawing a piece of boiled meat.' She guesses it is probably rabbit, because they are plentiful around here.

He smiles when he sees her heading towards him. A friend carrying a small plank stops her. "Desah, can you give my Anishnaabe friend's little baby a bath? We are helping my sister. The baby is ready for a nap. She needs a bath first."

Desah, without thinking, answers, "Hao`."

She turns back towards the shelter where the baby is crying. Swinging up her cranky new friend in the air, they continue to walk towards her older brother.

"Hasegá:dǫ:, I have been asked to give my new little friend a bath."

She places the baby in his free arm. "Can we talk before you leave for hunting?"

"We talk all the time."

"No, about your visions. I have questions."

"We can talk after the evening meal."

Seeing she is disappointed, he sticks out his chest and points to himself, saying, "The men are hunting today so that you can dry the meat all night."

The two siblings, close in age and spirit, constantly tease each other, especially about the amount of work they do or do not do. He points his chin at her, meaning it is her job.

"No, not alone, not tonight and not all day. We leave in the morning," she laughs.

Pointing to the men congregating close to the trail through the trees, she says, "They should bring back enough for the last feast this evening."

"Oh, there will be enough," he says with chewed rabbit sticking out of the side of his mouth and juice on his chin.

She squints at the sight. Smiling to herself, she turns her back to him as she walks to the temporary shelter where she found the baby. He follows closely with the protesting baby in his arms.

She pours the warm bathwater into a clay bowl, swirling the crushed dried flowers and pine needles with her fingers. She pulls the bowl into the temporary shelter and places it next to a soft skin mat. Behind her, Hasegá:dǫ: rolls the little girl into the shelter and she stops on her back, giggling. The smell of lavender and pine fills the air, soothing the baby and keeping her from struggling to get away from these familiar strangers.

Brother leaves her to her task to check the fire where they will be drying the meat, before he meets up with the other men.

Grabbing a corn cake on his way, he greets his aunt. "How are you, my aunt? Are you at peace?"

She responds with a smile and a nod.

As an afterthought, Gotsahniht reminds him, "Today is the last and shortest day for hunting and fishing; you will not need too much food for the feast. Did the men pack cornmeal cakes, and fruit for their travels?"

Hasegá:dǫ: shrugs his shoulders. "I will ask."

He saunters away from her and in the direction of the river.

Desah turns towards her little charge and hums her baby sister's favourite song, suddenly missing Star's smile. This is the first time Desah has been away from her mother for this long and the first hunting trip with her older siblings. The hunting camps can last one to three moons, depending on the success of the hunt. All the camps are drying meat for the winter. The youth gather nuts and berries, being careful not to squash them to juice. Some are left on the trees for the birds, and whatever is left at the end of season is gathered before they leave for home. Berries that are not used in the feasts are spread out in the sun near the fire to dry them. Gathering nuts off the ground and tying them in leather pouches is also the responsibility of the youth.

In their home territories, the mothers determine how much food, plants, squash, and corn to dry. The people look for winter signs from nature; usually the caterpillar or the bear give them signs. They can ration food if needed in unforeseen situations. The clans hold a ceremony for a safe trip before sending out the young men to hunt in the snow. There, the men are preparing for a winter hunt by checking and repairing snowshoes. Hatchets and stone tools are sharpened to cut the large kill into transportable pieces, such as a moose or buffalo. They can usually gather enough men to hunt, drag and guard the meat on their trip back to the village. They are quite aware that the fresh blood scent attracts bears, wolves, coyotes, and lynx, even when the meat is frozen.

Every able person in the village contributes towards making the longhouses warm for winter. The inner walls are covered with skins to keep the wind and cold out. The logs of the outer walls are packed with mud and weeds. Sometimes, siblings, parents and small children double up under their skins on extra cold nights. Enough wood is gathered and piled along the walls to keep the fires crackling day and night.

Her favourite part is after the evening feasts, when stories are told, songs are sung, and people dance through the night. Many clans visit each other's longhouses during the winter, a good time for bonding. Occasionally, men from other territories and nations, while out hunting, will stop in each other's villages to rest, or to bring fresh meat to share. They will participate in winter activities such as snowsnakes to compete against each other. Nearby frozen ponds are cleared of snow and used for games of strength and skill. The winter game is played in a similar manner to the stick games they play in the summer. The fittest men push each other out of the way or slide around the men on the ice to get the ball past guards of identified targets. There is always lots of laughter and tricks played on each other to score. Sometimes, the women are asked to gather around to distract the opponents. The winner's triumphant yells can always be heard throughout the village. Song and dance pass time and keep people inside in hard winters until storms pass.

Desah finishes bathing the little girl and says, "I must be lonesome for home."

She wraps baby in the soft leather that is laid out for her. She slides dried, clean moss in place and fixes her into a cradle board. Once outside the shelter, she carries her on her back towards the circle of women who are skinning animals and preparing them for drying. The smell of lavender and the swaying motion of the walk puts baby to sleep. Desasǫdręh hangs the cradle on a tree branch and secures it with a leather strapping.

"Akenhnhà:ke, your friend's sister is asleep."

Akenhnhà:ke puts down her project and walks over to Desah.

In Mohawk, her friend says, "Nia:wen. Who was that man holding her for you?"

"Hasegá:do:. He is my older brother. I should have asked you if it was proper for him to help. I do not know their customs. He helps me or my mother with our baby sister."

"I will ask and apologise."

The sigh and smile on Akenhnhà:ke's face bewilders Desasódreh. She turns to see she is looking at her brother, laughing and walking with her other brother. She does not see the attraction. She can only see the loose wisps of hair bouncing off his shoulders. In her mind she grumbles, 'He forgot to do something with his hair. I should have braided it or at least tied it back for him. It is too late to call him back now he is disappearing over the hill and into the woods.'

She turns to her new bold friend and asks, "Do the young people in your nation fast as they change seasons?"

Akenhnhà:ke answers quickly, "Yes, many of them."

She continues to tell Desasódreh about their village and its surroundings in Mohawk valley. While she talks, Desah's thoughts race back to her brother's story from last night. She wonders how he falls into such a deep sleep to be able to visit the generations to come. She will learn more tonight, but she is sure the discussion will be about hunting.

The work is lighter now in comparison to the first days of the hunt. Desah was delegated to rotate the strips to prevent tainted meat. Now she helps the women take down the A-frames that held smoked meat and fish over the last few days.

By the river, the fishnets are brought out and emptied of fish for the feast. The very small fish are returned to the water and the remainder are put in a basket and hung beside the canoes. Once they are done with the nets weaved from vines, they are rolled up and the best one will be kept out for the trip tomorrow. The older uncles stay behind and just before the men return they will demonstrate the art of filleting and cooking the fish. For practice, the youth take turns skinning and filleting them to see who can be the neatest and the fastest.

Gotsahniht, Desah's aunt, says, "Tonight is the last night of the camp in this place. Everyone needs to eat well and have a good sleep. There will be no dances. The men will share stories of the hunt, trade goods and present parting gifts before the night's sleep."

Desah knows she will love these trips because she met a new friend, Akenhnhà:ke, who lives in Mohawk territory. They learned each other's language enough to understand one another. They quickly became friends while picking and drying medicines, and they had fun dancing. Tomorrow they will work together dividing the seeds, medicines, and the dried meat and fish into the canoes for the trip home.

When the men return with fresh meat, it will be

prepared for the evening feast, along with beans, corn, nuts, and other local plants they have gathered for extra flavour.

When Akenhnhà:ke finishes describing her family, Desah asks, "Where do the girls fast from your territory?"

"We go into the mountains and in the summertime when it is warm.

"We are expected to wait for harvest ceremonies to be done before we can go. We leave when the men leave for the hunt. The next hunting camp and gathering will be in the south when they hunt buffalo."

"Maybe I will go there instead of fasting. Will Hasegá:dǫ: be hunting there?"

"I am not sure. I don't know if he plans that far ahead."

Akenhnhà:ke says, "Uncle says the men plan the next hunt while they are hunting, who is going, how many men will be needed and who will make the request to hunt in the territory."

"Good. Then maybe my brother knows if he is going after harvest."

Onráhdagǫ: calls, "Desah, come here."

"I will go. When my sister wants something, she uses my short name. She uses Desasǫ́dręh when I am in trouble. Talk later."

Her friend laughs, "Yes."

Onráhdagǫ: says, "Help me put the food out. The

men will be returning soon."

Hasegá:dǫ: and their older brother, Haihǫnyánih, walk up from the river, carrying five huge salmon.

Onráhdagǫ: and Desasǫ́dręh take the fish from them to the work areas where the men will scale and gut the fish. The nephews are anxious and ready to help.

When the fish and meat are finished cooking, the women lay out the feast under tall, colourful trees in the shape of a T for the people to line up and quickly fill their bowls. The elders and the children have already gotten their food by the time the men have cleaned up and are ready to get in line.

Once again, the men meet at their fires after the feast. Desah makes sure she chooses a fire close to Hasegá:dǫ: to avoid missing him after his story. There seems to be more men at his fire tonight. Some are sitting on the ground and along the top of the fallen trees.

Hasegá:dǫ: starts, "While visiting the seventh generation, I found that unlike our customs, few men hunt. They hunt in small bands, and they do not always walk near their territories to find the animals. They travel far north and ride in something."

"You mean they ride on something like the toboggan?"

"No. There are seats in a thing they call a 'car'," he says, motioning with his hands and walking out the length of the vehicle he describes.

"We have nothing like it. It makes a loud noise and smoke comes out of the back of it. Some old 'cars' have smoke coming out of both ends, causing the sky and clouds to be the same colour as the flowers. I fear the air smells as bad as the things they ride in."

"Do their animals have ears and noses to warn them of the hunters' approach? How can they sneak up on them if the car stinks and makes noise?"

The men at the fire laugh, discussing the future animals that have small or no ears and nose to notice the loud, stink thing that the men use.

"Can they ride the thing among the trees?"

"Sometimes the men ride far to hunt because there are few trees and animals near their villages. They leave their 'cars', then they walk into the woods. Some ride on smaller things that are as loud and smell as bad as cars. They catch one or two moose or deer and put them into or on their things to take back to their villages."

"Can a buffalo fit on the loud stink things?"

"They do not hunt buffalo. The few buffalo that are left are smaller than the ones we hunt."

Of all the information they have heard about the seventh generation, this news is the most astonishing.

"No buffalo? Where are they? Only one or two animals feed their village. How big are these animals? Are there fewer Ǫgwehǫ́:weh ?"

Hasegá:dǫ: sees he is confusing his audience.

"There are people remaining. Their hunting groups are small, and they only hunt for their mate and children, sometimes feeding their parents, grandparents, uncle, or an aunt."

The men look around the fire at each other. One of the men stands up. "One or two animals feed their clans? Are the Ǫgwehǫ:weh thin?"

He slides his hands down along his body. Some men laugh at his feminine description of a slim body.

"No, they do not feed their clans. They only feed the few people who live in their small shelter, not the whole clan. The clans are separated and do not live together in one longhouse. The small families live in little shelters that are spread out along well-worn paths made by their cars."

The men become silent.

"What animals are left to hunt? Are there beaver, rabbit, pheasant, moose, and deer left?"

"Yes. The people I visited do not hunt or eat many of those animals and birds. They eat fowl called chickens, and animals called pigs and cows. I did not see buffalo."

Hasegá:dǫ:'s story triggers tales of the hunt this year. A young man who has recently been allowed to hunt, boasts of the size of moose he helped kill and haul to the camp. The men nod with pride, adding their actions during the kill.

Desasǫ́drȩh loses interest in their hunting stories. She wants to know how her brother was able to visit the generations.

She turns to her aunt. "How did brother visit the future generations?"

Gotsahniht closes her eyes and says to herself, 'Help me describe the connection between spirits.' Then she answers her niece as best she can.

"Our spirits are eternal and connected through thoughts, dreams, and visions. As the spirits of our ancestors are always ready to carry us on their backs, especially when we need them, we must always be ready to carry the future generations on our backs if they need us."

Pressing her right hand into the open left hand above her head, she weaves the fingers to explain how a higher order of presence is available.

Looking up at the stars, and putting her palms together, moving them in sync, she says, "Our energies vibrate, causing an energy or a spirit in unison through thoughts, or dreams of messages to be sent and received connecting our two spirit worlds of energy. Everything that is alive has an energy or spirit. Some things have low energy and some things, like the stars, fire and people, have high energy. Connections between spirits happen stronger when we are still. You will learn that most women have this natural sense or instinct which is needed to protect their babies. In your next fast, explore these thoughts, and the generations to come. The experience will be your best teacher."

She adds, "Our ancestors used these gifts along with the stories of the stars for their survival in the old physical world. These gifts told them when to hunt and plant."

Desasódręh is overwhelmed with this teaching. Tears filling her eyes, she asks, "And brother knows this?"

Gotsahniht says, "Yes, your father has prepared all your brothers before their fasting time. When we get back to our waters and territory, it will be your time and other young women of the same winters to begin preparing for the two-nights, building up to the three-nights and four-night fasts in the hills near the waterfalls. On my fasts, as I was taught, I first think about how grateful I am for Creator, the Ǫgwehǫ́:weh , and all the gifts provided by Mother Earth: the wind, rain, sun, grandmother moon, stars and the four spirit teachers. Once this is done, I would sit or lay quiet, clear my mind of all thoughts and be open to any messages that may come."

Pointing to the direction of the sunrise, she says, "On our way home, think about what you learned while fasting the last time for one night. During this upcoming fast of two nights, it will be a difficult test with only your medicines and water, and no food. Be open to the answers you receive."

Desasódręh remembers the last fast, and the things she learned about herself, and the steps to a good mind. She also remembers her dream about a sad little girl on a raft in a shallow pond in the middle of an open field. Desah wonders why she was dreaming of this little girl, who she is and where she belongs. She did not recognise her from any of the local camps or villages. She was lying on her stomach with her arms down along her sides. Her head turned, with her brown hair covering part of her face. Her little brown legs poked out of her coverings. She stared into the clear water, watching the green grass flowing softly on the bottom of the shallow pond. The sunlight bounced along each tiny ripple caused by her raft.

Desah sensed that the little girl's spirit was low, as though she was carrying the world on her back. She did not say she was sad, nor was she crying. Her body did not show any signs of sadness at all. It was her little spirit that was dull, dense with so much sadness that it barely vibrated. She looked as though she had fallen asleep for a moment. Time suspended in the warm air carrying the soft sound and smell of the wind through the plants. The sun warmed her back. Desah sensed the little girl felt safe here, alone, enveloped in the warmth of the arms of Mother Earth.

Suddenly, the peaceful moment ended with the rustling in the tall, dry plants. She woke to see two pointed ears barely poking out and blending in with the colours that surrounded them. The little girl quickly sat up to get a better look at the being that was as curious about her as she was about it. Standing higher on its hind legs, the Jack rabbit stared at the little girl for a long moment, before it darted off without a sound in the plants through its secret path that closed behind it. Desah had not thought about the little girl or her dream until Hasegá:dǫ: talked of his visions of the future generations.

She never told anyone of that dream because she did not understand it. She wonders if the little girl was of a future generation. She must have been: her coverings were foreign to Desah. Through her aunt's explanation of the dreams, ancestors, and the past and future, she hopes to gain a better understanding on her next fasts.

Desah turns her attention to her brother's stories. Hasegá:dǫ: is winding up his vision stories and the men are out of their success stories. She grabs her bowl of water and takes it to him.

"Here is some water. Drink," she says, with her arm outstretched towards her brother's mouth.

He backs up smiling and takes the water, waiting to hear the reason for her generosity.

Desah starts right in with the discussion. "Our aunt explained some things about visions, dreams and fasting, but how do you know who or what generation to visit? How do you talk to them and how do they talk to you? How do you know if you understand each other? Did you visit the same Ǫgwehǫ́:weh every time over all your fasts?"

Hasegá:dǫ: blinks from the bombardment of

questions being fired at him. He holds his hand up. "I will try to answer your questions. I had the same questions when I learned of dreams and visions. I noticed that I visited the person that carries my name in the future generations. The person I met had a short name, Murray, and my name, Hasegá:dǫ:. I could sense his spirit understood my words and feelings."

"Did they speak in the Gayogohó:nǫ² language every day?"

Raising his eyebrows, he replies, "No, not every day. I heard elders and Murray's father speak their birth language with their family and with others as he grew up. His father had to learn the new people language. In Murray's day, the words are always spoken during ceremony and his father used a few Mohawk words to his children. I heard his father say that he did not want his children going through the abuse he went through for speaking his language. When I realised they did not understand me, I learned by watching and connecting through spirit or through images in their dreams or visions."

"Did you visit the same Ǫgwehǫ́:weh every time?"

"Yes. I visit the same time and person, not the same people around him every time. My next fast will be during the snow. This is the test of males only. Why do you ask these questions?"

Desasǫ́drę̨h begins telling him of her accidental visit and that she did not know what these images meant or why she was able to sense the little girl's feelings of happiness, fears, and heavy sadness. She had only one dream and it was short.

Hasegá:dǫ: hands her the empty bowl that contained the water. "I was confused at first. Wondering if these dreams or messages originated from our ancestors. Our father explained his ideas of how these visions happen. I have a better understanding today."

"Yes, our aunt explained her understanding of how it happens. I want to learn why the little girl needs my attention." She pauses, waiting for his input.

Her brother is already turning to walk back to the pit to check if the fire is out.

Over his shoulder he remarks, "Let me know when you find out, Desah."

Desah, satisfied with his answers, turns to help the women. For the rest of the day, they heavily wrap the dried meat to prevent animals from picking up the scent on their hike across the land to the next waterway. They evenly sort the heavy skins and tools in the canoes first. From the canoes, they will transfer the loads onto toboggan-like equipment for the men and youth to take turns pulling them until they reach the great waters before nightfall.

As the women work, one of the older women asks if Desah found a special friend.

Knowing what they mean, Desah wrinkles her

nose. "No, not this time. The boys are too young to hunt and their voices sound like girls or ducks."

Desasǫdręh leaves the women laughing and returns to her shelter to pack her belongings. She will be in the first group to leave tomorrow and wants to be ready as soon as there is sunlight, or earlier if the moon is bright enough. Her group will set up the next camp on the shore of the great waters and prepare the feast for the following canoes.

The hunting trip is officially at a close. The Mohawk, Onondaga, Cayuga, Seneca, and Oneida representatives will leave by canoes on the river tomorrow. The northern nations, Anishnaabe representatives that participated in the gathering for a couple of days, are leaving around the same time. Old and new friends have been giving their parting gifts over the last few nights of social singing and dancing. For many years, the people have been hunting here, loading canoes to travel the waterways, or loading the toboggans to drag along the ground to the next waterways leading to their home territories.

The hunting groups that leave later, stay back to disassemble the camps and take down the shelters. They will work to return the area as close to the way they found it, though the grass is flattened from the scattered shelters and the ground worn from the nights of dancing. The wood used for their shelters will be set aside for the next hunting group.

It is a long journey tomorrow, travelling by water

and land, transferring loads from canoes to tobaggon-like carriers, and camping for the next few days.

CHAPTER TWO – THE TRIP HOME

In the dark of early morning, the firekeepers have already stopped feeding the fires with wood. Desah wakes to someone's leather leggings scraping together as they rush past her shelter. She rises and peeks out to see the sun peeking back at her through the trees. The plants and trees smell wonderful.

As if waiting for her, Onráhdagǫ: points to the food set out and says, "Come and eat. You will eat again later in the day at the feast. When you finish that, help load the canoes."

Hearing Onráhdagǫ:'s request, one of the women looks at Desah and points to the bundles that have been wrapped and are ready to go. Desah washes quickly in the water set out near her favourite meal of corn mush, beans, and blueberries. She devours the food and washes and packs the small bowl in her bundle. As instructed, she heads to the river, dragging one of the bundles that the women had pointed out.

Desah and her siblings climb into the first five canoes carrying the evening feast food and the supplies and tools they need to set up the next camp.

As their canoes glide down the river, she has time to marvel at the beauty and protection of the huge trees lining the riverbanks. From their perches, big birds haughtily watch as the canoes pass. The blend of their songs and the splashing of the paddles soothes Desah's soul. She closes her eyes while she can. Every now and then, the men's voices are easily heard across the water between canoes.

"Is there ever a more soothing feeling as right now?" she asks her sister.

"Enjoy this moment. Soon you will have to paddle."

Interrupting her serenity, a splash, and some commotion come from the last canoe of the group. One of the men has caught a fish. Her older brother, Haihǫnyánih, turns and yells from his canoe, "Did Hasegá:dǫ: fly ahead to see where the fish were splashing?"

The men laugh, but Desah does not think the teasing is worth a laugh. She looks over to her brother and sees the hurt look on his face. One of the older men in another canoe catches his eye and slightly shakes his head. The eye contact is enough of a signal for him to ignore the words of his brother. Hasegá:dǫ: straightens his back and keeps on paddling.

The river trip seems shorter going home on the river than it had some moons ago, paddling against the current. Five canoes land on the north bank at the same location as before. Fifteen people quickly unload the supplies from camp canoes and onto the toboggan-like contraptions. They gather their belongings and tie them to their toboggans or on their backs. The men hoist each canoe above their shoulders, creating a huge caterpillar on the trail.

She notices Hasegá:dǫ: is one of the first young men chosen to drag the toboggans on the long walk on land to the great waters. Desah looks over at him and wipes her brow to show him she is working, too. Reading her mind, he smiles and shakes his head.

Walking alongside Gotsahniht, Desah visualises the next fast, forgetting the weight of the pack on her back.

Interrupting her aunt's thoughts, she says, "I think about my last fast and I am anxious for my next one."

"Good. How many days are you planning?"

"Only two. I wonder what we will do for two days. Last time the trip was short. We walked there, camped one night, ate the next day, and walked back to the village. We were kept busy walking there and back. We did not have time to think about food."

"Two nights are good for your season. The grandmothers will assign aunts to teach and uncles to lead the group. What happens on the trip and where you camp will be up to the teachers. They can choose a waterfall on our great water, where no permission is necessary. To travel to and camp near a waterfall in the territory of another nation, permission will be requested. Our people will know where to send you at the time of the announcement."

"The last time I fasted we camped near a waterfall that feeds our great water. The sound lulled us to sleep."

Gotsahniht's face changes as she tells her about her adventures during her days of fasting. She tells her about meeting her mate from the Seneca nation for the first time and how they would meet during each of her fasting trips. Her stories make the trek over land and the hard work a little more bearable.

When the group stop to rest and drink, the men rotate to drag toboggans and carry canoes.

She approaches her tired brother. "You are building strong muscles, my brother."

He answers with a smile and glances down at his sweaty arms.

She notices his hair is messy, again. It hangs loose, sticking to his face and back. "Brother, do you want me to braid your hair?"

Without answering, he turns his back towards her and crouches a bit so she can reach. Standing on her tiptoes, she braids his hair.

"Some day, your mate will braid your hair for you. I will miss it."

Knowing his sister hates discussing her future mate, he smiles. Turning his head towards her, he says, "Some day you will have a mate and children. They will need braids."

She laughs, tugging his head back by the thick braid she has in her hands and ties it with the leather from her own hair.

She slaps his back. "You are ready."

She walks over to Gotsahniht and together they watch proudly as he and his friend grab a canoe.

Almost in unison, the group rises to continue trudging on their way to the great waters. The lead men have to reclean a few areas of the trail that had filled in since they last travelled this way. Descending the mountain with their canoes and loaded toboggans turns out to be cumbersome and a bit treacherous. A couple of land loads overturn and have to be re-packed. One of the youths carrying a canoe on his shoulders slips near the edge of the slippery cliff. His partner grabs him. They almost lose the canoe over the edge. The youth and his partner are a little shaken. While the group stops for an unscheduled break, they switch the nervous youth and his partner with fresh men to carry the canoe. They continue their journey through the woods.

Desah loves looking around at the tall trees while they walk. She loves this part of the trip. The trees are so tall, and the trunks so long, most people can walk under the branches. Hasegá:dǫ:, who is six feet tall, just barely reaches the leaves. She is glad she fixed his hair, or it would be tangled in the bushes that grow under the trees along the trail. Her older brother, while carrying the canoe on his shoulders, occasionally ducks the branches. She wonders how tired her brothers get toting the toboggans and carrying the canoes.

She says, "How can I show my brothers I am grateful for their protection and the hard work they do for us?"

"That is nice of you to think that way. Haihǫnyánih has a mate. You can make him a sash or a bag to carry his hatchet and knife or his tobacco. Hasegá:dǫ: needs a winter covering for when he goes hunting. Tell him you want the hide from the next kill. He will make the request to the hunters."

"Thank you. I was hoping you would suggest something that would not take so long or is easier to make, like a hug and saying 'I love you'."

She bumps into her aunt's arm to let her know she is kidding. The mixture of sounds of the others chatting along the way, and twigs cracking under their feet, are familiar sounds to Desah. The group stop for a short rest to allow the men to change their tasks of carrying canoes with dragging loads.

Other than people tripping on tree roots or other minor mishaps, they finally reach the bay, tired and thirsty. After today's trip on land and down the mountain, they know there is easier work ahead, setting up the camp and preparing the feast for everyone. By the time the last group of canoes arrives, their loads will be transferred from the toboggans to the canoes.

Gotsahniht quickly finishes setting up a shelter. As Desah approaches, she turns and holds out some branches to her niece. Desah takes the branches and looks in the direction she's pointing.

"Hao`. I will help the others set up the next shelter."

Most of the materials and branches from the previous camp are still intact, which makes assembly quicker this time. The old boughs that are replaced with fresh ones will become kindling for the fires. While some people are assembling shelters, the other helpers prepare the feast.

Three teenagers bring some bundles up from the canoes. While the work is being accomplished, four youths take their spears to the edge of the great water.

Tired, Hasegá:dǫ: scrapes two flints together over a small mound of dried moss that their aunt had placed in the pit earlier. He begins to sweat more as he frantically strikes the thin pieces of stones together. A flicker of sparks flies out from the flints. Hasegá:dǫ: bends to gently cup his hands around the mound and softly blows life into the smouldering moss. A helpful youth waves a pine bough over the smoke. An older boy nudges the young one away and quickly waves a wing fan, helping the moss catch fire. Another young fire starter lightly places some dried twigs on the moss, producing a low fire which will eventually turn into a full blaze. An old log stands near the pit, along with branches from previous shelters and the old wood the youth have gathered and broken into smaller twigs.

Everyone fulfils the tasks that they have seen achieved for many winters as they set the fires, erect small structures, spreading reed mats and skins in their shelters, gathering and warming water, and preparing the fish. Everything is ready to eat when the last canoes arrive.

Upon their arrival, Gotsahniht announces to the workers, "There will be no dancing this night; everyone is tired from land travel. We will leave the decision to the singers if we dance on the remaining nights of our journey along the shores of the great water."

The camp comes alive as the last band of people arrive and gather around the feast to eat, each talking about their experiences on the way. The youth slipping on the edge of a rocky cliff and almost losing a canoe into the gorge is one topic.

"How long will it take us to get home, uncle?" a youth asks.

"If we have good weather, and nothing happens, it will take us six camps along the shores of the great water and three on land and the waterways to our village. We can take as long as we want, but we must be back in time for the ceremony."

The boy looks at his cousin and smiles. Desah notices the exchange of smiles between the boys, reminding her of childhood days.

Akenhnhà:ke asks, "Why are you smiling, Desasǫdręh?"

Desah says, "One time, I was pretending to be like my mother, placing big leaves on a tree stump that father sometimes uses as a seat. I was going to make mudcakes for my brother's meal."

Akenhnhà:ke spins to look at Desah, saying, "Hasegá:do: ate mudcakes?"

"No, he would pretend. Although in those days he usually did what I wanted him to do. He knew I was pretending. On that day, we were asked to gather fruit, cut wood, kindling, or clean the longhouse. Me and Hasegá:do: exchanged the same smile. We chose to gather fruit. Together, we grabbed baskets and ran towards the trees where two friends were waving us over to play in the pond."

Desah remembers the feeling of the breeze that blew through the shade of the trees.

"It was a warm day. We knew we could not play with our friends. We continued past them and found our favourite stream in the woods that had mud perfect for my mudcakes."

She pauses, remembering the shades of light grey and sunlight bouncing along the tiny ripples of water caused by the bug that scurried across the stream. Her favourite vines hung from the trees, causing eddies to swirl in the water.

"Hasegá:do: had disturbed a bug from its resting spot and it jumped into the water, landing near my foot. I moved quickly out of the stream and away from that bug.

"We laid on the soft moss and grasses beside the stream, watching the shadows move on the surface of the water. I dipped my fingers in the cold water."

The water had caused tingles to run up her fingers and little bumps to form on her arms. Desah got up and took off her moccasins. Ignoring the coldness of the water, she walked further, causing a smokey cloud to form. She remembers carefully collecting the right amount of ingredients for her mudcakes.

"I made a basket out of my skirt to carry the mud. I splashed past Hasegá:dǫ: and his new friends, the little bugs, to reach the right mud for my cakes. Blinking, he laughed, pointing at my legs and feet. I laughed, imagining mother's face when she sees the mud on his face."

The girls laugh at the image.

"Hasegá:dǫ: gets up to leave the woods. Remembering mother's warning to stay together, I follow close behind him."

She exaggerates ducking and blinking, saying, "I am always ready to duck the whipping branches that could swat me again."

Akenhnhà:ke and Onráhdagǫ: laugh.

Fondly, Desah continues, "Outside the woods, I make a couple attempts to put on my moccasins. I tried to sit down without dumping my skirt basket. Hasegá:dǫ: noticed and bent over next to me to help me squeeze my muddy, wet feet into my moccasins. He left me to follow a big orange and black flying bug that I do not care about. He trampled through the tall weeds until it landed on a tall swaying plant with tiny flowers sticking out the side of the stalk. I searched for more ingredients for my mudcakes. No. I mean I had to pick berries from the bushes for mother. I turned. No baskets. We left them by the stream. I ran back to get them. When I returned to where I left Hasegá:dǫ: and the bug, he was gone. I followed the path of bent and broken plants. I was scared when I could not see his short body in the tall plants. I knew I had to find him. We had already walked too far from home following that flying bug."

She describes his path through the tall scratchy weeds and the prickly bushes. Her stomach had tightened at the thought of losing him and being by herself so far from home.

"I was afraid that his path led to the base of the mountain."

Quickly, her sister says, "Base of what mountain? The mountain Mother says to stay away from?"

"Yes. At first, I could only see the top of Hasegá:dǫ:'s head halfway up the huge mountain. I dropped our empty baskets."

Showing them an angry face, she says, "I also had to dump my skirt to crawl up the side of the mountain. I kept slipping along a path of loose, large, flat, sharp stones that fell off the side."

She smiles. "Once I had climbed high enough, I turned to look back towards our village."

With amazement in her voice, she says, "I could see the whole village and our longhouse.

"He called me from above. I looked up to see Hasegá:dǫ: waving a big leaf or branch above the bushes. When he stopped hollering and disappeared into the mountain, my stomach tightened again. Tears came to my eyes. I did not know where he went. Did he keep climbing or did he fall into a hole, or did he fall off the other side of the mountain?"

She did not add that she did not want to lose her best friend, her brother. Her sister would be offended.

"I did not want Mother to cry. I moved faster up the path of slippery rocks, hanging on whatever branches of the bushes I could grab.

"I finally caught up to him. Ignoring my scolding for leaving me, he said he found a cave and a high mound of moss that we can use for sleeping mats. He told me to follow him and disappeared into the side of the mountain."

Holding her arms to demonstrate the coldness of the cave, she continues, "I followed him into the strange, dark, cold space. I could not see at first. I shivered, hoping the flying animals with big teeth would not fly out at me. At the same time, we noticed the mound of moss move!"

As a true storyteller does, Desah whispers for emphasis. She says, "'Hasegá:dǫ:, I think the bear is sleeping. We should leave here!' I grabbed his arm, dragging him away from what he thought was a mound of moss.

"We ran out of the cave and down the side of the mountain on the slippery rocks. I thought I could hear the sleepy bear let out a roar."

Onráhdagǫ: says, "Or it yawned?"

Desah smiles. "I remember us tripping over one another and tumbling down the hill, scraping our legs."

For emphasis, she shows them her knee and elbow scars from the flat, sharp stones and bushes.

"Brother grabbed my arm, hurting it, and dragged me running through the tall scratchy weeds back towards the village with no baskets of fruit and no mud for my cakes."

As she finishes her story, Desah notices her brother passing by them. She says, "Hasegá:dǫ:, remember when we saw a bear for the first time?"

He says, "Yes. You mean when you thought a mound of moss was a sleeping bear? Yes, I remember."

"That was you that led us up the forbidden mountain to the bear's cave. All I wanted to do was make your mudcakes."

Looking at Onráhdagǫ:, she corrects herself, "No, I mean to pick fruit for mother."

"Yes, I remember being glad that I did not have to eat your mudcakes," Hasegá:dǫ: says, rolling his eyes and wrinkling his nose.

The girls laugh.

Changing the subject to food, Hasegá:dǫ: says, "What is our aunt making us to eat? Mmmmh, maybe she will make corn and berry cakes for the feast."

Sister replied, "No, there is no time to make cakes. We will eat the fish you caught and the dried meat we brought."

Desasǫ́drẹh knows there is always enough food to last the trip, counting the food they have and the fresh meat caught on the way. The hardest part of the trip is the long routes of paddling, and the loading and unloading, and walking in the midday sun or in the rain on the old trails through the woods. The best part happens at the end of the trip in the village where her friends and family feast and dance together. She will finally see her mother and baby sister again. Then she will begin preparations for two days and two nights fast. She remembers the first fast did not last long. They walked half a day, learned how to make a temporary shelter, slept, and walked home the next day. She has many questions about the next fast.

At the end of the day, before bedtime, Desah, her sister Onráhdagǫ: and her friend Akenhnhà:ke make their way to find a good spot to sit on the shore of the great waters. The clear sky holds the moon and millions of stars that light their way. On the water, the moon reflects a stream of light that points directly at them, following them to their seat. They sit on the dry beach close to the last tide mark on the ground. The great water spreads out as far as the eye can see. They all take a deep breath. Desah is feeling very grateful for Mother Earth, the moon and the stars, the safe trip and her friends and family.

She knows that the following days will start and end the same way. The first group of canoes leave early to set up camp at the next site and prepare the evening feast. When the last group of loaded canoes arrive at the camp, they will be ready to eat. After the evening meal is done, the young men hang the dried meat high in the trees to avoid the natural predators. Some nights they dance, and the men sing. Later, everyone will crawl into their temporary shelters, except the men who take turns watching the fire, canoes, or toboggans for half the night and try to sleep during the day.

The following day the same thing: first canoes leave, while the last canoes tear down the site to return the area as they found it. Every day is the same and every day is arduous.

The girls head back up to the camp, wave at the firekeepers. Desah crawls into the shelter she is sharing with her aunt and Onráhdago:. Listening to the distant sounds of the night, she falls asleep.

Their family are the first to get up. In the half-dark morning they leave the shore in supply canoes. Desah takes her turn paddling. The wind picks up and she fights against the strong waves. Hasegá:do: sees she is having trouble, taps her shoulder and motions for her to stop and give him her paddle.

"When the waves calm, you can have your job back."

They do not calm before they land on the shores, and once the decision is made to wait, they begin the routine camp and food chores, preparing for the last canoes to land. The campsite gets louder and louder as the people arrive. Everyone circles around the food and fish, telling stories of their trip on the rough waters.

Hasegá:dǫ: says, "We were afraid that the last canoe would catch up to us when Desasǫ́dręh was paddling."

She laughs and says, "Yes. I was worried."

As an afterthought, she adds, "I am very grateful that I have strong brothers that do more than their share."

Her aunt proudly agrees with her.

Three days along the shores of the great water are uneventful, except the wind picks up and almost capsizes a couple of loaded canoes. The issue is remedied, and they carry on their way to the rivers where the different nations would take their own routes to their villages.

Gotsahniht says, "Before we separate from the Onondagas, Oneidas and Mohawks, the people will decide to camp with them for the night or travel on to their rivers back to their villages."

They decide that while everyone is still together, they dance and sing songs of gratitude to release the tension of the trip. They are grateful to do something different from the work they had to endure over the last few days. They burn tobacco to carry the thanksgiving speech, and gratitude for the bounty and a safe trip back home for everyone.

The next day, thunder is heard rolling in the distance, promising rain to slow down travel. Regardless of the threat of rain, the Onondaga, Oneida, and Mohawk take down their shelters. Their canoes set out along the shores of the great waters to the rivers that lead to their villages. They wave and holler last-minute promises to visit during the winter. The Cayugas decide to stay in their shelters and sit out the rain that has started to fall. Individuals visit relatives in each other's shelters to have a few laughs and tell a few stories before they retire.

Some time during the night, the rain stops. The next day canoes are turned upright, loaded, and they start up the waterway to their village.

After two days of travel on waterways and land, the Cayugas arrive at their village beside the great water. The typical sounds and smells of fire and food greet the tired travellers. The first canoe, including Hasegá:do̜: and Desas̜ǫ́dre̜h, search for familiar faces in the groups of families walking down to the bank to meet the canoes. Everyone hugs each other upon meeting and quickly ask too many questions at the same time.

"Who did you meet, did you make new friends,

what did you trade for my neck piece, did you find a future mate, Desasǫ́dręh?"

Desah wrinkles her nose in response, glancing sideways to her brother, who lets out an understanding laugh. He knows this is one question she dreads the most.

Pointing her chin towards her brother, and moving her hands to imitate his mouth, she says, "No men were near me. They were all sitting at the men's fire, listening to Hasegá:dǫ: talk and talk."

Their mother breaks up the conversation to remind everyone what they have to do. "We will hear about everything after we eat. Everyone is tired and hungry."

To the greeters standing around, the mothers say, "Help unload the canoes and sort the food. We will eat when the last group of canoes are unloaded. The travellers have time to wash up."

The able members, young and old, walk down the bank to help with the ladened canoes. They surround the canoes full of food and the goods that had been traded with the other villages. The baskets of medicines, seeds, dried meat, and nuts, along with the fruit, are taken to each of the longhouses. Desah notices the speed of unloading the canoes. Quickly, the fresh fish are on the fires for the evening feast. This will be the time for more stories to be told.

A large group gathers around Hasegá:dǫ: to retell his story of visiting the seventh generation, adding details of his fast and visions that he missed telling in his first story.

One of the other members at the fire asks, "Were there many representatives that had travelled to the trading and hunting grounds?"

Desah answers, "Eight fires," while holding up her fingers to demonstrate.

It is common for ten to fifteen representatives from each nation to keep a fire on the hunting grounds. The practice of hunting outside their villages in all directions is part of a well-known tradition to avoid overhunting.

Hasegá:dǫ: reported that the neutral grounds wampum ceremony was performed with the Anishnaabe present.

Haihǫnyánih adds, "Eight Anishnaabe were there to participate in the ceremony to exchange the Wampum. The meaning of the wampum was recited by the Hodinǫhsyǫ́:niʔ and repeated in the Anishnaabe language. The rest of the time, we hunted, danced, sang, and feasted together."

Before all the stories are finished, Desasǫ́dręh leaves the group and heads to the Wolf longhouse. Upon entering, her eyes begin to close. She sluggishly climbs the ladder to the upper level of the longhouse, slowly moving into her sleeping space she shares with her older sister. Onráhdagǫ: is awake when she gets there. They usually comb out each other's hair with their mother's comb. This time they use the comb made of quill and bone that Desah brought back from her trip. They reminisce about the hunting activities and laugh about Akenhnhà:ke bumping into the singers at one of the socials.

Deyawẹdǫh comes in and says, "I put baby to sleep and left him with his father. I want to visit the travelling sisters."

Her visit is welcome because they had missed her. They describe the people they met, territories and waters they crossed, and the scary canoe story on the mountain and on the trip along the shores of the great water.

Onráhdagǫ: recalls, "The trail was along the cliff of the mountain. One of the young fellows was more focussed on shifting the canoe comfortably around on his shoulders. He did not notice he was near the edge. He tripped and slipped, the canoe slid and could have pulled his partner with him over the edge. The partner was strong and quickly pushed the canoe forward and to the right, pulling the young fellow back on the path. Then, on the great water, the waves were too high and two canoes carrying the seeds and medicines almost tipped."

Onráhdagǫ: says, "After the canoe incidents, we landed early and made a fire for the night. The next day, the men separated the loads differently in the canoes."

Agreeing, Deyawẹdǫh adds, "I understand, to prevent losing all the same type of load in an overturned canoe. I am glad. What was the best part of the trip?"

That was an easy question for Desasǫ́dręh to answer, "Hearing about Hasegá:dǫ:'s visions or dreams during his fast. Have you had dreams during your fasts, Deyawę́dǫh?"

"No. I fasted once, one night. Then I was with baby and could not go again. I will some day."

Smirking a little, she asks, "Did you have visions and dreams during your fast last time, Desasǫ́dręh?"

Proudly, Desah says, "Yes. I dreamt of a little girl."

Deyawę́dǫh stiffly says, "Do not try to be like brother. You are making up stories to be important."

Desasǫ́dręh was surprised by her sister's words. "Yes, I saw a little girl on a raft in my vision."

Knowing she will not convince her sister her dream was real, she quits talking about the little girl. Instead, she answers the other questions people asked when they arrived on the shores.

"We met people from all directions. I made a new friend from the Mohawk territory, Akenhnhà:ke, or Oná'no is what Hasegá:dǫ: calls her. He teased her whenever they were together. I think she wants to be Hasegá:dǫ:'s friend more than mine."

The sisters smile and shake their heads, being aware of their brother's charm with the girls.

"We made lots of trades for baskets, and adornments for our necks, ears, coverings and combs," she says, holding up her new comb. "You will see the other items tomorrow when we lay them out."

Onráhdagǫ: says, "Beside the wide river, the Anishnaabe people visited to participate in the ceremony and trade the neutral ground wampum. The recital of the Great Law was heard over several days, and we ate and danced most nights. When the people were tired, we sat at the fires and heard stories from other lands."

Deyawę́dǫh changes the topic and asks, "Did you find a future mate, Desah?"

"Why do people ask me that? I would talk about it if I did. I do not want anyone there or here," she says in a huff.

She thinks of adding, 'I am more interested in visions and dreams of the future generations.' To avoid being scorned or being laughed at again, she stops talking and keeps the dream story to herself and her brother. He knows it to be true.

As her older sister gets up to leave them, she says, "You just wait, Desah. Some day you will want a mate. Enjoy your sleep, my sisters."

"I love you," the girls say in unison.

Desah does not agree or disagree with her older sister. She lays down next to Onráhdagǫ:, who is almost asleep, and her mind drifts to the little girl on the raft. In her mind she plans the next fast. 'I want to learn more about her and why she is so sad. Who is her mother, father, grandmother, grandfather, clan, and nation? Where does she sleep? Does she help the women of her village? What do they do? What is her name, why was she sad and alone on the water?'

Her sister interrupts her thoughts. "Keep still and cover up. I want to go to sleep."

Desah obeys, curling up against the warm back of her older sister. Onráhdagǫ: scolds her for trying to warm her feet on her legs. It sounds like their mother and father are settling into their sleeping space next to them. Hearing their father cooing to the baby, her sister turns her head towards Desah and raises her eyebrows. They both quietly giggle, shaking the hay mat they are sleeping on. Desasǫ́dręh soon falls asleep, smelling the leather and the sweet clover in the hay and listening to her parents' comforting sounds murmuring through the walls of the loft.

CHAPTER THREE – YEAR TWO –
TWO-NIGHTS' FAST

The next day, their mother places their sleepy baby under the skins with her sisters. Her name, Gajihsdǫdáha, means Evening Star, which sometimes is shortened to Jihsdǫ. As she curls up to her little sister in a soft leather bundle, she whispers, "Shhhh, we cannot wake Onráhdagǫ:."

Before their mother leaves the loft, she whispers, "Sleep as long as you want this morning."

With no protest, they go back to sleep until the sliver of sun is peeking between the crack in the logs. They hear grumblings of wet moss on baby's bottom, waking Desah for the second time this morning. At first thought of hearing Jihsdǫ's complaints, she hopes the moss is only wet.

Waking her older sister, she says, "Here, watch our sister."

Onráhdagǫ: keeps her eyes closed and blankly stretches her arms out for the baby. Instead of placing the baby in the arms of their sleepy sister, Desah gently lays Star next to her on the mat under the skins. Onráhdagǫ: puts her arms down and turns to curl up with her fussing sister.

"I will get the water warming near the fire for her bath."

She climbs down the ladder and out of the longhouse. Regardless of the blinding sun, she notices a couple of boys pushing and teasing each other near the fire. She worries they will get hurt fooling around, so she warns, "Watch now!"

Needing their help, she picks up hides and walks to the bowls of water near the fire, and says in a stern tone, "Help me."

Giving them a task away from the fire, she points to the bowls of lavender and cedar water that she needs help carrying to the longhouse.

The boys let go of each other, and at the same time answer, "Hao`."

Taking the hides from her, they pick up the hot, heavy bowls, carrying the splashing water behind Desah. They stop to allow their eyes to adjust to the dim light, before continuing a long walk to the fire where she stands. They gently set them down next to Desah. She tells them nyá:węh and gives them a grateful smile. They run off to collect more water to warm near the fire.

Onráhdagǫ: carries the baby down the ladder and lays her on the mat that Desah has prepared. Humming Star's favourite song, she bathes her and wraps her tight as a bundle.

Desah places her hand on her tiny chest. "Jihsdǫ,

you are such a special little heart."

Star makes a cooing sound in response and twists on her mat, trying to reach for the bowl of warm water.

Onráhdagǫ: says, "Lay still, my tiny sister, until our mother comes in to feed you."

As if Awę́hę? reads their minds, she comes in and sits next to her children, smiling as she thanks her daughters for helping. She hands them some bowls of mashed corn, honey, and berries. She picks up Star, and in seconds baby begins rooting around on her chest for her morning meal.

Onráhdagǫ: says, "Star has grown since we left."

Desah agrees. "I see that. She has grown sweeter, too."

Over the next few weeks, everyone in the village helps with harvesting and storage. The women begin preparing for winter and getting the skins ready to be hung on the walls of the longhouse. Summer is over and going by the weather fall is very close.

Desah has talked to some of the girls her age to see who is interested in the two-day fast. She has been preparing since the hunting trip and has encouraged them to do the same. The girls ask her when she expects to leave. She leaves them to find her mother.

Sitting by the family fire in the longhouse, her mother holds out a bowl of fruit and nuts to her as she approaches.

Looking seriously at her mother, she says, "On

last talk, I asked grandmother's approval to fast for two nights. Did she announce to the other grandmothers that I will be fasting before winter?"

"Desasǫ́dręh, talk to your grandmother."

With her bowl still in her hand, Desah rushes out to the side of the longhouse, where she hears the women talking and laughing. She finds her grandmother working on a fish basket under a huge shady tree.

Standing humbly in front of her grandmother, she says, "Grandmother, I want to begin preparing for two days, my next fasting trip."

"This late? The next trip happens after the harvest ceremony. Will you and the girls be ready to fit in the trip before winter? The ceremonies of gratitude should be your goals first."

"Yes. We will. I am excited for the fast as well."

As per protocol, her grandmother agrees, and says, "I will tell the other grandmothers your intention. An uncle will also be one of the firekeepers. We will find out who wants to make the trip. It usually happens at the same time the hunters go out."

In a little more serious tone she says, "You and your friends will travel together with the older brothers and sisters for a one-day walk and fast for two days. Do you agree, Desasǫ́dręh?"

Quickly, Desah smiles in agreement. She has been thinking about this day since the hunting trip.

"You will hear their answer in time. We will learn

who is going with you before you leave."

Only a few days pass when Desah approaches her mother and says, "Mother, did you hear if the grandmothers are going to approve our fast?"

"No. Keep busy until we hear. There must be enough girls in agreement to warrant the trip."

A couple of weeks go by, and Desah has gathered nine girls that have begun to prepare for two nights. Preparing early makes it hard for the girls to wait patiently for the elders' approval. The time goes by very slowly, when grandmothers ask for a meeting with the girls.

They wait for the confirmation question, then one by one they are asked, "Will you be ready to fast two nights, Desasǫ́dręh?"

"Yes, my grandmother, I am ready now."

"Will you be ready, Jiʔnhǫwę́:se:?"

"Yes, I am ready to prepare."

Her grandmother continues through the circle of eight girls with the formal question.

Then she explains, "There will be four men who will go for protection and to watch the fires, two during the sun and two for the night-time. Two women will be available to help and teach you to make something that the family can use."

Desah says, "Yes, last time we walked all morning."

Pointing to the lake beside their village, her grandmother says, "Correct. The last time you set up a camp by one of the falls in our territory. The next three times you camp, you will be set up in another nation's territory. The walk is long. We have agreements with the Seneca and the Onondaga Nations. They will know where you will camp to protect you and to avoid any interruptions in your activities."

Desah says, "My sister says we will make something. What do we do with the items that we make, because we will make too many to carry on our long walk home?"

Grandmother smiles at her ambitious grand-daughter. "I am sure you will not make too many items to carry once you see how far you walk. The teachers will tell you what to do."

They close the meeting and ask that the girls meet again closer to the trip.

After a couple of days, Desah asks Onráhdagǫ: to attend the regular girls' meeting.

Around the fire one night, Onráhdagǫ: asks the girls, "In preparation, did you add time between eating until you can go without food for two suns? Also, did you walk longer and longer every day? Have you gathered enough medicines? It is a long walk in the sun and through the woods and streams. Do you have something to carry enough water? Ask the lead teacher how much to take if you do not know. There will be water along the way and at the river near your camp. The other teacher could be my sister. We will take the tea and other supplies."

Ceremonies, gardens, gathering fruit and harvest go by faster than expected. Desah's grandmother approaches her the night before her trip.

"Sleep well tonight. You have a long walk tomorrow. No food for two days, starting in the morning of your walk and ending in the morning on the last day."

That night, Desah lays down on her side of the mat next to sister to avoid any scolding. It is hard to sleep. She is too anxious to learn more about the sad little girl on the raft.

The next day, their mother lays Star next to her. "Hug Jihsdǫ. You are leaving her again."

Squeezing her sister, Desah says against her cheek, "I am going away. Only two nights and two mornings this time. I love you."

The vibration on Jihsdǫ's cheek makes her giggle and squirm.

As usual, Desah and baby sister nuzzle until they are fully awake. Then she takes her down to bathe her. This time, Onráhdagǫ: is waiting with bath water by her mat. As Desah sings the baby song, she washes her head, eyes, ears, and the neck crease.

"You hide your neck, wee tiny one."

Onráhdagǫ: watches them for a while before she takes baby's soiled moss out to the field.

"I will find our mother so that you can get ready to leave. I am packed and have prepared for my two-nights' fast."

To Star, Desah says, "I will miss your bath time. Will you miss me?"

Instead of waiting for Onráhdagǫ: and her mother, she takes Star out of the longhouse. Both squinting in the bright sunlight at their exit, she finds her mother talking to some of the girls that are going on the fast.

"Are you going for a swim?" her mother asks.

She nods and kisses the baby, before she hands Star over to their mother.

In a short while, Desah comes up from the lake and hugs her mother. She looks across the village to see friends saying goodbye to their families as they leave to meet on the trail.

Her mother says, "Two men left in the early morning to set up your camp and fire."

Waving once, the remaining travellers line up on the trail west to the waterfalls. Everyone resembles tall turtles as they carry their bundles on their backs and skins full of water on their hips. The men carry slings, a hatchet, a bow and their arrows. The trees are still green enough to offer plenty of shade on their walk.

After many hours of walking, and two breaks, they can finally hear the steady splashing of water over the rocks.

One of the girls asks in a slightly whiney voice, "Are we close?"

Desah's uncle says, "We have to turn around; we passed it."

She begins her protest. "I am too tired to turn around. Can we set up camp here?"

Desah laughs, knowing that familiar twinkle in her uncle's eyes means he is teasing, and she says, "I do not think we passed it."

The group arrives at a camp site that has obviously been cleared recently for them by the two smiling men standing by the fire.

Looking around the small clearing, Desah asks, "When did you do this, uncle?"

Her uncle replies, "When you prepared, we prepared."

Desah rushes off to a large tree that has fallen. She plans to prop her branches against it. Two other friends claim their spots on each side of her, laying their bundles down.

Before the teachers pick their spots, they catch the girls' attention. "Silence. Wait."

The space is silent except for the sound of the water and the birds announcing the arrival of strangers to the area. One of the men places tobacco on the fire. He begins to point and express gratitude for the peaceful surroundings they share with nature, Mother Earth and her gifts, the young women that are present and the new faces to come.

As soon as he finishes the thanksgiving, Desah's sister Onráhdagǫ: motions to them and says to the girls, "Come here."

They look and follow her to the river. "We have until sunset to make our shelters. Find the appropriate size branches, and pine boughs for the tops of your shelters. You can sleep together or alone."

In a different direction, the men walk upriver to gather sticks and old logs for the all-night fire. One of the uncles goes to the river and fills clay pots of water for the camp. While the men are out of sight of the girls, they eat and plan who will stay awake to watch the camp and who will sleep.

Desah's aunt, Gotsahniht, eats as well. Onráhdagǫ: had decided before the trip she would fast along with two other girls, staying an extra two nights to complete their four days of fasting.

With their lean-tos finished, the girls rest under the bright stars glistening in the dark blue sky. Tired from walking and making their shelters, the girls retire early after their tea. In minutes, they fall asleep.

The faint chirping of the insects, along with the rumblings of the falls, fade into the background of Desah's reality. She falls asleep picturing the little girl on the pond. She does not understand why she knows the little girl has many older siblings and a younger sister. She just knows it.

In Desah's dream, she watches a busy little girl washing up in the morning time. Her father is outside getting water out of the ground. The little girl looks to be getting ready to go somewhere.

An old man, a stranger, comes out of one of the living areas into the kitchen where the little girl is washing. He looks around to see if anyone else is nearby. She smells his unwashed body and sour breath before he stands behind her, whispering in her ear. Desah cannot clearly understand the language but senses the fear and confusion of the little girl.

The little girl starts to cry, saying, "Don't," as she pushes away his old wrinkly freckled arm.

He keeps touching her. She cries and struggles free of his boney hands. Crying, frightened, and sickened, she gets away from him and runs up to another level in the shelter. She runs into a sleeping area. There, a boy close in age is awakened by her cries. Sobbing, she tells him what has happened. He comforts her shaking little body as an angry old man comes into the room. Her brother defends her, speaking angrily and calling the old man 'Dad'.

He must have learned of what had happened because the old man's, or Dad's, shoulders drop, and his jaw tightens. He turns and walks down to the lower level. Muffled angry voices are heard from below, fading in Desah's mind.

In another dream some time during the same night, Desah approaches an old shelter with two levels, one level where people eat their meals and another level where people sleep. There are children everywhere, some looking out the sides of the shelter and some running through the long grass that grows around it.

Upon entering a living space, she sees torn coverings on the sides where there are holes to let the sun in and keep the wind out. Hasegá:dǫ: had described the hard water-like material in his story. Where the two sides meet, a large dark thing stands smelling of ashes, pine, and another odor she does not recognize. She assumes that they use it to warm the shelter. Around the living space are thick mats, one long one and one short one used for sitting. A couple of old men are sitting, one of the men looks like an older version of Dad. The mats look to be used by the brothers for wrestling because they are tattered and worn. The two men appear to be looking at a black dream thing that Hasegá:dǫ: described in his vision.

In the kitchen, a woman sits, taking the skins off some ground roots. Desah thinks she is the family's mother. There is a pile of many ground roots on a flat wooden surface. Around the flat surface, there are smoothed wooden seats that she knows is used by the children. The noise of this space comes alive as the children run through leaving echoes of their laughter as they chase each other through and out of the shelter. Desah senses peace here but there is something the matter with the woman. Something has happened in her history that lives within her body. Desah feels there is sadness to come.

The woman hollers, "Sheyna, get a pot and wash these potatoes."

Sheyna comes down from the upper level to the kitchen to help her mother. The little girl's name is Sheyna. Desah recognises her spirit. She has grown since she saw her on the raft, and she has gotten older than when her brother defended her to Dad.

At another time during the night, Desah dreams that she hears the little girl Sheyna and her mother talking in their sleeping space on the upper level. Sheyna is lying on one mat. Her mother and little sister are lying on a bigger mat.

"Mum, where did you meet Dad?"

"I knew of him from around here," meaning their territory.

"Me and your auntie used to go to all the lacrosse games when we lived in St Catherines. Your dad played on one of the teams. One time, we were in line behind him going into the game. In those days, the wives got in free if their man played on a team. Just as he turned to give the free ticket to a white woman standing behind him, I walked up and snatched it out of their hands. Me and your auntie sat in the wives' box that day."

Sheyna laughs. "Holy, Mum. Who was the white woman? What did Dad do?"

"What could he do? I was using the ticket. He didn't know her. She was some woman in the line."

Her mum's serious face turns to a wistful smile, remembering that day.

"How come our older brother and sister don't live

with us?"

"When your brother was born, I was too young to care for him. Grandmother kept him so he could help her around the house while Grampa was in the army. We were poor. To help with bills, I had to work as a housekeeper for a family who owned a cherry farm. Your sister's father was rich. His family owned the farm. He had a nice car and a big house. He asked me to marry him when I was pregnant with her, but I said no."

Sheyna looks around the bedroom with three beds, board floors, no screens on the windows, and no paint on the walls. "Gee, Mum. How come you didn't marry him? You could have a nice house with nice furniture."

After a moment, she says, "I don't know. I guess because you wouldn't be born."

Desah feels the connection strengthen and love for her mother by the joy that shows in the little girl's face. She also senses something is wrong with the mother and wishes she could warn Sheyna. The spirits tell Desah that they are going to take that lump out of her mother's body. Desasǫ́dręh visits the structure where they keep the bodies of the people that have passed on. She does not see her mother there. She sees her mother in the place where they take sick people.

The next day at the morning meal, Sheyna says, "Mum, I had a dream about you last night."

Her mother stops what she's doing and says,

"You did? What happened?"

Sheyna answers, "You are lying on a metal table in the funeral home. I see your back and watch you get off the table wearing a hospital gown."

In a sigh of relief, her mum responds, "Oh, good. I must be surviving the operation."

When Desah wakes the next day, she thinks back to the dream. She wonders who told Sheyna her mother the good news that her mother is well now. The spirits that her aunt told her about had to have warned Sheyna. 'I wonder why I see Sheyna crying in the upper level of their shelter with an older brother crying and comforting her. This feeling must be the sadness I sense around her mother.'

The smell of smoke and the sound of the water resounding close by reminds Desah where she is and why she is here. She listens for other noises outside her shelter to let her know if there is anyone else awake.

Regrettably, she crawls out of her warm skins and then out of the shelter to find the other girls are also crawling out of their shelters, except Ji'nhǫwé:se:.

"Wake up, Ji'nhǫ. We are ready for the day."

Desah's spirit is low this morning, and the sadness from the dream lingers within her. She wonders why she feels this way. She walks over to sit on a rock that barely pokes out of the ground near the fire. The women are not in the camp. The other girls are huddled around the fire.

"Sgé:nǫ?," greetings are exchanged with the two men tending to the ashes.

"Sgé:nǫ? geh (pronounced skano gayh)?" Ji?nhǫ asks.

Uncle says, "Yes. We just woke up. The night firekeepers left to get some sleep."

The other man says, "The women walked down to the river this morning and said to send you down there when you wake up."

One by one, the girls wander down to the waterfalls to wash up for the day. Ji?nhǫwé:se:, last to catch up to them, finds an opportunity to push Desah into the water. Desah sees her out of the corner of her eye and moves away, allowing her friend Ji?nhǫ to slip by her, splashing into the cold water. All the girls laugh as they run into the water, splashing each other awake.

Cold and wet, the girls find the best spots to sit in the sun. Once they are semi-dry, they pull on their outer coverings and sit until they are fully dry before they walk back to the camp.

"Now what do we do?" asks one of the shivering girls.

Ji?nhǫ says, "On my way down, one of the women said to go back to the fire when we are finished. We have work to do."

The girls follow the winding path up to the camp, carefully holding the branches for the girl behind them. At the camp, the women stop talking and laughing with the uncles.

Gotsahniht, Desah's aunt, stands up, pointing to a pile of baskets. "Everyone grab one. We're going to find some reeds to make something to sleep on tonight."

Each girl grabs a basket and follows the older girls into the woods. They come upon a pond surrounded by bushes and greenery. They see wide, partially green reeds sticking proudly out of the marsh.

Gotsahniht, the lead teacher, says, "These will be good for what you are making."

A couple of girls try to snap the green reeds with their bare hands.

She holds up the two rocks she has and says, "It will help to find a flat thin rock and ask the men for something sharp to cut the reeds. Five go to the river to find flat rocks and the others go to the camp to ask the men for something sharp."

Without answering, five girls turn around and walk back to the waterfalls where they had bathed. They step slowly into the water that feels like it has not warmed up since morning to search for a flat stone as instructed. At the camp, the other girls gather enough sharp tools for everyone. They all wait at the marsh for the others to finish choosing the appropriate-size stones. Onráhdagǫ: bends the reeds across the flat stone and strikes them with the sharp stone. The girls find it a lot easier method of cutting them than trying to snap the rubbery reeds with their hands. They each bundle handfuls of reeds until the women say they have enough for their sleeping mats.

In the camp, the women lay out the reeds, sorting the various lengths in front of them. They begin weaving them over and under, over and under. The girls do the same, tightening the space between the reeds as they weave. Jiʔnhǫ looks at the other girls and begins to weave faster. The race is on to see who can finish their project first, occasionally glancing at their teachers' examples.

Onráhdagǫ: looks around at the girls, initiating a conversation. "How did you sleep? Do any of you have dreams to share?"

One of the girls says quietly, "I dreamt of a song last time. I did not hear it last night."

Gotsahniht says, "What is it about? Do you want to sing it for us?"

She hesitates, before she closes her eyes and sings as much of the song as she can remember. The men quietly move to the fire to hear the song better. Everyone is impressed, complimenting her on her singing.

"Do you know who brought you the song?"

"I think it was grandfather. I miss him," she says sadly.

Jiʔnhǫ says, "Share your charming song with the village."

Looking down at her lap shyly, the girl quietly

says, "I sing to my little niece. I am afraid to sing for many people."

Desah says, "I can picture your grandfather on the river singing the song. He sounds lonesome for his home."

After some silence, Gotsahniht says, "Nyá:węh for the song. Talk to me before you go to sleep. We will look at ways to get more words for your song while you sleep."

As each of the girls tell how they slept and talk about their dreams, they discuss the possible meanings. Desah is glad they do not notice her silence. She is not ready to tell anyone about the little girl after her sister Deyawędǫh accused her of copying her brother. She will confide in her grandmother when she knows more about Sheyna. When her mother has time, she will talk to her as well.

While they work, Jiʔnhǫ asks Desasǫ́dręh about the songs and dances they had on the hunting trip.

"You mentioned that you feasted and danced some nights."

Desah says, "Yes, many people attended the dances after the feast. Usually, the women danced. Some men sang and a few men danced. They were too tired from walking and hunting all day. A friend from the east wanted to learn our songs. Her name is Akenhnhà:ke. Hasegá:dǫ: called her Onáʔno."

Jiʔnhǫ laughs and asks, "Hasegá:dǫ: called her Cold to Touch? Was she cold towards him?"

"No. He teased her. We had many laughs teaching our dances to her and her Anishnaabe friend. Do you remember how the singers, men, and young men sit on two logs facing each other, keeping time with drums and turtle or buffalo horn rattles? At the hunting camp, in the centre of the clearing, there were two old narrow logs that had been smoothed for seats that the men sat on facing each other."

Smiling, she nods, imagining the men and boys lining the logs, holding their drums and singing.

Desah gets up to demonstrate the dance. "For the 'Shake the bush' dance, I asked my new friend to be my partner. You know the dance where two people take turns dancing backwards, kicking forward, and two people facing them dance forward, kicking forward. The people look like they are kicking each other and sometimes they do. Hasegá:dǫ: and his friend Hadahnyo came out to face us and partnering on the dance. I was the outside partner, and Akenhnhà:ke on the inside, the same side as the singers. We were dancing backwards and watching that we did not kick my brother and his friend. We could not see where we were going. Almost every round, she would be too close to the logs and bump into the first singer closest to the dancers. I think our partners steered us toward the singer so that she would bump into him. To avoid bumping into him again on the next round, we tried to watch where we were going behind us. We laughed when Oná'no, no,

Akenhnhà:ke, pointed out the singer we were bumping into had moved to the other end of the log and another singer was in his place."

After the girls finish laughing at the image of bumping into the unfortunate singers, Ji'nhǫ's face changes. "Does Hasegá:dǫ: admire your friend?"

"You know he likes everyone," she says, smiling and pointing her chin towards her friend.

Ji'nhǫ's cheeks turn red as she smiles and quickly looks down, pretending to focus on her project.

Desah knows her friend would like her brother for herself.

To reassure her, she says, "I do not want Hasegá:dǫ: to admire Akenhnhà:ke for a forever mate. He is not ready. Being her mate would mean he would move far away to our territory to live. I cannot lose him. No. We cannot lose him."

Ji'nhǫ looks satisfied with her answer. They continue with their work.

Once the mats are the right size, the girls begin to tuck in and braid the edges to prevent unravelling during use. One of the girls asks if they can make two for a better sleep.

Smiling, Ji'nhǫwę́:se: says, "I want to make one for my little sister."

Desah agrees with her, remembering the hunting trip and bathing her friend's sister. Mats made from reeds mean less animals killed, and they would be lighter to carry instead of more skins.

Abruptly, the older woman interrupts. "You can make more mats when you get back home. First, we will gather clay to take back to the village. Remember the long walk carrying everything you brought, what you make and the baskets of clay."

Desah asks, "Can we make more mats after we collect clay?"

Gotsahniht says, "We will see."

The girls follow the women to the creek that feeds the river where they bathe. Gotsahniht searches the sides for dense red clay. She points to the area and looks at Onráhdagǫ: to begin.

"This is the type of mud we will carry back to the village." Onráhdagǫ: smiles and shows a handful of red clay. "The mud is very dense."

The girls do as they are told, collecting their own piles and placing them in their baskets.

While they fill their basket, one of the girls asks, "What was it like on the hunting trip, Desah?"

Desah begins retelling Hasegá:dǫ:'s dream, and the things he described. She is about to retell her story about bumping into the singer when one of the girls breaks up her assessment of the trip to complain. She looks to the older woman for an answer.

"This mud is too heavy. How are we carrying this on the long walk to the village? The walk is mid-morning to near sunset."

Everyone turns to look at her basket that she cannot pick up.

Onráhdagǫ: smiles in response and ties her basket over one shoulder. "In our baskets. Take only what you can carry back to the camp. Night-time comes early and the sun leaves sooner."

The girls stop piling the clay into their baskets, testing to see if they can carry it on their backs, throwing some back into the creek. When everyone is satisfied, they wash their hands and feet as best they can, before they insert their feet into their moccasins.

When they return to the camp, the teachers sit their baskets down by four bowls of water that the men have gathered. One woman points out two girls to do the same while the others watch. They begin massaging the clay and adding water until the mud is the right consistency to work with. She divides her ball in half, giving one half to Onráhdagǫ:, and places the other ball into a clay bowl. With her thumb, she presses a hole into the top of the ball, ensuring it does not crack. She reaches into the water, cupping enough to keep her project manageable. Slowly, she presses out the insides with her thumbs and fingers, stretching the clay, cupping water on it and forming the mud into the shape of a pot or bowl. The other girl does the same.

Onráhdagǫ: takes the clay handed her and flattens it in a thin round shape, constantly adding water to keep it from drying out. She divides her ball of clay into quarters, rolling each quarter into thick oblong coils. She folds up the edges of the flat round piece of clay, placing it inside the first coil. She smooths the seams with water. Then she lays the remaining coils on top of each other in a circle. While she does that, she keeps adding water and smoothing the creases to seal the coils. The girl beside her does the same.

The women and girls constantly rub the water along the sides, stretching and smoothing their clay. When they are satisfied, they take their projects to the clearing to bake in the sun. While the teachers and the girls look for a spot for their bowls to get the most sun, four more girls do the same process with their clay, until all the girls have bowls. Their projects are all different sizes, thicknesses, and shapes. As the girls proudly place their projects in the sun, the other girls and women admire each other's work.

Onráhdagǫ: says, "Tonight we will have a good sleep and tomorrow we will have food and water, clean the camp, pack our bundles, and prepare for the walk home to the village. We may get back in the dark. Hope for clear skies."

All day, the women have been sipping their water and medicines. Sitting around the fire, they talk about their experiences of sporadically fasting in preparation for these days.

Onráhdagǫ: and Desasǫ́dręh talk about the hunting trip, the feasts, the dancing, walking and canoeing for days and the hard work. Soon, the moon shines down on their camp.

One of the girls says, "I have been so busy with

my work today, I forgot about eating."

All the girls let out a groan in unison.

One says, "Why did you mention that?"

When the girls quit laughing, Gotsahniht tells them to go to their shelters for a long sleep. "Tomorrow, we will clean up and have nourishment before we leave this peaceful place."

As Desah heads for her shelter, she says, "It is the second night already. It is too soon to leave." She lies down on her new mat, covers herself with her skin to keep off the slight chill in the air. She is surprised how tired she is from the day's activities and is soon lulled by the steady hum of the waterfall. As the darkness fades in her awareness, Desasǫdręh hears Sheyna crying in the upper level of their shelter. An older brother is holding her, his chin shakes, his eyes fill with tears that will not fall. They are unaware of the sounds of the many people in the lower level of the shelter. Desah's being fills with an overwhelming sadness at the sight. Her own chest aches from the heart space.

Tears fill their eyes to overflowing and down their faces. Sheyna cries on her brother's shoulder; no words are spoken. The silence of their space is broken when Sheyna hears a little one's voice behind her. She turns to see their four-year-old niece standing on the stairs.

She asks, "Where is grandma?"

Sheyna quickly turns back to her brother for an

answer. She is not prepared to answer this question from the grand-daughter who calls her mother, 'the soft Grandma'. When no one answers, the little girl says, "Did she go to the moon?"

The brother chuckles and says, "She's gone. I don't think she's gone to the moon."

Desah hears the people on the lower level saying, "They are too young to lose their mother, and there are so many of them. What will happen to the young girls, Sheyna and Lindy? I cannot imagine their lives without their mum. I know I couldn't bear it."

It seems like time has passed when Desah's spirit feels their father's despair. He is doing his best in his new role as both mother and father. She observes Sheyna and her sister visiting with one of the aunts or the older siblings while their father is away enjoying the drink that Hasegá:dǫ: describes as 'boiling like a sour spring'.

Desah watches as Sheyna is taking care of the children of her older siblings or as she gets into trouble in a large village away from their home. There is a boy around Sheyna that Desah wishes she could warn her about. Desah's spirit knows that Sheyna is powerless and grieving the loss of her mother, and the life before her mother passed. She sees the changes Sheyna is making in her life: new friends, drinking the sour springs and quitting going to the Longhouse where she got her name, Desasǫ́dręh.

Desah sees Sheyna in a huge structure, standing

in a line with other young people. They are the 'new people' that Hasegá:dǫ: talked about. Standing in front of Sheyna is a strange man that looks like he has a nest on his head. His hair is curly and grows only around the sides. His head has no hair on the top.

The man is angrily speaking to Sheyna, saying, "What are you going to do, *re* school?"

Sheyna looks at him, puzzled. "What?"

The young people turn and stare at the scene as the man's voice gets louder with every word as he repeats his question.

Sheyna's face turns red, and her jaw tightens as she finally realises what he means, and she says, "Nothing."

Without another word, she drops what she has in her hands and walks out of the place, shaking with anger and embarrassment. Desah feels what Sheyna feels: that this action is a mistake. She cannot turn around and change it. Sheyna has not been happy since her mother passed, reducing her sense of security forever.

The sad little girl on the raft flashes in Desah's memory. She vows to help this Desasǫ́dręh to reach the path she is meant to travel.

The next morning, Desah opens her eyes to a cloudy day and the smell of cornmeal and honey. In the next shelter she hears Jiʔnhǫ exclaim as a question, "We get to eat today?"

The girls rush out of their shelters.

Onráhdagǫ: says, "They are coming out of their shelters and going to the water faster this morning than they did last sunrise."

When the girls walk back up from the river bath, Gotsahniht says, "Do you have your bowls ready?"

Two girls are in line to fill their bowls with the food while the others upturn their bundles, digging for theirs.

Jiʔnhǫ notices the images on Desah's bowl. "Who made your bowl, Desah? It is very nice."

"Deyawę́dǫh when I was a baby. See, here is my mark."

Desah shows the girls the drawing her older sister had scratched into the sides. It is two circles overlapping each other.

The girls enjoy their meals, savouring every mouthful. One of the men stands and begins speaking the words of gratitude as he places tobacco on the fire. As soon as he finishes, the girls run to collect their new mats, clay pots and bowls to pack in their bundles.

Onráhdagǫ:, four young women and two men are staying to finish a four-day fast. The other girls who only stayed two nights begin their trek with two male chaperones and her aunt. They should arrive before dark if they take less breaks. In a very happy mood, the girls look forward to seeing their families, their clan, their longhouses, and the familiar surroundings of their village.

CHAPTER FOUR – YEAR THREE – THREE NIGHTS' FAST

Arriving home way before sunset, Desah is greeted by family. They walk together to the Longhouse of the Wolf clan to see if she feels like talking about her experiences. They sit on the shady side of the longhouse, where baby sister is playing with her two-year-old niece. Desah unravels her bundles to show the projects they made. She does not have much of an appetite, but she takes the food handed to her. She sits beside her baby sister on her soft leather.

In a tender voice, she says, "Look, little heart. See the bowl I made for you."

Her sister's chubby little hand touches the side of the bowl. Desah says, "I agree. I should have scratched some images there. On my travels I stopped at a wonderful waterfall. I can still hear the water rushing down the mountain to fill the river where we swam every day. I will scratch the image of the falls and a star for your name."

Mother asks, "How are you doing, Desasǫdręh? You are not eating much."

"I am good. Time will go slow waiting to go on

the next fast."

Mother and grandmother smile at each other.

"Good, you are not discouraged from this trip."

"No. I am excited."

Getting through winter, spring, and maintaining the summer gardens speed by quickly for Desah and her friends. The group is in a different mood, more confident than last time. They know what will happen. They set off to the waterfalls after practising their fasting over four moons, adding more hours until they can last three days without eating. Desah learns that Hasegá:dǫ: and his friend Hadahnyo are the firekeepers and had left a day earlier to set up camp. Desah is thrilled about the prospect of discussing her visions with her brother.

Ji²nhǫ catches Desah coming out of the longhouse. "Do you have everything?"

Laughingly agreeing, Desah says, "We look like turtles again."

They turn to see two women standing with the girls at the beginning of the trail, waving at them to hurry. Two men disappear into the woods, with the two teachers and girls following.

Desah looks at Ji²nhǫ, saying, "Hurry. Run, we are late. They will leave us behind."

The two girls dash off with their bundles swinging on their backs.

When they catch up with their group, Desah says to Ji²nhǫ, "This could be our last trip together. You could find a mate and have to stay behind next time."

Smiling after Desah's comment, Jiʔnhǫ says, "This could be true. Last fast, I dreamt that I was standing on a hill among many trees, looking across a wide body of water at a village on the other shore. Many trees surrounded the village. I could see their tall shelters made of skins with smoke being released through the tops," she says, showing the shape of a teepee and a point where the smoke is released.

She continues, "The people are not Hodinǫhsyǫ́:niʔ. The men wear their dark hair tied in braids on both sides of their head. I can see me at the entrance of one of those shelters. I am with baby."

Desah's mouth drops open. "Who is your man?"

"I do not know this from my dream because I see him from his back. He is tall and has broad shoulders. This fast I hope to see Hasegá:dǫ: in my vision."

Desah smiles. "You will see him in real life. He is one of the firekeepers on this trip."

Jiʔnhǫ lets out a little squeal and clasps her mouth. "How will I be able to go to sleep with him so close?"

Desah laughs. "You will be able to sleep. We have eaten very little food since the evening feast and taking all day to walk to the waterfall and then the work to build our shelters."

"Maybe I will not see him. I will think of my vision last time and make myself sleep."

"Yes, you will sleep well. Listen."

Both stop to listen to the sound of crackling twigs

and dry leaves.

Desah gives her observation. "This group would not make good hunters."

After six hours of walking, there is moisture in the air and the faint thunder of the waterfall is heard in the distance, which means they are approaching their camp.

Ji'nhǫ cheers up. "I can hear the waterfall."

Desah places her hands on her face and her chest and says, "I can feel it."

Finally arriving at the camp, they know the ritual of claiming their spots for their shelters by laying down their bundles. The two guys that had arrived earlier have already cleared the area and made their shelters. They hand hatchets to the girls to begin constructing their lean-tos. Desah and Ji'nhǫ see that this time they cannot get their same spots next to the log.

Desah says, "Nyá:węh, Hasegá:dǫ:, for making my shelter for me."

Smiling, her brother says, "No, that's mine."

Changing her focus and pointing to other spaces in the opposite side of his shelter, he asks, "Did you see we cut away the brush for your shelters?"

There was no answer necessary. The girls went about the tasks of making shelters and gathering reeds and making mats, taking the rest of the afternoon. The girls take a break around the fire, talking about their dreams during their last fasts. The firekeepers and the teachers are planning the programme for the next three days.

It is night-time when one of the women says, "How is everyone doing? Is there anything anyone needs before we go to our shelters?"

Since the tired girls are silent, she adds, "Hao`. Enjoy your rest. Tomorrow, you can tell us your dreams and discuss the meanings. When you want to tell us, it is not a rule."

The girls begin making their way into their shelters, tired from the walk and the work.

Ji'nhǫ and Desah say good night to Hasegá:dǫ:.

"Do not fall asleep, brother."

He returns the smile and says, "I had a sleep already. Go to sleep."

With sweetgrass by her head, Desasǫ́dręh's last thoughts are, 'I wonder about the little girl's life before the sickness takes her mother's body. I remember Sheyna hating the times her parents and siblings drink the sour springs.'

Desah wonders why Sheyna is sneaking down to the lower level. She watches as her parents get ready to leave. Before they are finished getting ready, she runs to the thing they call a car and hides in the back of it. Desah watches as her parents get in. They direct it down the well-worn path. After a while, Sheyna pops up and says, "Where are we going?"

Her mother abruptly stops it, dust flies in the windows and the dream fades as they take her back to their shelter.

There are other times Desah sees Sheyna running behind the thing they call a car, screaming and crying for her parents. One of the older brothers, the one that is as pretty as a woman, runs out and drags her back to the shelter, scolding her for chasing them...

At another time during the night, Desah approaches the shelter where Sheyna's family lives with the youngest siblings. Winter cold keeps the family confined to one small space on the lower level. There are large coverings on the entrances to hold in the warmth coming from a small black thing that holds fire and controls smoke.

Five boys are wrestling, when Sheyna's mother scolds, "Watch now, you boys. Someone will get burnt on the stove. There is no room in here to be wrestling. Go outside and milk the cow."

Four boys quickly don their outer coverings and run out the door. The oldest son who is visiting, remains sitting on the long black mat, watching the dream thing.

The mother asks, "What are you doing in here? Why didn't you go out with the boys to milk the cow?"

He says, "The cow has only four tits."

Whatever he means, the mother laughs and lightly swats the back of his head. While he scrambles out the door, the father is hiding his laughter behind a thin white thing that is shaking in his hands.

The mother returns to making the bread. "I see you laughing behind the newspaper."

Desah feels comfort and security within this space.

Her mind moves into another part of Sheyna's young life. She watches the two little sisters in a shelter in the upper level. Sheyna's little sister of five winters, Lindy, is helping her take care of two crying little babies that are the same size. There is no one else in the shelter except the four of them. Although they seem to be managing, Desah feels their frustration.

"Bounce the baby on the bed, Lindy. Maybe that will help put him to sleep. I will change this little girl. Maybe that's why she's crying."

Lindy bounces her little body on the mat, trying her best to move it, but she is too light to make a difference. Sheyna changes the wrap on the little girl. The baby begins screaming louder. Just in case, Sheyna checks the wrap to see if she did something wrong.

"Oh, no. What did I do?" Sheyna hurries to unfasten the wrap from the baby's hip. She cries while she hugs and rocks the baby, trying to console her. She refastens the wrap and lays the baby girl on the thick mat next to her little sister and the cranky baby boy. The girls' little faces are red, and their hair is wet from sweat as they both bounce the crying babies on the mats. There is no air blowing into their space from the holes in their shelter.

Finally, the mothers arrive home. Seeing the sweaty scene, they pick up their babies and laugh until her sister-in-law, Joyce, asks, "Why are they crying?"

Sheyna cries in frustration, "I don't know. We changed them and they won't take their bottles."

"Where's mum?" asks the worried little Lindy.

Looking around her baby boy, Marlene says, "They were in a bad car crash, and are in the hospital. We will stay here until they come home."

Sheyna is too tired to ask questions. She just wants to sleep. Marlene tells them that Mum is in worse shape than Dad, while giving her attention to her baby. As the sister describes the accident, Desah can see flashing lights and hears their mother moan. She is pinned inside that thing. She cannot breathe. The father is sitting in the grass. He calls out for his wife, but someone holds him down because his leg is straight out from his hip.

An officer says in an authoritative but comforting tone, "Don't move, sir. You might make things worse. Your wife is okay. The men are working to get her out of the car. There is another ambulance on its way."

The vision, the sounds and the scent surrounding Sheyna's parents fade in Desah's mind. Her dreams move her from one event to the next.

She sees Sheyna at thirteen or fourteen winters,

standing in a seat basket high in the sky. Down below there are many people, tents, and she smells food cooking. Sheyna's friends are with her. The boy is grabbing her arm and telling her to sit down. The people on the ground are looking up at Sheyna, shaking their heads.

Desah's heart is racing when she is awakened by the sun peeking through the leaves of the trees and cracks between the pine boughs of her shelter. Desah does not understand what she sees in her dream. 'What was that huge thing she was standing in? I will ask brother.'

She crawls out to find that Ji²nhǫ is also crawling out of her shelter. Pointing to her roof, Desah says, "I would be wet if it rained last night."

Ji²nhǫ laughs and suggests adding the boughs from her shelter to her roof and they can sleep together. Desah did not hear the whole suggestion because she was already scrambling over branches and twigs towards the waterfalls. She can never get enough of this place of beauty, soothing sounds, and the smell of the water, plants, and trees. She wades in with a handful of lavender and flowers in her hands. Wetting the plants, she rubs the juice through her glistening dark hair, then along her arms and legs. She stands to watch bits of the flower petals swirl down the river.

To the Creator, she says, "Nyá:węh."

The girls trade places so that Ji²nhǫ can wash the

night sweat off. From the water, Ji²nhǫ asks, "Did you dream of the little girl last night?"

"Yes. I cannot believe she is the same girl I had seen at any of the times during the other fasts. She has grown. It seems I am watching her past and future at the same time. I am confused right now."

Ji²nhǫ says, "I wish I could dream like you. You smell and see in another time."

"You told me you see another time and that you are pregnant by my brother."

Ji²nhǫ gasps and giggles, shrinking her head into her shoulders as if to hide while she looks to see who is around that can hear Desah blurt out her secret.

She says in a lower voice than Desah used, "No. I am with someone and about to have a baby. I did not see Hasegá:dǫ:. I was teasing you when I said his name to see if you like the match."

Desah says, "I always like the match of friendship. I am not sure about the children and Hasegá:dǫ:. Both of you are too young. We have many things to learn before that happens."

Ji²nhǫ looks disappointed with her friend's response.

The girls quit talking about Ji²nhǫ's love life when they hear, 'Come here' from the top of the hill. Now they are dry, they scramble up the hill. They find all the girls lined up in front of the teachers.

Teacher says, "We are going to make moccasins. By summer, you can give your used moccasins to the younger ones. The men brought skins of deer and rabbit, sharp tools to cut and make holes for the sinew. Gather a flat rock and a heavy rock for hitting the sharp tools. Lay the skin on the flat rock and cut the leather along the marks."

After the description, the girls go to the river to find their tools, returning to watch the women demonstrate the process for making moccasins. Using cold wood ash, the women trace their feet on the best spot of the inside of the rabbit skin. The girls take the coal and trace their feet.

As the hours go by, the girls work diligently, concentrating on their projects, taking breaks to ease muscles they did not know they had. One of the women gets up to make teas for everyone. Desah is disappointed her brother, the night firekeeper, is missing. She wants to talk to him about her dream.

While the girls share their dreams, one says she heard a voice or someone singing when she was at the falls this morning. The two women smile at each other.

"You are correct. The old people say a young woman loved the falls so much she dived in and never came out. The story is that the girl continues to sing near the falls."

Nightfall comes quickly, making it too dark to continue with the winter moccasins. Most of the girls have finished the inner rabbit-fur lining.

Onráhdagǫ: says, "We have the next two days to

finish the deer skin for the outside."

Although the girls' backs and hands are tired and sore, they clean their areas and take their half-finished projects to their shelters.

At their shelters, Ji?nhǫ's shoulders drop. "We did not combine our shelters."

Desah, anxious to get to her vision, says, "We can do that tomorrow. I am sleepy."

Desah crawls in, dragging her bundle behind her. She places the sweet grass by her head, curls up under her skin to prepare for the second night. Her thoughts transfer into a deep sleep, searching for Sheyna. She approaches an old stone house on a hill overlooking a river. Sheyna and her little sister huddle in bed with three little children. Sheyna shivers, getting out of the bed to warm a bottle for the baby. She puts the bottle in the baby's mouth. He turns his head away from the bottle and continues to cry.

"Taste this, Lindy, to see if the milk is sour."

"No. You taste it. I am cold. Maybe he is cold, too."

Sheyna laughs, but she looks worried. "I don't know how to make a fire. Vinny is too little to be in this cold house."

Her sister says, "I am hungry, too."

"We don't have any more bread to eat. We have cereal, but we don't have milk."

"We don't have cereal left; the girls ate it last night for supper."

Sheyna makes a twelve-year-old decision. "Put the girls' coats and boots on them. I will get Vinny ready. Let's walk home. We can't stay here again tonight. It might be too cold and we don't have food left."

Sheyna bundles the baby, and says, "I will take a diaper," that she puts in her covering. She looks around, "I will take his bottle." She picks up her heavy little baby, holding him tight to her chest. She turns to see if the girls are behind her. The little sister who looks like she has seen seven winters holds the hands of the two little girls who look to be three and four winters. The young group set off, walking down the hill to a well-worn path. They are almost to the top of the hill when the thing that breathes smoke comes over.

Just as Desah worries about the littlest girl who is far behind the group, Sheyna turns to see the smallest girl is by herself on the side of the road.

She yells, almost crying, "Tauni, get off the road!"

Lindy leaves the one she has with Sheyna and runs back to get the little girl. Sheyna is crying now with a little girl hanging on her leg; she stands in front of the people to keep it from hitting them.

Gravel crunches as the car rolls to a stop alongside Sheyna. Smiling, an elderly couple calmly ask, "Where are you kids going?"

Sheyna turns towards them, rubbing her face on

the baby's wrap to wipe away the tears, and says, "We're walking home to Bert and Trude's place."

"That's too far for the babies. Get in. We will give you a ride there."

Sheyna hesitates, before she hands the baby over to the woman and nudges the little girls to climb in. She holds Tauni on her lap, hugging her until she stops shaking. They go past the old stone house and down the worn path beside the river, when Desah is awakened during the night, her heart thudding in her chest. It is still dark outside her shelter. Hearing her brother whispering and his comforting laugh lulls her back to sleep and into another scene.

She returns to Sheyna's generation, noticing she has been through fourteen winters. She, her older sister, Marlene, oldest brother, Dean, and her little sister, Lindy, are visiting their mother where they take the sick people. She feels Sheyna's spiritual connection to her mother: both are worried, lonesome, and confused. Her mother has purple marks on both arms.

Pointing to his wrist, Dean asks, "Where did you get the bruises?"

The mother looks at the object on her wrist and says, "It's half past two."

The siblings laugh, except for the little sister. Desasódreh does not see the mother walking away from the sick place this time.

The next day, Desasódreh awakes to an overcast

sky. As the girls go to the water to wash themselves, Jiʔnhǫ notices Desah's mood has changed since the last night.

"What is the matter, Desah? You look unhappy today."

"It is my dreams. Sheyna has lost her mother."

"That is awful. Is she young or old?"

"Does it matter whether a person is old or young when they lose a mother? In my dream everyone is sad, and I feel Sheyna's emptiness and confusion like I lost my own mother."

"I cannot think about losing my mother. Does she have a father?"

Sheyna looks off at the falls; slowly she answers, "Yes. He is very sad, too."

"Talk to the women to see if they can help you with your sadness."

With an agreeing nod, she says, "I could. I want to talk to grandmother."

Rain threatens their work. They continue. Throughout the day, the women and girls are talking and laughing while they work, except Desah.

Her sister, Onráhdagǫ:, takes her aside. "Have a break. Walk with me to the river."

When they are alone, she says, "What is it, Desasǫ́dręh?"

Without hesitation, Desah cries, "I cannot forget the image of my little girl's family. Her siblings and her father are sad and alone with their feelings. I fear my sad little girl is on a dark path without her mother's guidance."

Onráhdagǫ: lets her cry for a while, then says in a comforting tone, "I see your saddness. Try to remember you see Sheyna's life, not yours. We can talk more about it when you want. Are you ready to finish your big moccasins? You cannot walk with one side."

Desah smiles at her sister's attempt at humour. She dries her eyes. When she is ready, they return to find that most of the girls are almost finished; at least, one of their decorated boots is lined with rabbit fur. Each of the girls slip on one and model it for the others to admire.

Two of the girls have prepared tea for the others. Hasegá:dǫ: joins the women to have tea. He sits down, squeezing into the small space between Desasǫ́dręh and her friend, Jiˀnhǫwę́:se:.

Moving over, Desah groans under the weight of his hand, and says, "There is no room here."

Not moving, Jiˀnhǫ laughs, "Hasegá:dǫ:, what are you doing? There is space over there for you to sit."

"I feel like the flower between two thorn bushes."

His comment earns him a couple of elbows on each side from both girls. The other girls laugh.

"I will finish my tea and watch the fire all night."

"Yes, you do." Desah teasingly adds, "You woke me during the night with your whispering and laughing."

"I did? How did you hear me over the sound of the waterfall, coyotes, owls, and Ji?nhǫ making that noise we hear all night?"

He makes a snoring noise, earning another elbow from Ji?nhǫ.

Desah continues, "I did not hear her. I heard you laughing and talking. I was too tired to complain and went back to sleep."

Looking back and forth at the girls, Hasegá:dǫ: asks, "Did you dream?"

Excited that he asked, Desah answers quickly, "Yes, I dreamt of the little girl on the raft again."

"Good. You answered one of your questions about visiting the same Ǫgwehǫ́:weh from the seventh generation every time. Did you find the answers to the other questions?"

Desah is glad he paid attention.

"Yes. Her Ǫgwehǫ́:weh name is Desasǫ́dręh, like mine. She does not speak Cayuga. The spirits around her help me understand what I see and hear. Do not ask me how that works. I am still unsure why she needs my attention. I think it is to guide her to her path, to a happier path."

She goes on to describe the life she sees in the seventh generation. Ji?nhǫ keeps silent. She does not want to tell him her dream. She hopes Desah keeps talking with no mention of her story or draws attention to her silence. She looks on with interest as Desah's story unfolds, pretending this is the first time hearing about her dream. Desah and her brother continue to compare notes about the things they have seen and heard, assigning reasons for the incidents.

Much to Ji'nhǫ's sadness, Hasegá:dǫ: is done with his tea and his stories. He gets up, leaning on their shoulders extra hard before standing. The girls grumble and laugh as he heads to the fire to talk to the other firekeepers.

Gotsahniht, the lead teacher, says, "Tomorrow, we have the morning to finish our moccasins. We will eat and clean up the camp before we head towards home. Do you have questions about anything?"

Ji'nhǫ looks up at the sky, then at Desah. "Do you want to combine our shelters to keep us drier when it rains tonight?"

Afraid her energy would disturb her sleep and dreams, Desah says confidently, "It will not rain."

After a pause, Desah looks up at the cloudy sky barely showing the stars. "It is too late to fix our shelters. We will sleep better by ourselves." Smiling, she adds, "When it rains, I will drag my mat into your dry shelter."

"Yes. You and your mat will be wet, making my shelter wet."

The girls laugh. Finishing their teas and medicines, they retire earlier. Desah is having a hard time falling asleep. She crawls out to find her brother at the fire.

Her brother whispers, "You should be asleep.

This is the last night. You have a lot of work to do before we leave: finish your moccasins, eat, and restore the grounds. What keeps you awake? Are you excited to go home?"

"No. I am happy to go home. Not excited."

Pretending concern and mocking a snore, he says seriously, "Is Jiʔnhǫ making too much noise?"

His snoring noise and her laughing too loud wakes a grumpy Gotsahniht to suddenly appear at the fire.

She whispers, "Sssshhh. Quiet."

Hasegá:dǫ: explains, "Desasǫ́dręh cannot sleep."

Gotsahniht is fully awake now and is genuinely concerned. She whispers, "What is the matter?"

"I am tired. Sleep will not come. I am afraid to go to sleep."

They listen to Desah tell Sheyna's sad story.

Once she finishes, the teacher says, "Try to remember to watch Sheyna's life separating your spirit from her feelings. You are learning things about her that you will need before you can help her."

The elder disappears into the dark; returning, she hands a small bunch of lavender to Desah. "Take this to rub in your hair. It is too late to make lavender and sweetgrass wash. Do you have some sweetgrass?"

On her way to her shelter with the dried lavender in her hands, she nods yes to having sweetgrass.

Lying down, she says to herself, 'I wonder what her father was like. I only heard him a few times, once when he was mad at Sheyna, and later in the accident with her mother.'

Her mind drifts to a happier time for Sheyna when the boys were sent out to milk the cow with four tits.

The father gets up, smiles, and says, "What time is supper?"

The mother says, "Usual time, around five or six. Why? Where are you going in this cold weather?"

Without answering, he gets on his outside coverings and grabs a long black and brown object behind his seat. Sheyna and her little sister watch their father get ready to go outside. Sheyna smiles brightly at her little sister. She knows he is going to hunt rabbits. Sheyna rushes to put on her outer coverings with the little sister right behind her. They sneak out the door when their mother is not looking. They are walking behind their father through the snow and into the bush for a few minutes before a branch swats Sheyna.

"Ouch. Dad!"

He turns around to see his ten-year-old and six-year-old daughters barely dressed for winter, walking in snow almost to their knees. The littlest one is wearing jeans with a tear on the pant leg, rubber boots and no socks. Both girls do not have mitts, scarves, or hats on.

Knowing their mum would be mad at him, with a half-smile on his face he says, "Where did you two come from? We got to get you back to the house before your mum gets mad."

He takes something out of the weapon and picks up Lindy in his free arm. Sheyna walks behind him, trying to follow his footprints in the snow.

There is silence until he sings to distract them from the cold. "Lindy, it's cold outside. Lindy, it's co-ho-ho-ho-old outside."

Sheyna looks at her little sister. "Lindy smiles every time you sing that song, Dad."

Images of fun times and scary times with their family flash through Desah's mind.

Desah jumps in her sleep when she hears a loud lonesome wail. She cannot wake up to stop the sound. Instead, she finds Sheyna's shelter dark.

The wail comes from her father on the lower level, crying, "Why did you have to leave me here? I didn't know I would miss you this much. I love you. I did not know you were so sick. Why you? Why did you have to go? It should have been me."

Sheyna feels sorry for him and covers her head to drown out his sorrowful cries.

Time and dreams shift into another life change for Sheyna. She is telling her older sister she loves her art class and remembers Mr Smith buying her painting in grade six for twenty-five cents. Her school days story is interrupted.

"What are you going to do with art? You can't get a job with that. How come you aren't taking Home

Economics?"

"Mr Thomas suggested I take art in high school because I am a good artist."

"Oh, change it to Home Economics, silly. You don't have a mother to teach you how to cook now."

Desah sees and feels Sheyna's disappointment. She feels like choking as she does as she is told.

Next, Desah hears her father waking Sheyna up. "Are you going to school today?"

"No. I quit Monday."

She can tell he is mad because his jaw is set when he says, "Well, you have to go back to school or get a job. You are not lying around here to do nothing."

Sheyna knows she cannot and does not want to go back to school.

She gets up and calls Marlene. "Dad says I have to get a job."

"Okay. Get ready then. I will be right there."

They drive to various buildings in the big village close to their territory. They end up at an ominous old building by the river. Reluctantly, she gets out, takes a deep breath, and walks in.

Sheyna disappears into the building for a little while, before she comes back out to her sister's car. "I got a job! I start Monday. I said I have experience running a sewing machine."

Sister says, "Good. I think Helaina works there, too. You can ask her for a ride."

Sheyna is happy to hear that; at least she will

know someone working at the scary place.

Desah notices that once Sheyna gets to know some of the people there, most days she has a fun time at work.

While Sheyna is having lunch, Helaina and the supervisor approach her. They look very serious. The supervisor asks Sheyna to walk with her to the coatroom.

Helaina's chin is shaking. She stands in front of Sheyna. "Your dad has passed away."

Sheyna is immediately confused by the news. It must be true, seeing Helaina cry like this. She starts to cry, leaning on her sister-in-law. Together, their broken hearts cause tears to stream down their faces.

"No. No. No," Sheyna cries.

She tries to rationalise what she has heard and backs away from Helaina, shaking her head. "Maybe they are wrong or you heard wrong. Maybe someone got the message wrong. Maybe he's in the hospital and they are trying to bring him back to life."

"No. He was at your brother's place in Buffalo. He died in front of your brother, right there on his couch."

Her supervisor comes back to the space where they are talking. "I'm sorry to hear about your loss, Sheyna. You can go home now. You, too, Helaina. I will punch your timecards at quitting time."

During the night, Jiʔnhǫ crawls into Desah's shelter and wakes her, whispering, "Desah. Desah, you are crying out. What is the matter?"

After she realises Ji'nhǫ is in her shelter, she says, "I had another sad dream. I cannot help her."

Ji'nhǫ holds her friend until her sobbing subsides and waits for Desasǫ́dręh's next words. "She has lost her mother and now her father."

"Do you want to talk to one of the women, or Hasegá:dǫ:?"

"No. Not yet. It is still dark. We should try to go back to sleep. Can you stay with me?"

"It might rain."

"Do not tease me. I do not feel like laughing. It will not rain."

"Hao`. I will sleep with you."

When Desah goes back to sleep, she follows Sheyna through her memories of her father. She sees him fishing in the creek behind the Longhouse where Sheyna got her name, Desasǫ́dręh, announced. A little Sheyna is with him, watching bugs bounce on the surface of the creek. She fits perfectly on the little tree that bends out over the creek. She can see the roots of the tree under the clean, clear water.

"Dad?"

He does not answer. She repeats his name, adding her question, "Dad, where did you meet mum?"

After a moment, he says, "I don't know. At the Longhouse or around the reserve. I used to see her and your auntie watching my lacrosse games."

"How did you know you wanted to marry her?"

"I saw her sitting on a blanket at the fair. In those days, the fair wasn't like it is now. They had horse races. People brought their vegetables to see who grew the best ones. There was a merry-go-round for the kids and the Ferris wheel for the adults. Not many people sold cooked food. People brought picnic baskets."

"Who was Mum with at the fair? Her sisters?"

"No. She was by herself except for a little baby girl lying on the blanket beside her, your sister. I asked her, 'Who is this?' She started to cry, saying, 'Your daughter.' Right then, I knew I wanted to marry them."

Sheyna is about to ask another question when he says in Mohawk, "Be quiet now. You are scaring the fish away."

At another time during the night, Desah sees Sheyna and her sister as little girls. Their mum has just finished bathing them and put fresh sleepwear on them.

She hears their mother say, "Go see Dad, let him see how good his girls smell."

The little girls run into the living space, standing in line to let their father smell them, saying, "Daddy, smell us! We are clean. We had a bath."

Their father holds each of them in his arms in turn. Pressing his nose on their head, he gives an exaggerated inhale, saying, "Mmmm, my girl smells good."

Then the next one, same thing, "Mmmm, my girl smells good."

Happily, they climb the stairs to their sleeping space above, glad their father is happy with them.

The next morning, Desah is startled to find her friend next to her when she wakes up. "Why are you here? Is your mat wet?"

Ji'nhǫ explains, "No. Remember? You were crying in your sleep. You asked me to sleep here."

Stretching and yawning, she slowly recalls the night. "Hao`. I think I am good now. How did you sleep?"

"I am good, too. Are you going to talk to your brother about your dream?"

"Not yet. I am fine. I will feel better after I swim and eat."

The girls crawl out of Desah's shelter. They greet those that are at the fire on their way to the river. Ji'nhǫ is quick to go in the water. Desah takes off her outer covering, shivering in the morning end of summer breeze, and wades out into the cold water. When she is done, she climbs up onto her favourite spot, a rock that barely reaches the surface of the river. She looks up to see an unconcerned eagle sitting high on a branch that is bending under its weight.

Desah says to the eagle, "Yes. Your life is not difficult. Not as difficult as the furry little meal you see hopping around under that tree where you sit."

Her friend beside her asks, "Do you always talk

to eagles?"

Desah hurriedly turns away from the eagle and rabbit. She does not answer. She is distracted.

Jiʔnhǫ says, "They will tell us to eat something today. I am too tired to close the camp and take the long walk home."

"We will survive. I was thinking about Sheyna's story. Once I sort it all out, I will talk to my grandmother. She will make sense of it. I believe my aunt when she said I must learn as much as I can about Sheyna before I can help her."

The girls join the group working diligently to close the camp, taking down shelters and gathering their belongings and projects. They rest and eat before heading out on the trail home. The three-day fast is finished.

CHAPTER FIVE – FOURTH YEAR –
FOUR NIGHTS' FAST

The group is relieved to be back at the village. Desah's mother and siblings are there to walk her back to the longhouse.

Awéhę? turns to notice her son is being detained by the young women from the village, saying patiently, "Come and eat, Hasegá:dǫ:."

She gives a knowing smile to the grandmother as they turn towards the longhouse.

Desah looks over at Hasegá:dǫ: and the girls. "I do not know what they see or what they like about him. He is a pest. He is always teasing them."

Mother says, "The girls like the way he pays attention to them."

Looking at her daughters, she asks, "Did you enjoy the trip?"

"Yes. Look," Desah says, reaching into her bundle to produce her new moccasins.

"Nice; they look like they are good for winter. Your cousin will fit your summer ones. During the wintertime you can make new ones for the summer. You know how."

Desah removes her giggling little sister from her mother's arms and sits her on the skin that is waiting for them.

She sits, takes a summer moccasin off, and holds it next to her sister's tiny foot. "I want to give them to Jihsdǫ."

Her mum smiles. "It will be many winters before your baby sister can fit them."

Onráhdagǫ: takes her turn, talking about the walk, work, and waterfalls with no life-threatening events to report.

Desah's eyes get her grandmother's attention. "Grandmother, when I know more about the little girl on the raft, I will need your advice to see how I can help her."

"Yes, any time. You both look tired."

"Nyá:węh, grandmother."

Yawning, Desah gets up. Onráhdagǫ: agrees and follows Desah. They climb the ladder to the upper level.

Onráhdagǫ: says, "What is the matter? Your energy is low, Desasǫ́dręh."

"Yes. I am as tired as you."

The next morning, their warm, comfortable mat is hard to leave. She is alone. Onráhdagǫ: must be up already. She scampers down the ladder to start her day.

Desah organises the girls to meet that afternoon to plan the next fast. It will be the most important test as young women. They will ask Onráhdagǫ: for suggestions to prepare for four days. Each moon they plan to meet to encourage each other to keep to their schedule of preparations and fasting. Once they agree, they join the whole village in preparing their longhouses for winter.

They keep busy, hanging skins and patching holes in the side of the longhouse where the mud has fallen out. They carry in logs of wood, gather and pile kindling, gather flint and moss for the fires. They pound corn and store what they need for the clans, and potential guests. The winter turns out to be long and fun, with many visitors stopping at the Cayuga village to eat, sing and dance, or to participate in the ceremonies.

Mid-winters and spring ceremonies are completed with everyone focusing on the planting season. Work and harvest seasons keep the girls busy while they are fasting sporadically. The time goes by in a blink.

The village is talking about the upcoming ceremony and hunting trip. Desah has prepared too long for the four-day fast to think about the hunting trip. She is surprised her friend Ji'nhǫwę́:se: is undecided.

"Why are you staying back? You have only this time to finish your fasts."

Smiling, Ji'nhǫ says, "I want to go on the hunting trip. Hasegá:dǫ: might go because they will be hunting buffalo in the west."

A frustrated Desah says, "Listen. Do you want me to ask my mother if you and Hasegá:dǫ: are a good match? If he is, she will ask my grandmother to talk to the elders of your clan and request a match. If everyone approves, they will promise you to him."

Pouting, Ji²nhǫ quickly responds, "That will take too long! He and Akenhnhà:ke will fall in love before she talks to the elders."

Pulling her friend's face close, Desah looks straight into her eyes, and says each word purposely, "Hasegá:dǫ: is not ready. I told you. We do not know if Akenhnhà:ke is going on the buffalo hunt. We do not know if Hasegá:dǫ: is going for sure."

Believing her friend, Ji²nhǫ rushes back to her longhouse, coming out with her prepared bundle. Together, they follow the group into the woods to walk a different path that they have used over the last years. It is the opposite direction. Their camp is chosen near a new waterfall to the east in the Onondaga territory.

The girls know the camp routine. After sundown, they take a break for tea and a round of introductions. Four Mohawk girls and two teachers have met up with them and are staying for only two nights.

The Cayuga teacher, Gotsahniht, looks at all the girls around the fire. "Everyone looks tired. We can go to our shelters when you finish your tea."

The Mohawk teachers translate the comment to

their girls. Everyone rises and leaves for their shelters.

In her shelter, Desah wonders how she can help Sheyna as she drifts off to the fading sounds around her. Desasódrẹh finds Sheyna in a noisy place where people are dancing to loud music. Everyone is drinking. Sheyna and her niece are standing in line to buy some sour springs. She draws her niece's attention to the well-dressed man standing in front of her. Out of the side of her mouth she says, "How did this guy get past me?"

Sheyna looks down and steps on his heel and waits. The guy turns around and flashes the handsomest smile she has not seen since her early twenties. She says, "Oh, sorry. Hello, Damon."

He answers, "Oh. Hi. Where are you sitting? I just got here."

She squints at the tables to see where her friends are sitting. "Third table from the front on the right side of the band."

Her and her niece get their drinks and look for their friends. Soon after, Damon comes over and hands her a drink. He starts them off by talking about the changes he has had since they were twenty-two. He owns a roofing business, he's single and his son lives with him in a house in Brantford.

She tells him that she never had children and where she works as a camera operator for a silkscreen company just down the street from where he lives.

She says, "Isn't it weird that we are from the same reserve and never run into each other? I thought you moved away."

As the night wears on, they run out of things they care to share. Damon looks down and laughs to himself.

Sheyna says, "What's so funny?"

"If you go on a honeymoon, where would you want to go?" He looks to see her reaction.

Quickly, Sheyna turns to face him, shocked. "Honeymoon? Please don't talk about marriage. My relationships go downhill every time the topic comes up. I do not want to get married. I've seen marriages around me. No, thank you."

"Okay. Sorry. Then where would you like to travel?"

Wistfully, she answers, "I always wanted to see Hawaii."

This was the beginning of their dating, drinking every time they meet with their friends in some bar or at a dance. Sometimes they stay overnight in each other's homes. Eventually, he invites her to live with him and his son, Jason. The small family of three move to an old house in their territory.

Desah watches how Damon controls their lives and Sheyna seems happy to let him. Over time, his other children enter their lives; the two girls regularly visit on the weekends. The oldest son pops in and out. Desasǫdreh feels Sheyna's spirit lift as she develops relationships with them. She has made a type of family that seems normal for their generation. They organise a vow ceremony the way he wants, leaving her to worry about how they will pay for it. She cuts corners by making her own bouquet and dress. At the dance, everyone seems to be having a good time drinking sour springs, eating, and dancing to loud music.

Desah senses what Sheyna feels: a familiar knot in her stomach as she searches for her new husband, asking people if they have seen him recently. One of her nephews says, "Yeah. He's outside."

Sheyna goes out and sees her husband passing a bottle of wine around to his circle of friends. A redheaded woman is standing too close to him, laughing and whispering too close to his ear. Defiantly, Sheyna grabs the bottle from one of the people in the circle and takes a drink. Tightly gripping the bottle, her eyes shoot daggers at the redhead, who slowly moves away from Damon. Looking at her new husband through gritted teeth, she says, "It is time to make speeches."

Damon cautiously removes the bottle from her hands and jokingly says, "Yes, dear."

He takes his angry new wife by the hand, leading her back into the hall. The band leader says, "Let me introduce you to Mr and Mrs Lovitt."

People are clapping as the couple walk towards the stage. They thank everyone for sharing their special day. As Damon is making his speech, he sees Sheyna's older brother walking across the floor with some drinks.

"Murray, do you owe my wife something?"

Murray's shoulders jump as he stops in his tracks. He makes his way to the stage, with Sheyna explaining Murray's five-dollar bet that she would get married before him. He hands her five dollars.

She says, "Your wife wouldn't let me mention this bet at your wedding, which is okay because I had no intentions of getting married at that time."

Desah's thoughts fade into a new dream. Angry voices jar her nerves.

It is Sheyna screaming, "She saw you and her coming out of a motel. Why would she make that up? I should have listened to your other girlfriend who called the day after our wedding. The day after!"

Damon walks around the place like a caged animal looking for a way to escape.

He stops to say, "The only people who can break us up are me and you."

"Well, you are doing a good job of it. The only reason she goes with you is to break us up. Can't you see that?"

"I told you I wasn't with her. Maybe your friend was drunk. She's the one trying to break us up."

He leaves Sheyna at the entrance of the house sobbing, her face showing her heartache.

The next time Desah sees Damon, Sheyna, and

his two sons, they are driving out west away from her family and his girlfriends.

Desah is confused. Although Sheyna quit the printing job where she loved to work, she seems happy leaving it to work on roofs beside her husband and stepsons through a scorching summer and below-zero winter.

She watches as the couple walk among many pairs of boys wrestling on mats. Her stepsons saunter towards them.

Devin says, "I pinned the guy in four minutes."

Damon teases, "Are you done your match already? We haven't even sat down yet. You pinned your opponent too fast. We missed it."

Her stepson reminds her of her husband. "Good job, Devin."

Three whistles blow, signalling for the next set of matches to begin.

"Devin has a body like you now," she says proudly to her husband.

"Yeah. He can carry thirty-four bundles up three storeys. He wanted to see how many he could carry. I told him not to do that again to save his back."

After Devin pins his opponent in nine minutes, he walks up to his father and says, "What about that match, Pops?"

"It looked like you had a hard time pinning that guy."

Sheyna laughs with pride in Devin's wit. "You

said you wanted to see me wrestle."

On many occasions, Devin has shared stories of stealing cars with his uncles. Her stepsons already got caught stealing white out and glue at the Canadian Tire. Sheyna encourages Damon to talk to Devin about his stealing.

"Why? Who am I to talk? I used to steal cars."

"You are their father. You have a right to teach them good things."

During one of Damon's parenting speeches, Devin says, "Yeah, right, Pops, you were worse than me."

Sheyna, quick to defend her husband, snaps, "That's why he's telling you. He wants you to live your life, not his." She lets that sink in before she says, "And he's in yours."

One morning, Damon hollers at the boys to get up for school. Sheyna is in the kitchen when Devin comes in and asks for a ride.

"I thought your dad was taking you to school."

"I want you to take me."

She looks at his charming smile suspiciously. "Okay. I'll get ready."

Almost to the school, out of the blue he says, "Tracey is pregnant."

Sheyna's heart sinks, and she says sadly, "Devin, you are only sixteen. You worked so hard to get into a high school with your dyslexia and hearing problem. What are you going to do now?"

"I don't know. I am only sixteen. I thought if I went out with an older woman, she wouldn't get pregnant. She's eighteen."

"Eighteen? That's not an older woman. That's hardly a woman. I have to talk to your mum."

"Go ahead. She won't care."

"Good heavens, Devin. Yes, she will. You are doing good in school, your reading level is up, and you are the top wrestler in your grade. Yes, you work on the weekends, but you don't make enough to keep a baby and your girlfriend. I'm telling you right now you are not quitting school."

"Tracey's parents want us to visit."

"Who? Me and your dad, or just your dad?"

"All of us."

"Oh, no. Tell them to give us time to talk to your mum. They do not want to know what I'm thinking right now."

Visit day comes. Damon, Sheyna, and Devin are let into the house of Tracey's parents. Phony smiles are exchanged all around. The three guests barely sit down when Tracey's mother starts talking without pausing to breathe.

Desah can feel Sheyna's anger seething while the nervous little new people woman goes on and on about money. "A crib costs $800, clothes cost $100, and food costs..."

That's it! Sheyna interrupts the list and says, "He is not going to quit school. He is only sixteen. His mother says you can have his baby bonus."

"Oh. Wow. $8 a month."

Ignoring Sheyna, the woman looks at Damon. "And a car seat costs $150."

Through a clenched jaw, Sheyna's anger flies out. "Yeah, and how much does the pill cost?"

The little woman spins around and says, "How much does a condom cost?"

Sheyna stands defensively. "He has condoms. What do you want me to do, put it on him?"

Damon knows that look and stands in front of her, saying to Tracey's father, "We will be in touch. We are not solving anything today."

Looking at his wife to stop talking, her father says, "Agree."

The next time Desah sees the family of four, they are heading across the flat lands and hills back to their territory in the east. There is no Tracey and no baby.

Desah wakes to a cloudy day, recalling her dreams of the night. Pieces of the events fade in and out of her memory, leaving an unsettled feeling in her stomach. Sheyna seems happy with her mother-in-law and surrounded by Damon's family, living in a big house near huge, magnificent mountains. 'Why did they leave?'

Keeping much to herself throughout the day, Desah goes through the motions: bath, working on a pot, leaving it to start a corn basket, leaving that to work on the pot. Desah remembers Sheyna's excitement as Damon and his friends build their new shelter. A regular event is drinking the sour springs with their friends. Sheyna's dark times and mistrust bother Desah. She wonders why she does not have children with this man. Then she remembers when she was younger, she lost a baby before it was born.

Noticing the fidgeting, her aunt asks her in private, "What is the matter, Desasǫdręh?"

Releasing her breath, she replies, "I cannot find what haunts the little girl on the raft. I see the effects of it on her life, her partners, and her decisions. She seems lonely. She has no children of her own and her actions lead her to more loneliness."

Gotsahniht says, "You have three more nights to find out. Think of those questions before you go to sleep. Try not to worry and keep busy for now."

Desah agrees and listens to the other girls decipher their dreams. Some dreams seem prophetic, some are everyday life and other dreams are confusing with a mixture of images. Desah believes her dreams are lessons. The day goes by fast with work, conversation, and friendship.

The sun is going down behind the trees when Ji?nhǫ brings her pot over to where Desah is working. "No sleep, again? You have been silent all day."

Desah concentrates on her pot. "I am always quiet. Yes, I did not sleep well. What was your dream?"

"My dream was clear and not a good one. I

dreamt that Hasegá:dǫ: was with a girl, sitting by the river, watching men compete with their canoes."

Smiling, she says, swooning, "Were they touching or looking at each other with love in their eyes?"

"No. Listen. They have a connection of energies. He looks happy around her."

"That does not sound like him. Quit intruding on his relationship. You might see something you are not ready to see," Desah says teasingly.

"You can intrude on Sheyna's life," Jiʔnhǫ says, teasing her right back.

"No. I visit Sheyna for her benefit, not mine."

Sadly, Jiʔnhǫ says, "You are right. I will worry about my future, not your brother's."

"Good. I will worry about sleep, blissful sleep."

Gotsahniht and Onráhdagǫ: begin to clean up their work area, which is a signal for the girls to do the same.

Desah places her pot by the fire pit to dry. Then gratefully crawls into her shelter, preparing herself for the second night with lavender and sweetgrass by her head. Her thoughts go over the scenes of last night's dreams. She cannot sleep. The circle of her thoughts will not stop. Without waking anyone, Desah slips out of her shelter in the dark to be alone on the shore of the river.

Alone at the pit, Hasegá:dǫ:'s friend, Hadahnyo, acknowledges her nervously, "Sgę́:nǫʔ Desasǫ́dręh."

She answers quietly, "Sgę́:nǫʔ."

She does not notice her effect on him. She continues to the falls and climbs on her favourite rock, wondering, 'What is bothering me?'

Flashes of Sheyna and her mate float back to Desah. Damon's lies about his connections with his past girlfriends, stories of those affairs, and having five charming children with five different mothers where one of the mothers is a constant in his life. Then she sees it, an empty shelter, no sounds, no laughter, no children, and no cooking. Why is she without children of her own? The answer comes to her: he will leave her. 'Is this the reason for not having children by this man?'

Desah returns to her shelter to attempt sleep. The sounds of the night and the firekeepers fade. 'I want to warn Sheyna of a major life-changing event,' is her last thought.

Desah hears Sheyna and a friend talking while watching a lacrosse game. Gawf asks, "Why didn't you have children of your own?"

"I always wanted children, but I have not been able to conceive. The only time I had a conversation about pregnancy was when I was with my first boyfriend. For three months my moon lasted for ten days every month. My boyfriend took me to his doctor in Cayuga. When I told the doctor what was happening, all he said was that I must have been pregnant."

Gawf asked, "Then what happened? Did he give you a D&C?"

"What's that?"

"It stands for dilation and curettage procedure, or something like that. They usually scrape your womb after a miscarriage."

"No, nothing. I think he prescribed antibiotics."

"I can't believe they didn't do that for you. Did they test your blood?"

"No, I don't think so. When me and Damon first got married, he wanted to have a child with me. We went for tests and I had surgery to see why I couldn't conceive. They said they found scar tissue and asked if I had been pregnant before."

With a lonely heart, Desah's thoughts of Sheyna's situation fade into a phone call between two women.

Sheyna calls Lindy as soon as she gets her coffee ready. "Hey, do you have time to gab?"

Lindy says, "Sure, I was just going to call you. I already have my coffee. This is the third call I got this morning and the third time I knew who it was and what they wanted."

"Oh, yeah. I don't know why I keep forgetting your gift. Anyway, you must know the reason I am calling is to tell you about a weird dream I had last night."

"No; only that you wanted to talk to me. Go ahead."

"Well, I am upstairs in an old house, sitting on a wheelchair. My hips are fractured. I think it is because I was trying to give birth to a baby. It's our old house on First Line. There are big holes in the floorboards and tattered and wrinkly curtains hanging on the windows. I open them to look out at the back yard, but I can't see past the windows because they are smokey or dirty. The things I can see through the window are murky or blurred."

Lindy teases her, saying, "Your hips crack trying to have a baby. Holy. How old are you?"

Smiling, Sheyna says, "My bones were not too brittle to have a baby. Sheesh."

"Oh, sorry. I don't dream the same way you do. My dreams are clear and meant for other people."

"That's true."

"Remember when our niece was pregnant? I knew she was going to have a boy because I saw her in the park with a three-year-old boy with long dark hair, wearing a blue jeans jacket."

"Oh, yeah, I remember you telling me about that dream. I used it when she and nephew were sick with worry for their little guy who was scary sick with a severe fever. I reminded her of your dream. I told her he is going to come through this because Lindy had that dream about him in the park, at three or four years old. She remembered it, too, and thanked me for reminding her."

"Oh, yeah, I had that dream before she told us she

was pregnant. You don't dream like that. Your dreams sound cryptic, or something. Okay, your hips are good, you're in your new house now, you are working, your stepkids are on their own and everything is good with you and Damon, right? Maybe it doesn't mean anything. Did you eat too much pizza the night before?"

"No. Maybe it is warning me of something coming. I'm going to watch what happens next."

Desah feels Sheyna's loneliness. She knows Sheyna aches to have children of her own. The connection to other spirits, the spirits of the helpers in her territory, are strong. They come in and out of her paths through other people. People like Jen.

"I wonder if it is warning me about having a baby. After that dream, I kept running into Jen, an elder who I had not seen for years. I always think that people are in our lives for a reason. Either there is something I need to learn, or they need to learn something from me. I remembered that she knows about herbal medicines, so I asked her if she makes medicine to have children. She told me she did, but I never visited her to get some."

Desasǫ́dręh sees Sheyna getting medicine from another woman to help her conceive. She does not finish taking it.

Desah is confused as she watches an anguished man storm around their new shelter, ending up in the space where they sleep. It is Damon angrily throwing clothes into a small bag. The woman on the bed wakes and slowly sits up, focusing on the intruder. The woman is Sheyna, with messy hair, barely aware of her surroundings and unaware that Damon is mad. Squinting, she says, "What are you doing?"

"I am leaving, of course," he says with his back to her.

"Why are you leaving for Sarnia so early? You usually leave after supper."

He continues to pack without answering her questions. Fully awake now, she gets out of bed, barely dressed, and stands behind him, wrapping her arms around him.

"Come to bed," she says softly.

He moves away and pushes past her. Realising he's not kidding, she gets scared and grabs the duffle bag he is packing.

"Where are you going?"

He doesn't answer. He tries to yank the bag from her hands, refusing to look at her face.

Stiffly and firmly, he says, "Let go of the bag."

Finally, he lets it go and walks away. She drops the bag to the floor and follows him. She's crying loudly by this time.

From the closet, he wrenches a leather jacket from a hanger, leaving the rest of the hangers and coats swinging from the force.

She gets in front of him to stand firmly at the door, and pleads with him. Her hair is tangled, her lids puffy from crying and her face is red and blotchy from the night before.

Through a clenched jaw, he warns, "Get out of my way, Sheyna."

Sheyna grabs the front of his shirt.

"Please, Damon, don't leave. Let's talk."

"Let go," he says, prying her fingers from his shirt. "I told you if you get drunk one more time I am going to leave."

"Oh, take it easy. You never said that."

"How would you know what I said? You were drunk."

Rationally, she tries to come up with solutions. "I'll quit drinking. We can get counselling, couples counselling."

"There's nothing wrong with me. You're the one with the problem! I am done. I don't care any more."

He moves her limp, sobbing body away from the door and leaves. She sinks to the floor, crying until she has no voice. She feels ill. Slowly, after a few moments, her self-pity turns to anger.

She gets up and wanders around their shelter, screaming and pounding her thighs with her fists. "Nooo. Nooo. Nooo!"

Sheyna sits on the couch, trying to remember last night. They were at a birthday party outside her brother's house. A lot of people were dancing on the grass under a tent. Foggy thoughts of him asking her to go home faded in and out. Her husband and stepson, Jason, were in front of her with her coat.

"Let's go home," he demands.

Sheyna slurs, "You are always telling me what to do. We never get to visit my family."

Jason says, "Let's go home, Sheyna. We're your family now."

This is the last semi-clear memory of the night. The rest is blurry, more dancing, more laughing, more faces, and more beer.

Desasǫdrẹh feels sorry for her. In the next dream, she watches Sheyna make nest-like beds on the floor in front of the TV. Sheyna seems to look forward to the regular little visitor who eats vegetables dipped in an orange creamy substance and watches the dream thing until they fall asleep. Sheyna is awakened by a knock. She looks out. Her oldest brother and her husband are outside on the deck. Without waiting for an answer, her brother walks in and says, "I came over to pay you the $10 I owe you."

Sheyna slams the door behind him. "Yes, you can come in, but he can't."

"Hey. You shut the door on him."

"How many times does he have to leave and come back?"

Her brother laughs. Reaching for the door, he says, "I better go with him."

Desah's dream fades with Sheyna crying as she watches the lights drive down the lane in the dark. She realises Sheyna still loves him.

When Desasǫ́dręh wakes up the next day, she can still hear Sheyna's voice and the angry screams resonating in her head. She feels as helpless as Sheyna. She slips out too early to start her morning routine. Her aunt sees her and walks with her to the river.

To avoid waking the others, she whispers, "Sgę:nǫʔ Desasǫ́dręh. What's the matter?"

Desah holds it in until they are at the river. "A spirit tried to warn Sheyna that her mate would leave her. She did not listen. Now she is alone." Desah cries into her aunt's shoulder.

"Desasǫ́dręh, you did not warn her?"

"No. I wanted to help her. Another spirit helped her through a dream. I can only watch her make mistake after mistake."

Giving Desah a moment to cry out her tension, she says, "She will be fine. It appears she has the spirits guiding her. She will or must have got through this or you would not feel this connection. It sounds like Sheyna's vow is broken. She wants it. Her mate does not. Like any ending of a match, one person cannot fix it alone. You must learn that."

Still crying, Desah says, "Sheyna's spirit has been weak since she was the little girl on the raft. I am afraid for her. She loved this man. She loved her little family with all their problems."

"Listen, Desasǫ́dręh. Have your bath, do your work today, keep your hands busy, not your mind.

Stay among the other girls, which will help lift your spirit. You will be fine."

Desah wipes her face and takes a deep breath, "Yes. Nyá:węh."

"The girls will be up soon. Prepare a bowl of cedar and lavender water. After you swim, cup some of the medicine in your hands and rub it on you from the top of your head to your feet. Make sure you wipe your eyes, mouth, ears and heart. Pour the remainder over your head. Feel your gratitude to the Creator for Mother Earth and her gifts. Tonight, do the same thing. Do you have everything you need?"

Feeling better after a long cry, Desah says, "Yes, in my bundle."

The girls come down to the river and take their time returning to work on their outer coverings, moccasins, pots, or mats. A couple of girls pick medicine to dry by the fire.

Once the girls are settled with their projects, Gotsahniht asks, "Who wants to tell us about their dreams or warnings for our people?"

As each of the girls describe their dreams, Desah listens intently to avoid thinking about Sheyna. She realises the day has gone by as quickly as the last two days. One by one, the girls leave to crawl into their shelters. Desah prepares for the third night, putting some lavender and sweetgrass into a bowl of water and placing it on the edge of the fire. She wonders why she does not dream of her own future and why she is connected to Sheyna. Desah takes her bowl and wipes down with her medicine wash as she did in the morning. Finally, sleep comes.

Desah watches as Lindy paces around Sheyna's shelter. Her face is tense. Walking beside her is an ancestor.

Sheyna is sitting on a long yellow mat. Her spirit is dark purple. Her eyes are blank as she stares at the dream thing.

Lindy is talking into a black object that she is holding to her ear.

After a few moments, she hands it to Sheyna. "Here. Bethy wants to talk to you."

She reaches for the phone slowly. Cautiously, Sheyna says, "Hello?"

Bethy, in a soothing tone, slowly asks, "Hello. How are you doing?"

At the sound of her nurturing voice, Sheyna's chin begins to shake and her voice waivers. "I'm okay."

"Are you sure? Lindy said you are having a hard time since Damon left."

There is silence and a long pause. Bethy is waiting for more information or confirmation.

Finally, Sheyna says, "To tell you honestly, I don't care. I quit caring about him, and about our marriage. The only thing is, the house feels empty without the kids coming over. Without the kids, I feel worthless and useless. Do you understand? I cannot feel…" Sheyna's voice lowers as she finishes her sentence with, "anything else."

"Yes. I have been there. I don't feel that way now, but I felt that way before. Sometimes we naturally protect our spirit by not caring."

After a pause, Bethy says, "I want to try something with you. Can I? It is called spiritual counselling."

Confused, Sheyna says, "Yes. I suppose. It can't hurt any more than I have been hurting in the last month."

"Good. Turn your TV off, okay?"

Sheyna gets up slowly and turns the dream thing off, placing the object back to her ear. "Okay. It's off."

"Okay. Are you sitting on the couch?"

"Yes."

"Close your eyes. Think about the 'not caring' feeling; let's think back to the first time you did not care about anything or yourself. Tell me the age you were when you felt like this."

"After Mum died, I was fourteen; after Dad died, I was twenty-one; after I realised I had lost a baby, and every time after I drank since I was seventeen, many, many times."

"Okay. Then tell me the earliest time you felt this way and what age you are."

Sheyna thinks of her helpless, worthless, and hopeless feeling she has had over the years. "I think I was two or three years. I know I was little, maybe four or five."

"In your mind, go back to that time and watch the little girl as if you are watching a movie. Can you picture the little girl? Tell me what she is doing and where she is."

Sheyna nods, saying, "She is in Dad's house in the living room. Mum is gone somewhere. My Dad, brothers and their friends are outside under the pear tree, drinking. Someone comes in the kitchen door by the stove at the back of the house. He comes into the living room where I am; he is an ugly friend of the brothers. He smiles at me, picks me up and carries me upstairs to the room he uses sometimes. He smells like booze. I don't really know what he is going to do. I don't know why, but I feel sick to my stomach."

Sheyna starts to cry uncontrollably, pitying herself. Trembling, she says, "I cry out, but no one hears me. I must black out, because I don't know what happened. When I woke up he was not there."

Letting Sheyna cry, Bethy continues gently, "I am so sorry that has happened to you at such a young age. That sounds like an awful thing to happen to a little girl. He awakened your innocent spirit way too soon."

Sheyna feels like a little girl again, tears streaming down her face, listening to Bethy's soothing words. "It is okay, cry as long as you want. Cry as long as you need."

Once Sheyna's sobbing wanes, Bethy says, "You are okay now. You are safe in your living room. The little girl is safe. That man can never bother you again. You are safe now."

As Sheyna begins to calm down, Bethy says, "I want you to imagine the little girl in her safe space. Can you see the safe place?"

Taking a deep breath, Sheyna says, "Yes. I see her on a cot behind the woodstove. She and Lindy are warm and safe where no stinky, ugly person can get at us because Mum is near us doing something: cooking, or doing dishes. Our Dad and brothers are near us, sitting at the table, eating or playing cards. No one is drinking beer."

"Okay. Now, imagine you approach the little girl. Sit next to her and put a comforting arm around her. What is she doing?"

"She can't quit shaking. She's cold and sick to her stomach. She is not sad or scared."

"Okay. What does she need?"

"She needs to throw up."

"Okay. If she needs to throw up, take her outside to throw up. If you have some place for her to throw up, take her there."

"What is she doing now?"

"She is back on the cot."

"Is she crying?"

"No."

"Hold her, then. Hold her for as long as she needs.

When you are ready, look around you. There is a blanket beside you."

Sheyna looks beside her on the couch. There is a blanket beside her. Sheyna is surprised that Bethy could see the blanket.

Without question, she picks it up. "Okay, I have it."

"Good. Now wrap that warm blanket around you and the little girl. When you know she feels safe, let her have the blanket and grab her hand. Lead her out of the house to a place on this earth where she will be safe. To a place where you know no one can bother her again."

Bethy waits a few moments. "When you arrive at the safe place, take three big breaths. Fill your lungs with fresh, cleansing air."

Sheyna does as she's told. In her mind, she imagines grabbing the little girl by the hand and leading her to the field across the road from her dad's house. The boys' raft is floating on a little shallow pond under the willow tree. She lies on it and feels the warm sun on her back and she falls asleep. Sheyna smiles, remembering the safe warm place.

"If you have arrived, what do you want to say to the little girl?"

"That she is safe now."

Sheyna cries again. Wiping her cheeks, she says, "I feel a lot better. Like I am lighter. I think the lump in my throat and chest that I felt for months is finally gone."

"Good. This exercise is only the beginning. You might need a little more help. Can I suggest you see a psychologist or therapist? Soon, so you don't bring the little girl back."

"Okay. Nyá:węh, Bethy. Wow, that was cool."

"You are welcome. Is Lindy still there?"

"Yes, making coffee."

"I wonder if she can stay with you tonight. Let me say good night to her."

Desah feels great when she wakes up the next day. The sun is bright and the air warm. Stretching out the lazies, as Mother would say.

Her first thoughts are about her experiences through the night and she asks herself, 'What did I learn?'

She watches moments of Sheyna's life in her thoughts, surviving her days as a child of trauma. She hides her pain that lives just below the surface. Nothing ever seems to be in balance for her. All the pain she feels through her life is brought to the top as each life-changing event happens, like the fresh blood that comes up from an unhealed wound. She still needs help healing that first cut. She lingers in her shelter, still thinking about the changes and events of Sheyna's life, when Ji'nhǫ pokes her head in her shelter.

"You were crying again last night. I was going to wake you, but one of the firekeepers stopped me. He told me your aunt said not to wake anyone when they are sleeping. It is important to finish their dreams."

"I am glad you listened. I feel very good today."

She crawls out and motions for her friend to follow as she walks towards the river.

"I am learning many things through my little girl, and I am not afraid to dream again. I was scared to go to sleep the first two nights. It seems like I only visit her during her life changes, which always seem to be sad or turn sad."

Sitting on their favourite rock is her aunt. Smiling, Desah and Jiˀnhǫ crawl up beside her. "Sgę:nǫˀ, I heard you cry last night."

"Yes. It was refreshing. Whatever happened to Sheyna when she was a little girl blocked her natural senses. That is why she cannot understand the ancestor's messages. She sees them. They are not clear to her. I am glad that her sister and her friend helped her naturally."

"Good. I am glad you got through that. Now, when you are ready, we must get our work done."

The girls slide off their stoops in the water and run up the hill to finish their projects before they leave tomorrow.

The girls go about their work, laughing and talking about their experiences with their dreams. One of the girls asks Desah what she dreams about.

"I visit a girl that has my name, Desasǫ́dręh. I first met her when she was a little girl sleeping on a raft. I could see a Jack rabbit watching her for a long time. She wakes up when she sees its ears. I could barely see it. It was brown as the plants around it. The little girl sits up to get a better look. She must have startled it, because it stood up on its hind legs and darted off through the tall plants. Every fast after that I watched her grow into a woman. She dreams. Ancestors send her messages and warnings about the same things I see are going to happen to her. I want to help her. Now that she is a grown woman, I am not sure I have the experience to guide her."

Onráhdagǫ: says, "I cannot help. I do not have the experiences of a woman in relationships."

Gotsahniht says, "Do you have a plan to help her?"

"Yes. Grandmother will know how I can help her. She is wise. I will tell her the little girl's story. I still have more to learn about her before I finish this fast."

"Who has work to do on their projects? Tomorrow, after we eat, we will show all the things we have made. We hope they are complete. Is there anything anyone needs to finish?"

There is no answer from the girls, who are working diligently on their projects. They continue to chatter about their dreams. Desah is loving their last full day here. 'I wonder what my little girl will be up to this last night?'

The girls sip their tea while they sit by the fire, listening to the sounds around them. One by one, they say they will see everyone tomorrow and leave the fire to crawl into their shelters.

Desah quietly leaves Jiʔnhǫ talking with one of the night firekeepers and crawls into her shelter. In no time, she falls asleep, thinking, 'Why does Sheyna need me? She has an ancestor helping her. Why am I involved?' Desasǫ́dręh is determined to enter Sheyna's dreams. 'Her friend Bethy told Sheyna to talk to someone. It is time. What does she mean?'

As she falls asleep on the last night, she watches as Sheyna is talking to a woman who will be good for Sheyna's mind. Desah listens as Sheyna tells the woman the message the spirits sent.

Sheyna tells the woman she dreamt of her.

"Helen, you were in my dream. I drive my car up to a building. You come out and put a big basket of red apples in the trunk of my car. Then you get in the driver's seat."

Desah sees that she is becoming aware that her dreams mean something to her. She continues to listen to Sheyna's therapy sessions that include her childhood trauma and the separation from her mate. She blames herself for the people she hurt since childhood, and for Damon leaving.

"I was miserable when I drank too much. I chased him out."

Helen knows Sheyna's story and her episodes while drinking.

"We talked through your childhood experiences,

learning that you knew no different. It is only through an adult's understanding that carries the shame of the past. Shame that is overt while you drink. Were you drinking when you and your husband first met? Does he drink?"

"Yes. I was drunk when we first met. Yes, he drinks, but he doesn't get drunk."

"You have mentioned while drinking you black out on occasion. Is he drinking along with you?"

"Yes, but he remembers things that I do not remember."

"If you don't remember, how do you know he remembers? You once told me that sometimes you and your husband do not remember who drives home after a party?"

Sheyna's silence is confirmation for her counsellor to continue. "Okay. Over the marriage of seven years, were you in an unfamiliar condition from the first time you met him?"

"Not really."

"You quit drinking for three years. He left, again. Do you still think he left because of your drinking? How many times has he tried to come back? Do you still think he left because of you?"

"No. I guess not."

"Your parents stayed together until your mother died and after your father mentioned her several times, which tells me he was still married. You know their life was not perfect, but your father stayed with her until she passed."

Sheyna looks up from her hands.

"No. He didn't leave you. He was not strong enough to help you. He wanted to leave the marriage. He may have blamed you, but really, he did not want to be in a marriage where partners rely on each other. Not in a marriage where two people grow together. He sounds like he acts before he thinks. What was the shocking question he asked before you really got to know each other again?"

Sheyna thinks about all the shocking questions over the last ten years. Finally, she remembers. "Where do you want to go on a honeymoon?"

"Yes. He thought he wanted to get married without considering what marriage means and everything that goes along with it, like you and your issues, and he and his. You knew how hard a marriage can be for a couple. Your parents stayed together until your mother died; and even after, your father mourned her death. You have seen some family members go through similar situations and they stayed together because the two people wanted to stay together. The partners worked on staying together."

Their conversation fades.

Desah sees Sheyna sitting in her house with Helen, talking about the event that Sheyna had organised involving the various departments. The event seemed to be a success, according to her counsellor, yet Sheyna seemed upset.

"When I walked into the gym, I could not believe how many people were involved in the exercise. You mentioned the upcoming event during a couple of sessions, but you never mentioned how important it would be or how many departments would be involved. You did not seem excited about it at all."

Sheyna seems to be somewhere other than in this room with her counsellor.

"Sheyna?"

"Oh, yeah. It was my job. I cried when the TV reporter interviewed me. Damon was home. I told him about my job. He did not care. He seemed jealous and made some demeaning remarks. He told me to quit talking, saying he had to work tomorrow. I couldn't sleep. I went into the living room to watch TV. I will never do that again."

"What won't you do again? Was stress the reason for lack of sleep?"

"Maybe it was stress. Maybe it was me and Damon living in limbo since I quit drinking. I will never have an event where the children will be scared."

"Who told you that?"

"Damon said he was talking to one of the counsellors and they said the children got scared because they heard one of the ambulance, fireman or policemen talking on the radio."

"No. They were fine. I was one of the counsellors that organised debriefing for the children after the event. We took pizza to their school. We questioned and assessed how well they managed their involvement. They were fine when we left. One of the counsellors called all the parents of the children involved and provided a number if they showed any signs of stress. They were fine when we left, according to our assessment. We never heard from the parents."

"Why didn't anyone tell me this?"

"Who did you ask?"

Desah can feel the red energy rise in Sheyna. In a strained voice, she says, "The whole reason for the debriefing is so that people would not be impacted by the event. I was worried that the event I designed had affected the children. No one informed me that they were okay."

"Are you still worried about the children?"

"No, but I couldn't sleep for days. I grouched at my husband. My stepdaughter was over, and I am pretty sure she wasn't having a good time. I went through the motions for days. My husband stayed out all night and then acted like nothing was wrong when he finally came home."

The counsellor and Desah watch as Sheyna relives the anguish she went through during that time.

Allowing Sheyna time to process, the counsellor says, "Do you see how you focussed on the one thing that went wrong, and not the hundreds of things you did right?"

"Yes. Now I can also see the importance of organising two debriefings following an incident."

"You are right back at work in your mind, aren't you? Your energy is still visible. Your emotions are ignored, and you are mentally back to work."

Desah can see how the counsellor has become a trusted friend. At another time during the night, she sees them discussing one of her dreams.

"Whatever house I was walking around in, my sister and her little daughter were there, too. They did not say anything. I had two bedrooms that I could choose to sleep in. We were upstairs, because my niece and I looked out the window down at the green lawn below where the animals were. I can't remember what kind of animals. I think one was a cat, but that could be because they have a kitty. Each bedroom had a nice bed to sleep in. Seems to me we rummaged around for some pyjamas for me. We ended up going into the back bedroom."

Helen says, "I am sorry if my guess is wrong. Since you have been telling me your dreams, I looked up a few interpretations. Do you mind if I share what I learned?"

"No. Go ahead."

"I assume you have a good relationship with the two people in your dream, so that must make the dream a good one. Or the sister and the niece can represent you. It sounds like you have two choices to lay your head, because there is a choice of two bedrooms. It depends whether the lawn is green and fresh, or dried or bare."

"The grass was green and freshly cut. I am glad you help. Dreams are not interesting for everyone. Some people say they don't remember them, or they say they don't dream. I was okay in my dream. The next day was when I became confused about the dream because I remembered the details. Sometimes my dreams are fuzzy or very abstract."

"Let me know what happens next or keep track of your thoughts in a journal. Take time for yourself and look at how your emotions and thoughts affect your behaviours."

"Okay. I can do that. When I was a little girl, my older sister gave me a diary. I used to write things in that. Dreams must mean something, because I remember when I first started working for the Council I dreamed that *I was in a huge building with lots of people where I was standing and walking around above me. There were windows all around us. I was standing on the ground floor, looking up to the second level. In front of me there were stairs to the right and escalators on the left. Between me and the upper level, there were levels or shelves in between the stairs and escalators where a couple of people stood looking at me. I walked up the stairs.*

I recognised the girl coming down the escalators. I got her job, and she got my temporary job as a secretary."

"The job you are talking about, is it the job you have now?"

"No, that job was a couple of years ago. It was my first full-time permanent job with the Council. At that time, the girl on the escalator took the job I knew I didn't really want. I liked my boss, but it was too stressful in that building. I was worried about getting another job when the contract was done. I did not know what I was going to do or how I was going to pay off all the marriage debts myself. Damon left me with house payments, a bank loan payment, water filter and credit card debts from our trip to Hawaii."

"You seemed to be managing, now."

"Yes, I am chipping away at the debts a little at a time. Just mad at myself for not listening to my instincts when he was getting deeper into debt with those credit cards. I thought he would pay his credit cards, at least. My family helped me, especially my older sister and brother-in-law, who were always there for me."

Desah is half awake and half sleep thinking about the history of Sheyna's life. She can see the many relationships that Sheyna dealt with through her years and watches as she buries the root of the issues deeper and deeper under new relationships. 'She has not dealt with those root issues.'

When she wakes up the last morning of her fast, she still wonders what the reason is for her connection to Sheyna. *My grandmother will know.*

She crawls out of her shelter, dragging her belongings behind her. She heads to the fire to close the fast with the others. The girls are asked if they have any questions about anything that happened over the four days. No one says anything, anxious to get home.

After they have eaten, they tear down their shelters, laying the pine boughs next to the fire pit. They pack their projects and throw their bundles over their shoulders. One last check of the site, and the group lines up to walk to their home, their village.

CHAPTER SIX – CONFIDING IN GRANDMOTHER

The families greet the weary travellers with cakes of corn, beans, and honey. Desah's mother, Awę́hę̨ʔ, is there to greet her sister and daughters. The women in Desah's clan invite the other girls to their fire to talk about their experiences during their trip.

A smiling Gajihsdǫdáha runs over to Desah when she sees her. Desah crouches and sticks her arms out to hold her, kissing her head all over. The little girl giggles when she reaches her neck.

Jiʔnhǫ walks up to Desah's mother and asks, "Awę́hę̨ʔ, when will the people come back from hunting?"

Smiling, Desah looks up and says, "She wants to know when Hasegá:dǫ: will be back."

Jiʔnhǫ laughs and swipes at the top of Desah's head to be quiet.

Her understanding mother says, "He will be back in time for the midwinter's ceremony."

Looking at her sister and the girls, she says, "Get a little food to eat. I want to hear about the trip and the dreams. What do we have to watch out for? Was there anything unusual about your dreams or the trip?"

The women quietly sit down with their food. Each of them, in turn, describes the trip and their dreams of mates, and children, and the various lands they had visited.

"What did you see, Desasǫ́dręh?"

Desah begins, "During the first fast, I saw the little girl on the raft that was floating on a little pond in the middle of a field of dried plants. I could smell sweet grass in my dream. I am not sure if it was growing near our camp or if it was part of my dream."

Looking at her friend, she says, "That night I slept with some sweetgrass from Jiʔnhǫ's bundle. Nyá:węh, Jiʔnhǫwę́:se:. I keep it with me in memory of the trips."

Desah, still holding her sister in her arms, answers as if she is talking to her baby sister, "There was a little girl in my dream from another generation. She has one name in our words, Desasǫ́dręh, the same as me, and a short name in her language. They called her Sheyna."

Her mother asks, "What does Sheyna mean?"

"They did not say the meaning of her short name. She does not speak Gayogǫhó:nǫʔ. The people talk in new people's language. They speak our words during ceremonies of gratitude and song. Sheyna was a little girl when she got her name, Desasǫ́dręh, during the naming ceremony in a place they call 'Longhouse'. I felt I was sitting next to the little girl during the ceremony. One of the Faithkeepers asks her mother her name. Another woman sitting next to her mother tells him, 'Desasǫ́drę̜h'. He nods and tells the people assembled there our name. We watch as they continue to name the other babies and children. The boys are carried around the room, introduced to everyone by one of the men from the baby's clan."

Grandmother asks, "What does their 'Longhouse' look like?"

For the next part of her story, she lets go of her baby sister and says, "The Longhouse where they hold ceremonies is like our longhouse without sleeping places."

She stands. Moving her hands to show the logs that run sideways, she says, "The wood on the sides runs from north to south and not from ground to sky. The trees in their time are smaller than the trees we have. There are holes in the sides that let the sun and air in and keep the cold out. The trees are smoothed flat for the people to sit all around the Longhouse, and the ground is covered with the same flat trees that are smoothed for walking and dancing."

The stoves or fire pits are harder for her to describe, so she shows them. "They make fire in a black thing that controls the fire and smoke. At each end of the Longhouse, the black pits hold wood, fire, and ashes. They call it a 'stove'."

One of the girls pronounces it "stoff?"

"No. Stovvvvve."

Desah uses her hands in the shape of the stove and pipe, moving them up and sideways along the top in the path of the pipe, then shows the release of the smoke to the air. She says, "This pit controls the fire and directs the smoke along the top and out of the Longhouse."

Desah sits down next to her mother and little sister. Putting her finger in her sister's hand, she says, "Sheyna has many older siblings and one younger. In another dream, after a few winters, their mother gets sick."

Onráhdagǫ: asks, "How do you know?"

Pensively, Desah looks up from her sister's face. "I could feel sorrow around her. Her spirit told me there was history growing in her body. It is hard for me to talk about. I feel what Sheyna feels at those times, and wake up with a feeling of sadness and dread. I felt like crying during the day. I cried during my sleep. I know it was Sheyna's story, the little girl on the raft."

Grandmother says, "I see you have become attached to the little girl, and you are afraid of the pain you feel for her."

The women and girls are silent while they sip their teas of herbs with thoughts of visions on their last fast.

Ji'nhǫ turns to their grandmother and asks, "How do we dream of the past or future people?"

The grandmother looks up and around at the trees and sky, thinking of a way to explain the higher level of self. She describes it as best she can.

Touching her heart space and clasping her hands above her head, she says, "Our good energy allows two spirit worlds to merge on a higher space than self. The dialogue and connection are energies outside of our bodies. When there is no physical support to hear, there is always spiritual support to feel, or a good energy to relay guidance as they need it. Let the messages flow naturally. Try not to control your dreams. Try to remember important elements in the dream that might mean messages such as scents, colours, light, dark, going up or down, sounds, and quantities."

When the women become silent again, Ji²nhǫ's mother motions for her to come to her family's fire.

She thanks their grandmother and says, "Mother has something for me to do. Can I talk to you later?"

Grandmother, who always seems to be glad to help, agrees.

Desah asks if she can leave the fire.

Her mother looks up and says, "There is tea made in the longhouse."

Then she hands her a piece of cooked squash.

Standing up and following Desah, Grandmother looks at her daughter and says, "I will see if she needs anything. Join us when you are done."

Awęhę² agrees. The sound of the voices of

Onráhdagǫ: and Star blend in with the other noises as Desah and her grandmother approach the Wolf longhouse.

Once inside, Desah says, "Can we talk?"

Her grandmother tells her she can always talk to her. She motions for Desasǫ́dręh to follow her to her sleeping space on the lower level. On their way, she tells Desah to bring tea with her. After placing her bundle near the ladder to the upper level, Desah goes over to the fire to a large pot to scoop out some tea into their bowls.

Desah holds in her emotions until they are sitting. "They tried to warn Sheyna that her mate would leave her. She did not understand the warning. Something deep haunts her throughout her life, affecting her love with her parents, siblings, nieces, nephews, her mate and for herself. Now she is alone." Desah cries into her grandmother's shoulder.

In a soothing voice, grandmother says, "We can talk as long as you need. Continue."

Desah tells her how the little girl has grown into a woman since the first dream.

"Throughout her life, I learn the reasons for her sadness, from her first mate to the mate she makes vows to live with forever. The beginning of her reasons is hidden deep within her energy."

"How many winters has she seen?"

"The first time, on the raft, she looked like she had lived seven or eight winters. Other times, I see her at ten, fourteen, and twenty-one winters, and older. She was eleven when her mother and father got hurt in a car, a thing they ride in, as Hasegá:dǫ: had described. She had seen fourteen winters when she lost her mother, eighteen when she lost her baby, and twenty-one when she lost her father. I always see her in the times of life changes that sadden her. I felt so helpless watching her go through them."

Desah begins to cry again, remembering when they got hurt.

"The mother and the father had an accident. Their mother was hurt and bleeding. They took her to the place where they keep the sick people. She stayed there for a while. The older siblings took care of the younger ones. The little girls were sad and lonely without their mother."

Crying, Desah continues to describe that part of Sheyna's life.

Finally, grandmother says, "What do you think you could have done to change the outcome?"

With little conviction, Desah says slowly, "Warn her."

"Let us say that you are at the same time as she is experiencing these life changes, and she can understand you, your language – would a warning change the accident? Would she be less sad? Could you have prevented the accident that made the mother sick?"

Desah, realising there was nothing she could have

done, leans helplessly into her grandmother's arms and cries until there are no tears left. Her grandmother puts her arm around her and places her head on Desah's head.

Desah finishes her cry with a heavy sigh. She described how that accident was the beginning of her mother's pain in her chest. When Sheyna was a little girl, she was innocently open to messages. Her mother was worried she would die if they removed the lump of flesh from her body. Her mother could not receive messages, she was too busy with all her children.

"That thing in her body grew and caused her to go to the place where they take sick people. My little girl was able to reduce her worry. She received a warning in her dream and told her mother. Her mother was happy to hear it, and my little girl was happy she could lift her mother's spirit. She was too young to be aware the message was meant for her mother; her mother knew it was."

"Did you warn them? Did the spirits warn her?"

"It was not me. I could only watch everything that had happened."

Desah tells grandmother of the search in the funeral home and the hospital.

"The message showed her that her mother would get up and walk away from the place where they prepare their dead. Her mother was happy when Sheyna told her the dream."

"Was her mother's illness the reason for the little girl's sadness?"

In Desah's reflection of all the dreams, she says, "The sadness comes from many things. It starts when she was a tiny girl. She does not remember what had happened, but her spirit does. Another time is when her father's friend disrespected her. Her father was angry at her. She was crying and scared when she told her brother. Her father's anger was confusing to her. She loves her father. She could not understand why he took the stranger's side."

"Where was her father? He should have protected her."

"He was outside getting water. He did not know the man was touching her."

"Why did he get mad at her? He should have been mad at the man."

"Yes, he was mad at the man. I see him grab the man and push him out of their shelter. Sheyna did not know what her father did. She was with her brother on the upper level. They were planning what they would do to avoid the man. Her brother told her he would stay with her until she leaves their shelter, and he would take their little sister to their mother."

"I am glad that her father defended her. Was she a young woman?"

"No. She was only six winters. I see her at different winters when men disrespected her. She had only seen seven winters and younger when the first man disrespects her at two or three winters. When it first happened, she was so young she did not know what was happening. She grew up too early. She is nine winters when she takes care of babies without the adults around."

Before she finishes her story, grandmother says in a questioning tone, "She has babies at nine winters."

"No. She is often left alone with the children of her older siblings. Not by herself; her sister of five winters helps her. They are too young taking care of the babies by themselves."

Desah stares into her bowl of tea. "Sheyna's childhood life when her parents are there feels secure and happy. Her brothers, Clark, Douglas, and Murray, Sheyna, and her little sister, Lindy, are the younger half of the family. There are five older siblings that have mates and children living somewhere else. Her father has great love for his children. She is happy and safe when she is with the whole family, and they are not drinking the sour springs."

Grandmother asks, "Where are the elders, her parents, her siblings, and their parents when she is left with the babies?"

"I do not know. Their shelter is too small for everyone. I think the older people are away with their friends. In her time, the Qgwehǫ:weh are unaware that they have problems with the sour springs that Hasegá:dǫ: described from his dreams of the seventh

177

generation. As I started to learn more about her, I was burdened with Sheyna's sadness. I cried out in my sleep during those times. I never knew from one dream to the next where my little girl would be or the number of winters she has seen. As one life-changing event fades, she is in another situation. The life-changing events that bother Sheyna bothered me. At times, I was afraid to go to sleep."

Desah's chin shakes as she takes a drink of her tea. "After her mother passes, she has seen fourteen winters; her being is in turmoil for three winters. She feels like there is no one to talk to. The three youngest do not have mates and do not know who they can lean on. The people she usually talks to, her siblings or her father, cannot help; they are hurting and sad, too. Their family splits up emotionally. The same closeness of the family is gone, leaving the girls with the father who tries his best to take care of his daughters who are growing into young women. He leaves the girls home alone while he is away drinking the sour springs. When the siblings and their mates are away, the girls are responsible for their little nieces and nephews. Sometimes the siblings come home angry and yelling at each other. The girls and their children huddle together on the upper level, hoping the angry people stay on the lower level until they fall asleep. I feel awful."

She goes on to explain how everyone in Sheyna's family is suffering from the loss and struggle to return to normal. Everyone drinks the sour springs to escape or hide their pain, which causes them to become happy or agitated. Sheyna tries to find happiness with her young friends. They begin to drink the sour springs when their bodies are too young. Sheyna tries to be happy when she is with her siblings to prevent her father from knowing her sadness. She does not tell them the truth about what she does when she is supposed to be in school. Some days she is not in the place where they expect her to be.

"I hear her older sister and father talking. They are worried that she quit school."

"School?"

"In the new times, the parents do not teach their children life skills. The young people attend school, where strangers teach them skills to survive in their world. Sheyna likes to learn the skills to make images. Her teacher often compliments her on her work. She does as she's told and asks to change from art to cooking and making outer coverings. Now, she is very unhappy at school because there is no reason to go. One of the new people who learns alongside her, tells her that the art teacher wishes she had stayed in his class. Sheyna wishes she had, too. Finally, she leaves that place of learning and the mean 'man with the bird's nest head' behind. She would rather be with that boy and her friends who lift her spirits. She calls him to pick her up from school.

"Losing her mother, quitting school, learning to

drink like an adult and finding a mate are important turning points in Sheyna's life. I learned from the adults talking in her village that too many changes are not good for her physical, emotional, mental, and spiritual being to get better. Sounds like she finds some comfort with the boy who makes her laugh."

"How do you know he is not a good match? You said she calls this boy to pick her up. Does he live near this school? Does he go to that school?"

"He lives with his mother in their territory. It is close to Sheyna's territory."

"He can hear her calling him. He must have good ears."

Desah realises that she has not explained what 'call' means in the seventh generation.

"No, Grandmother, they do not yell. They put a black object to their ear and talk to it. I believe her words are carried over the black vines that are all over the place."

Grandmother does not fully understand, but she nods to encourage her to continue.

Desah explains, "I could see her leaving her life's path and her father to be with him. He is not a good match forever. They were too young for this path. Her body has grown to seventeen winters, her mind and spirit are still nine winters, and her emotions are five winters. There is something about the boy that reminds Sheyna of the sadness she carries within her. She is too young to be aware she is with baby."

"Where are her older siblings? Why did she not tell her sisters or father?"

"She was unaware. The medicine man told her after she lost the baby."

"Did she tell them when she found out?"

"No, she was afraid to disappoint them."

"Did you feel her sadness? What is bothering you?"

"I do not understand her feelings of good and bad within herself through this boy's attention. I have a feeling she needs my care to guide her when she is weak from the inner sadness she carries. The issue will be getting her to understand my messages. As a young woman, a spirit tried to show her that her security was going to change for the worse. Her life mate left her. She was shown her being was confined to an old shelter, confined to her history, that she would be crushed, unable to move without being pushed. Outside of her confinement, her vision was clouded from seeing the future. To show how this change of security would affect her, she was seen sitting in a seat. Her movement is affected due to trying to give birth. It means that when she tries to take the medicine to have a baby, her mate would leave. He left. The children, his children, left her. She was very close to giving up on life."

Desah's voice trembles, making it hard to finish her story.

Grandmother lets her finish her cry before she

says, "You are a good person to ache for this person who came to earth as a pure being. You are filled with a lot of love for her family, Desasǫ́dręh. I feel your generous love every day, here, with us. It is because of this love that you will not let her self-destruct. Remember, people come to earth wanting to learn something and needing to teach someone something. It is life that has changed her. This is the path she is to bear. How dangerous is her life now?"

Desah answers slowly because she understands her grandmother's question. She tells her about Sheyna's experience with Lindy and Bethy's spiritual counselling.

"Without knowing it, she was close to ending her life. The negative thoughts in her mind and feelings were mixed up, leading her to more negative actions. Her spirit was crying for help. Since talking to the spiritual counsellor, she seems to be out of harm's way; no more crippling feelings of worthlessness. She seems to have enough means to continue a path of healing."

Awęhę' walks in, and, seeing their bowls empty, she offers, "Do you want more tea?"

Grandmother says, "Not right now," and pats the space next to her.

She looks at Desah. "You have witnessed her receiving guidance from our ancestors through her young life and as a woman. She may not have understood the warning before it happened. Her spirit understood the messages. They prepare her spirit whether she understands the messages or not. When the incident happened, it did not affect her as much as it would have without the guidance of the messages she received."

Desah's mother adds, "You will have many ways to help your little girl. Work on opening a connection between you and her; she will get used to you helping her. At first, make a connection to the spirits around her."

Desah says, "Yes, I have seen this. In a way, it was Sheyna's sister and her friend that seemed to be open to the spirits around them."

Mother says, "Yes, once you learn how, you can transfer your messages and warnings through their spirit helpers until she understands."

"Her family, especially her sister, seems to be close to their spirit helpers. When Sheyna was a little girl, she experienced the same connection. When something happened to her, the messages were blocked. She became unaware of her dreams."

As Desah tells her grandmother the stories of Sheyna's life, she cries as if she is physically there with Sheyna, going through her life changes. Grandmother watches her grand-daughter without interrupting her story. She does not know all the details of Desasǫdręh's dream friend.

She knows her grand-daughter. "Is Sheyna happy?"

"On the surface. It helps to bury or overshadow the pain. It is this forced happiness that helps her survive."

Her mother, glad that Desasǫdręh has come to terms with her spirit friend, says, "I believe the gift of connection will come back, and she will learn to trust her gift some day. You will learn a way to strengthen the connection. Until Sheyna is aware that you are available to help her, the spirits around her will be your connections. Until she is well enough, they will let you know when she needs you."

Grandmother adds, "You have witnessed the changes in her life. Now you can help her or direct her to her helpers in her village. Allow her time to find and learn the tools to survive in her own time when she is ready."

Looking less anxious, she expresses her gratitude with a smile, and says, "Nyá:węh."

As she reaches for her grandmother's empty bowl, Desah says, "I am tired. I can wash our bowls."

Grandmother says, "I will wash them when I am done talking to your mother. Before you go to sleep, I want you to think about one thing you learned is good in Sheyna's life, and something that is good for her. Tomorrow, think about everything you have seen, heard, and felt during your fasts. Depend on the spirits involved to guide your dreams from now on."

Desah looks at her mother and then her grandmother. "Sheyna cannot love herself. She is unaware of the love that surrounds her because she does not feel the same love for herself. She has love for others and that feels good to her. She has learned to shut that part of herself off. How can I help her when I dream of her older self? I do not have the experience or the knowledge to help her deal with what has happened in her life: losing her parents, and her baby. She continues to deal with her mate leaving her and losing the family they shared."

After a while, grandmother says in a solemn tone, "Sometimes people must take their own journeys to learn the lessons that they were meant to learn while they are here, or she is meant to teach her experiences to help others. What did she learn when her mate left her?"

"She learned to live alone, be strong, defend herself, and the ability to quit things that harmed her health. She returned to learning new skills and gaining more knowledge about her world."

"You can guide her to the people who can help her. You know her and about the people around her. You can ask me, your sisters, or your mother to share our experiences."

"Everyone is always too busy with family. Deyawẹdǫh gets angry when I talk about the little girl. She says I am trying to be like Hasegá:dǫ:. Onráhdagǫ: and my friends are too young and have as much experience with mates as I do."

"Do not forget you have great love, Desasǫ́drẹh.

185

Love is the greatest power in this world. You will know when she needs you. You will feel she needs you through that love. Their world may be different to ours; love among people is not. Once she learns to understand her dreams, she will come to your mind when you are awake. Talk to us when you have questions. We will make time."

Desah is quiet and feeling a lot more relieved.

Her mother says, "I am glad you are available to her for now. There is no guarantee the little girl on the raft will not return."

Knowing her daughter's compassion is beginning to show, Awẹ́hę̣ʔ asks, "Are you tired, Desasǫ́drẹh?"

As if this is a cue for everyone, the circle breaks up. Desah smiles tiredly. "I love you."

Each express their love in return, as well as their pride in her accomplishments. Desah hugs her grandmother. As she hugs her mother, she says to Desah, "Check to see if your little sister is sleep."

Desah climbs to her space, sees her sisters are asleep and lies down beside Star, covering up with the skins. With no trouble at all, she drifts off into a deep sleep.

Grandmother tells her daughter, "Awẹ́hę̣ʔ, Desasǫ́drẹh's energy will be very low for a few sunsets. Be gentle with her emotions until she heals from her trip. Keep her working, giving her more small family responsibilities. Let her practice making decisions and planning. Give her five tasks that you want accomplished. Let her choose which two tasks she can do. Ask her how long it will take her to do them."

"Nyá:węh, Mother. Yes, it is time. She has been through eighteen winters."

Desah does not wake when her parents come in to carry her little sister with them to their sleeping space.

The next day, a thin strip of sun peeks through the crack in the wall near her mat, waking her. She hears her mother and baby sister coming towards her. As usual, mother lays sister down with her so that they can sleep longer. Desah curls around her tiny body, smelling the lavender from her bath. They both fall back to sleep.

She wakes up feeling as if someone is looking at her. Opening her eyes and turning her head, she looks into the two big brown eyes of her little sister.

She smiles and presses her face against the soft skin of her cheek. "Good morning, little heart. Did you have a good sleep? I did. No dreams to remember."

Desah makes her eyes big and looks at her sister, who laughs at the face she makes.

"Shhhh, Onráhdagǫ: is sleeping."

They get up. Desah takes her sister by the hand, leading her to the ladder. She climbs a couple of rungs down and motions for her sister to come to her. She refuses. Onráhdagǫ: wakes.

"You can carry her down. They do not want her to learn how to go down the ladder by herself until she is big enough."

With one arm around her nervous sister and one hanging on the ladder, they get down the ladder.

Grandmother and one of her cousins are kneeling in front of a worn smooth log, twisting corn husks into shape.

Grandmother motions for the girl to take Gajihsdǫdáha outside. "Your cousin must be hungry."

Her cousin rises and hands Desah some meat and takes Star to find her mother.

Grandmother asks, "How are you today? Did your dream friend appear?"

"No, grandmother. No dreams. I think I will no longer be tormented with the little girl's sadness."

"Good. You can always check in on her now that you know how that happens. When you are ready, help your mother with the winter preparations, sort seeds and other dried foods."

"Hao`."

She looks at the food in her hand, saying, "I am not hungry yet."

Jiʔnhǫ enters their longhouse, trying to focus her eyes to the semi-dark space. She walks towards Desah and her grandmother by their fire.

"Sgę́:nǫʔ. It is a beautiful day. Did you swim in the great water this morning?"

"Not yet. I just woke." Looking at her grandmother, she says, "I want to go with her."

"Hao`."

Seeing her grandmother look at the food in her hand, she eats it while she watches. As soon as it is down, she takes a drink of the water that is there. The two young women wave before they run to their favourite secluded space on the lake to bathe.

Ji²nhǫ asks, "Are you going on the next hunting trip?"

"No. I will go on the one after the next hunting trip."

Smiling and pointing to her belly that she has puffed out, Desah says, "One or both of my sisters will be with baby and will need help in the spring and summer."

Laughing, Ji²nhǫ says, "How will that happen? Onráhdagǫ: does not have a mate and Deyawędǫh has many little ones already."

"I am not ready to go on the hunting trip. I am still tired from our fasting trip."

"Not tomorrow. When they go in the fall."

Desah gives a sigh. She cannot think of doing anything else right now. She is too tired. Changing the focus, she says, "My grandmother asked me to sort seeds. Help me."

"Are the seeds too heavy to carry?"

"No, too many." She laughs.

Desah and Ji²nhǫ quickly dry themselves and set off to find the seeds.

CHAPTER SEVEN – CRUSHES OR DESPERATE

Sheyna wakes to a gorgeous day in Connecticut. She hears the door shutting and brother starting his car. 'Is he leaving for work already?'

She gets up, anxious to write down her recent dream.

In her journal she writes, 'A man wrapped his arms around me and held me. I don't remember where we were, only that I felt held. He took me to flashes of places. I know he was beside me. There was another guy present but not seen. I only felt observed. It seemed like he wanted to be with me, but he didn't approach me, just followed me. He seemed to wait for his chance. The guy I was with was energetic, sure, handsome, full of ideas, athletic. It seems like I knew him to be quiet at times. I felt I knew him. The other guy I didn't know; he was quiet, too, and followed me around.'

'This is a dream that I definitely want to discuss with my sister,' she thinks to herself.

Desasǫ́dręh feels Sheyna's happiness as she drives down the hill to the work trailer beside the river. She has a new job and new friends in a different location far away from her territory, and memories of her mate. She feels her gratefulness and how privileged she is to be working in this lush countryside of trees, rocks and water.

On her way to work, Sheyna stops at the local coffee drive-through to get her coffee and something for her brother. She cannot get over how grumpy the servers are here. She lets on she doesn't notice and picks up her order at the window, smiles and drives away.

As she approaches the work site, her thoughts wander as if she is talking directly to Desah. 'Every day I get to see this breathtaking sight; that's if I can block those twenty to twenty-five office trailers from my mind's view. Too bad, eventually this spot will be a secondary parking lot to the casino and the hotel on the hill. Nice spot for the hotel that will eventually overlook the view of the pristine Thames River. I hope I will get to stay there when it is finished.

'It is Monday, eight twenty a.m., and it looks like everyone is already at the office. The new car on the lot must be Evan's, the big boss.'

He is one of the partners from Canada, which means there is a site meeting today with all the construction companies under the main contractor. As usual, Sheyna is delivering Clark's morning refreshments, one of her biggest and most unappreciated responsibilities of this job. She smiles to herself. 'Ehhh, this company would fold without me.'

Remembering a conversation with her sister, Lindy, Sheyna says, "This type of job does not remind me of any of the jobs I have ever done, and it is exactly what I need at this turning point in my life. It is certainly a different type of stress to my previous job with the emergency services on the Rez."

Lindy asks worriedly, "How's brother doing?"

"Why? What does your senses tell you?"

Desah knows Sheyna's family has strong spiritual ties and accepts their sharp intuition as natural. Her sisters have varying levels of intuitive strength, especially her youngest sister, Lindy, who is open to messages through another sense. She was born with a gift the family inherited from their ancestors.

"No, I don't sense anything. Shanana says he's not well. He has high blood pressure or something."

Sheyna says, "He seems okay if he remembers his pills. He needs them to keep calm managing all these guys on this job. Seventy-five employees are erecting the steel of the casino. You should come out and see him in action. It's pretty cool to watch. There are too many companies on site at once. We are only one of many companies here; close to one thousand two hundred employees, including first aid, secretaries, safety officers, ironworkers, and heavy machine, and crane operators all working on the site at the same time. I have to laugh when I hear Clark refer to the ironworkers as the 'guys', because of his common gender-biased description of ironwork. We signed up women and the guys say that they are handy for carrying bolts, dragging cables, and getting into spots where the bulky guys can't fit. It's just that brother is nervous about women working on the site. What's happening on the Rez?"

"You know, the same things," Lindy says. "I'm going out with Phil. He's okay… funny. When he asked me for my cell number, he asked what name he should use in the contacts list. I told him 'Bambi', my stripper name."

Sheyna laughs. Lindy is so comical, and comfortable with herself. She never seems to care what people think as long as she gets a laugh out of them. She's the baby of ten in the family, which means over the years the brothers – five of them – pay a lot of attention to the conversations of their sisters, their young sensibility and limited experience. She has watched families and it seems that the youngest learn early they are the entertainment for the rest of the family.

Desah feels Sheyna's lonesomeness; as she reminisces about her conversations with her sister, her mood changes.

Sheyna shakes off the feeling and rushes into the office. She is not acknowledged by her brother, who is busy memorising the blueprints. The other two relaxed guys in the room are leaning against the desk and say, "Good morning, Sheyna."

Evan, the big boss, is on his phone and nods acknowledgement of her entrance.

Placing her brother's coffee, egg sandwich and orange juice next to the drafting table full of blueprints and sticky notes, she asks, "What time is the meeting today?"

"Eleven thirty a.m. start. They'll feed us before the meeting." He flashes a second of a smile, then he says, "Did you finish the list of the monthly expenses for Evan to review before the meeting?"

Without answering immediately, she turns to her office in the front half of the trailer.

"You know I did," she mutters to herself under her breath.

She knows she is a good secretary, always thinking ahead of what he needs; but, of course, because she's the younger sister, he takes her assistance for granted.

Thinking back to her conversation with her younger sister, Lindy says, "Remember how you got this Connecticut job?"

Sheyna says, "Of course. Shanana gets right to the point, 'Hire Sheyna, Clark. She doesn't have a job, or a husband, or kids.'"

The girls laugh because Shanana is so blunt about the facts. She does not know the depth of suffering Sheyna went through when Damon left or what it feels like to lose the security of kids, a husband, and a permanent job.

Over and over, Desah recalls the scene, repeating it in her mind, where Sheyna is begging Damon to have a baby with her and his constant refusal, coming up with a different excuse every time.

Her husband said, "I have my children, we're too old to start a family now. We're just getting to the age where we can do things without worrying about the kids."

She finishes the herbal medicine to have a baby after Damon left her for the second time in ten years. They had been married for seven years the first time he left, which had left her devastated, practically crippling her being. She was not prepared for him to leave at that time, becoming gravely ill mentally, emotionally, and spiritually. On the advice of family and friends, she signed up for counselling. Five months later, she took him back because she knew what it takes to stay married. Her parents stayed together until death parted them. Damon did not think much of marriage because both his parents remarried a few times. She blamed herself the first time he left. The second time, three years of counselling later, she quit drinking. He left her again. She was prepared the next time. She pretended to be okay. She quit blaming herself for him leaving.

In a conversation with Lindy, she said, "Now, here I am in Connecticut with house payments and his credit card debts in Canada. Nice husband I picked, huh?"

Desasǫdręh discusses Sheyna's new life and her emotional status with her mum and grandmother. "After a separation, Damon came back home. Sheyna's trust and security were shaken. I am sure she still loves this man. She knows people make sacrifices and fight to stay together if there is interference. She thinks about her happy days with the children, the trips they took and the laughs they had. Her heart aches for those days. She loves him because of the children and the happiness he brought to her life."

Grandmother says, "Do not worry. After some time, she will be fine."

Mother says, "She thinks of those days because she is lonesome for that happiness she experienced. Did she want children?"

Desah's face turns sombre. "All her life. She was very young when she got pregnant by the boy that made her laugh. The spirit passed before it was born. She was too young to know she was pregnant. She visited a medicine man they call 'doctor' about the irregularity of her moon. He told her she must have been pregnant. He did not check the issue. Her womb was scarred from what I later learned they called a miscarriage."

Her mother asks, "Did she talk to her mother?"

"No. Her mother had passed three years before.

She was afraid to say anything to her older sisters, and she thought that her father would not know anything about her moon. She was afraid to disappoint them."

"Near the end of her relationship with Damon, he gave her a choice: to quit her Fire Department job to move with him to New Jersey, or he was leaving without her. Desperate to hang on to a toxic marriage, and based on those beliefs that all was lost, she left her work to be with him."

As if she is talking to Desah, Sheyna says, 'What a fool I was? It took me five years of counselling to realise we are two people who should not have been married in the first place.'

"Married or marriage means a ceremony in front of people to vow to stay together. I remember her telling Damon when they met that she did not want to get married. He was more determined to marry her."

Mother says, "She got her wish. He left her."

Desah remembers Sheyna talking to Lindy, saying, "Good thing Bro was in a bind and needed a secretary."

Smiling to herself, she says, "Here I am gratefully working in Connecticut, getting to know my serious brother as an adult. The old fart is ten years older than me. I did not really know him before now. He was always so serious as he was turning into a man."

Sheyna tells her sister, Lindy, "It's kind of cool watching our brother in action on a daily basis and learning about his work as an ironworker, and now as a Superintendent. The guys respect him. Although the casino requested the ironworkers be natives of North America, a call went out to the local steel union in Connecticut, as well as the unions to attract ironworkers. The word travelled fast through Six Nations: Akwesasne, Kahnawake, Snye, Cayuga, Oneida, and Onondaga. The guys from the local union are good guys, too, brother says. One of the local guys admitted there's only a few that have experience climbing or raising iron. This is why Clark put a call-out for gangs from the other Indigenous communities in Canada and New York. Most of them have worked with him on various jobs over the years, or heard of him in the field."

Lindy says in a questioning tone, "Oh, so there are a lot of Rez boys you can mess with?"

"Not a chance. I think most of them are married or have children."

"Clark said he was looking for a smaller, short-term job, and he almost turned down MIDI because of his health issues. He admits he loves the challenge of working a fast-tracked job this size. The many conflicting deadlines are not easily synchronised with the other companies on site. Then there is also the safety equipment up the 'yin yang' to contend with, as Bro would say."

Taking a deep breath, Sheyna adds, "Timing deliveries of supplies and equipment rentals, iron beams, cement, rock, sand, stone, decking, and tie rods, along with the manoeuvre of cumbersome cranes, lifts and scaffolding around in such a small area, causes minor conflicts among companies. At one point, there were thirteen cranes and one tower crane sticking out above the trees on the hill."

Desasódreh understands her amazement. She can see the back of a giant porcupine on the hill where the many cranes are sticking up in the sky.

Lindy laughs, saying, "Okay. He's busy. Your job is important. I get it."

"I wish you could come out to visit us, see where we work. Maybe I would not be so lonesome if I have memories of you being here."

Clark and Evan leave the trailer to check the site to prepare for the meeting with the main contracting company that is responsible for the billion-dollar budget. Richard, a stiff, or maybe better described as professional, and Louis, a confident little Frenchman, stay behind at the trailer.

Sheyna writes in her journal, 'Louis was probably hired to assist Clark or learn from him; either way, I suspect he is here to report to Evan in French. He sure is a big comic relief for me and my Bro.'

Sheyna tells her brother, "I think Louis' translation of English through his French brain makes him comical. I like him."

Her brother says, "Yeah, me, too. He's a funny little guy. There are no words to describe Louis."

Louis starts with his normal way of storytelling

with swearing, 'F' this and 'F'ing' that.

Teasing him, Sheyna asks, "Who on earth taught you how to speak English? They should have taught you more adjectives."

Richard, MIDI co-worker, snidely replies, "He taught himself."

Just then, a voice comes over the radio. "Sheyna. Clark. Office, come in."

It is Jake, the General Foreman, in his usual grumpy tone, and hard to tell if his manner is due to his personality or professionalism. Either way, he seems to always get on her brother's last nerve.

Using her usual response, she says, "Go ahead. This is the office."

"Can you order two gallons of clear paint?"

Sheyna's brows furrow as she looks at Louis with an inquisitive expression that says, '*What the heck does he mean...?*'

Louis confidently saunters over to the radio and says, "Jake. Come in, Jake."

Without waiting for a response, he says, "Jake, what the hell is clear paint... paint that don't paint?"

Sheyna is not expecting that question! Of course, she bursts into her loud cackle and most unladylike laughter. Once she recovers, she is shocked at his poor use of English on the radio. She does not tell him that his 'h-word' is a definite no, no for a radio communications licence if the authorities had heard. For a moment – there's dead air.

From somewhere on the one hundred and fifty-acre site, they hear Clark's serious voice come over the radio, saying, "It's okay, Louis. We'll be back at the office in ten."

As she flips through the supplies catalogue looking for the paint-that-don't-paint, Evan and Clark arrive back at the trailer to check the blueprints one more time before the site meeting. They are discussing the status of construction, expenses, list of needs, issues, and the scheduling conflicts that Clark's crew has been experiencing with the other companies. Once Evan is briefed, he, Clark, and Louis head to the contractor's trailer.

To Richard, an employee from Montreal, she says, "I have worked many places with various levels of stress. This type of workplace is nothing like any I have ever experienced."

"Yes. We get regular reports at the head office. We don't hear about the other companies unless they mention it in the big meeting, and only if it affects scheduling."

"Maybe they will tell you that one morning they found a guy in his office dead from a heart attack. It had to have happened after supper that night, because one of the guys asked him to go to supper with them and he turned them down. Another time, a worker is blown off or pulled off the steel by a strong wind. The sheet of decking was yanked from his hands, pulling him off the second floor. He lands and rolls on the ground without getting hurt, but the sheet of decking comes down after him and lands on his leg, breaking it."

Richard says, "He should have been tied off."

"Yes, that's what Paul, the safety inspector, investigated. Apparently, he wasn't placing it into position, nor was he on a beam. He was on a floor, picked it up to move it and the wind took him by surprise, pulling him off the iron."

"That's right. We read all of Paul's reports. Evan complains that there is always a line-up for the First Aid trailer."

Sheyna thinks, 'Oh, oh, did I say too much?'

Out loud, she says, "What does the nurse look like? There are few women around here and the guys are away from their Mrs... Maybe she is too pretty."

Richard laughs. "So you say we should hire an unattractive nurse for the job to lessen the safety issues?"

The guys come back from the meeting. Clark puts his handwritten notes on her desk for her to type out. She asks, "Is the meeting over already?"

Clark says, "No. Evan is still in the meeting. Louis got us kicked out. We were laughing too much."

Brother seemed nervous before the meeting and is much more relaxed now.

She asks, "How did it go? Did you get access schedules approved?"

Clark answers with a bit of a smile. "The meeting was great. That Evan's calm manner always amazes me when he's in those meetings. He usually has an answer for everything. Yes, we got our ingress/egress schedule approved. Evan sent us to check on the crane that sank into the cement. They should have it removed by now."

"I'm going back to the apartment after work. You'll probably have supper with the guys, right?"

With a nod, he leaves for the site.

After another tense day, she arrives at the two-bedroom apartment the company rents for Clark. She benefits indirectly because she does not have to pay for her section. The layout is they share a kitchen and bathroom in the middle, and from their bedrooms they have their own entrance to the outside. Clark turned the living room into a bedroom, which meant she couldn't watch TV in there. She brought her own TV and VCR from home, so she wouldn't have to bother him. She loves her cosy little part of the world. It is only a bedroom big enough for two dressers and a bed. When Clark works late or goes to the bar with the guys, she spends her time sitting outside her room, smoking, and writing in her journal; a mental exercise she gained in counselling that she has come to love.

To Desasǫdręh, she says, 'I like to write my silly romantic thoughts down. This way I don't bore people and I can slowly chip away at my garbage.'

Sheyna moans, 'I have to get a life! Maybe I

should join the gym. There is one in Glastonbury which is not far from here.'

Thursday afternoons and Saturday mornings she has set aside for her physical exercise by going to the gym. Clark usually drives home on the weekends. Sheyna, who really has no reason to go home, stays put in Uncasville most of the time, turning down the eight-hour drive home with her brother. Some of the guys go to the bar on Fridays after work and some drive home to their families. The guys that stay, and local men, ask her to go to supper and the bar sometimes. Still carrying the pain of being separated from her husband, she politely refuses. She figures there is no use getting to know these guys too good if the estimated completion or plan to 'roll up' is calculated for January 2001.

Sick of being without the love of a man, she writes in her journal, 'The next time one of those guys from work asks me to go to dinner, I might consider it.' She smiles at her brother's famous words: "Don't go out with an ironworker," he says, while rolling his eyes with exasperation.

"Why not? Shanana did." To which he had no reply.

The morning comes fast. Sheyna wakes with a fuzzy dream in her head. 'What does that dream mean? The kiss was familiar, which means it is one of many.'

Sheyna writes down her kissing dream in her

journal. 'I am sitting at the computer in my office. A man wearing a white hat gives me a goodbye kiss on the cheek. The kiss feels comfortable. It feels good because whoever he is will be back after work.'

'Great, the only kiss I get is on the cheek and in my dreams. That's it, I am sick of being alone. The next time one of those guys asks me to go to dinner, I will consider it.'

Maybe her dream means the guy in the white hat is Jake, the green-eyed, handsome General Foreman on the job. He caught Sheyna's attention from the moment she met him. She looks forward to him lumbering into the trailer every day. One of the best things about him is he loves his Ǫgwehǫ́:weh mother.

That night she calls Lindy. "Oh, my gosh, I think Jake, the General Foreman, is one big, hot dude," she says, emphasising the big. "I mean, he's huge! His frigging shoulders are about four feet wide! He doesn't seem to get along with our bro, though, probably because he is insecure about his skills as an ironworker, or a foreman. I think he and Clark had a heated discussion about hiring the guys from Six Nations. Clark tried to tell him he's more comfortable working with a raising gang he knows and has worked with many times for many years. He trusts them."

Lindy agrees. "Yeah, I heard a couple of the guys from Six Nations dragged up on their current jobs just to work with Clark; and, of course, the American money is good right now."

"Yeah, I wonder who they are. Anyway, Jake's mum is native, but I'm not sure of her Nation because they live in Massachusetts. I think he said she is Sioux. Anyway, he is so big. I bet he is way over six foot and probably his bulky body is inherited from his dad."

"Okay, he's physically big. We got some big guys," Lindy says, defending the men from their community.

Without acknowledging Lindy's comment, she returns to her own topic. "Bro said he heard Jake is going home to Massachusetts for the weekend to see his mother. You know how I always like a man who loves his mother because it means he respects women. Maybe I'm too obvious about my feelings because he seems agitated when he's around me. All I want is those huge arms around me, just to see how they feel to my hands or my teeth," Sheyna moons.

Trying to slow down her sister, Lindy says, "Is it worth having a relationship with this guy? He gets agitated when he's around you and Clark."

"Hey, I have to get off the phone. Here comes Jake. Love and miss you always."

She gets the message and understands her sister's exasperation, but there is no time to discuss it.

Jake comes into the office big as life to write out timecards. Why she bothers with this grumpy-no-sense-of-humour guy, she does not know. Maybe the reason is that he is single.

She says in a playful way, "I heard you're going to Massachusetts this weekend."

Still going about his business in her side of the work trailer, he says in a surprisingly friendly tone, "You heard right; leaving Friday at noon."

Wondering why he's in her office, she walks over to the table where he's working. He stands about a foot taller than her five-foot-two-inch frame. Those shoulders seem broader up close. He always smells good, too. He must not work up a sweat.

Feeling the heat between them, she asks, "Are you taking me with you?"

"No. I am not."

"Why not? I don't take up much space. I could fit in your suitcase."

"I imagine you could, but you're not going," he says as he folds his paperwork.

Looking sideways at her, he adds in a questioning tone, "We can go for supper when I get back, if you want."

Livening up, Sheyna says, "Okay."

He leaves her office but not before he gives her a wink. She almost pees. The wink is enough to set her mind whirling. 'Wait until I tell Lindy! Either he's teasing me, or we are going to dinner when he gets back.'

Sheyna calls Lindy that night, excited to tell her about her and Jake's conversation.

"Today was a heck of a lot better than yesterday

when everyone was picking on each other and taking out their frustrations on me. Jake came into the trailer, nagging and insulting me and my brother. He says he is teasing, but it really hurts because I don't want him to see me as a bumbling idiot. It's just because I am so nervous around him. Louis said Jake knows I love him. I wanted to laugh because it is an 'L' word, all right, but it's not love. I am freaking sexually attracted to this guy. It's frustrating. When he's around I mess up, lost for words, basically a mess. I know he thinks I'm stupid."

"You? Lost for words? You are not stupid, and, of course, you don't love that grumpy guy! He's probably the only single guy around. It is no wonder you have the hots for him."

"Yeah. I would have to put up with his grumpiness and the guys in the trailer, but I overheard the guys from Montreal talking about me. Dana said something about not believing I am still single. Louis said I'm not married because I didn't keep my mouth shut. I walked into their office and told him, 'No, I am single because I kept my mouth shut. Where did that get me?' I left early that day and dared them to say anything. I barely talk when I am at work. He probably had a recent fight with his wife."

"Yeah, probably. Besides, I don't think you wanted to get married, did you?"

"Not really. One time I told a friend I would get married when I found someone that loved me more than I did. I wanted to see what he would say."

"What did he say?"

"He said that's why he hasn't asked anyone to marry him."

Changing the topic back to Jake, Lindy asks, "What do you see in this Jake guy, anyway?"

"I don't know. He's handsome, brown-skinned, and big-chested, with huge arms and shoulders I could ride on. He can be funny, once or twice. He's smart, doesn't mess with married women, fun to be out with, sticks up for me, and those green eyes twinkle, making his smile the greatest soul warmer around."

Lindy says, "Maybe that's it. He is the only guy you see other than bro and Louis?"

"I realise I'm looking too hard to find the good side of him. There are seventy-five guys out there that I could go after, but the one guy that rarely pays attention to me, I lust. Yes, it's confirmed. I am starving for attention. Before I was married, I always had someone on the line. This can't be my life, Lindy. I wish Jake would be around more like he was today, playful. He knows I have a crush on him, and yet he has never made any moves in my direction. Last night he went to the casino. Did he ask me to go? Nope."

"He winked at you," Lindy says, teasing her.

In her journal, she writes, 'Ben, one of the ironworkers, bounces into the work trailer and asked to use the phone to call Lainey, his girlfriend.'

Desah can't help but hear him say, "I have VIP tickets to the boxing match tonight. Do you want to go? No? Oh. Okay. Can I come over after the match?"

Ben turns to Sheyna and asks, "Hey. Do you want to be second fiddle and go to the boxing match at the casino?"

Sheyna, without thinking, says, "Yes. Now isn't that the story of my life being second fiddle, even in my marriage. Why not, I would love to see that fight."

Beaming, Sheyna adds, a little more excited, "My Dad and my brothers were boxers. They trained in Brantford and competed in the Golden Gloves. My brother, Douglas, said he would gag when he saw the US border, he was so nervous. The only live fights I watched were my brothers, and Nick, my sister-in-law's younger brother. What time should I be ready?"

Ben picks her up at five thirty p.m. at the apartment in Uncasville. They have supper in the casino, where he shows off his comical, confident, and charming self. After a great buffet, they find their seats in the huge tent next to the casino. They are so close they can hear the flesh being hit by their opponent's gloves and see the sweat splash off the boxers' hair as they dance around the ring. One guy is almost knocked through the ropes. The crowd parts, knocking over chairs to get out of the estimated landing spot. They both gaze at each other with a sick look and big eyes. Ben says, "How can you stand this?"

She is surprised at his wimpy question and laughs. "Hopefully, they are well matched and have trained for months or all their lives before a fight of equal or better skills and strength. They should know what they are getting into before they step into that ring."

It is a good night. Sheyna is full of supper and wins $10 after she watches one of her favourite sports, and she didn't have to pay for any of it. She is glad Ben is a gentleman. He's comfortable to be with. Butting in on her summary of the night, Ben asks, "Do you want to hit the bar before I take you home?"

"Thank you for the exciting night, but I don't think so. Seven a.m. comes too early for me. Besides, you asked your honey if you could visit later."

"I thought I would ask." He drops her off at the apartment. Ben cracks the ice.

The next morning, instead of noting a dream she had, she writes about last night's outing in her journal.

Sheyna calls her sister. "Lindy, I finally went somewhere without bro last night."

"Really? Did you go to the gym or casino?"

"No. I mean with someone, a man. Ben is one of the ironworkers that kisses-up to Clark. Anyway, he took me out to dinner and a boxing match."

"Sounds like he's kissing-up to you."

"No. He has a girlfriend that he wants me to meet. He said we would hit it off."

"Sheyna, isn't there one single guy there?"

Almost as if her sister didn't say anything, Sheyna says, "All I want is Jake's huge arms around me, just to see how it feels. I know I would be a good woman for him. I'd rub his huge shoulders and kiss his chest."

"That's okay. I don't need to hear any gory details of your fantasy. I mean another single guy besides Jake."

Sheyna giggles. "Yes, you're right. I have to forget that guy. I asked him out and he said he was busy."

"Maybe he was."

"Yeah, I don't know. I peeked at Jake when he was working in my office again, and we smiled at each other. Yes, today was a good day; he shot an elastic at me."

"Oh, wow, the elastic proves you two are meant for each other."

Sheyna laughs at her own silliness. This is why she writes in her journal.

"You don't understand. He hardly ever talks to me directly and he never fools around. This is a big step. The other day he came into the trailer with Ben, the only other guy that's brave enough to visit during lunch. Ben asked me to go to lunch with him and Jake. At the same time, Jake asked Louis, which meant I had to stay in the office because Clark wasn't around. That was my chance to be with Jake without bro and away from the office. Fate is not fair sometimes."

"Yes, it's fate. Get the hint."

"That's true. Louis told me Jake wants me to go out with Ben!"

Lindy, sounding a bit frustrated with her sister, says, "Sheesh. It is funny how you wrap your love life around a guy you see maybe once a day, who took you to dinner once only because you bugged him, and he's mean to you most of the time."

"You're right! I put him in my set of pictures, I can take him out. When are you coming out to visit?"

"Before the end of summer, I should be able to get away. If not this year, then next year."

"Really? We are supposed to roll up in January."

"Well, whenever. I'll try to get there."

Desah senses a change coming to Sheyna. From her conversations with her sisters and friends, she seems to be slowly coming alive. Sheyna calls her friend Collette in Teterboro, New Jersey. They met as sisters-in-law, and bonded as sisters. "Hey. You have to come out to visit me before we move back to the Rez."

"Okay. I will ask John, again."

"Great! Let me know, so I won't go home to the Rez, or commit to work that weekend. Get an Amtrak to Old Saybrook or New London stations."

"I'll call your office when I know."

Sheyna's older sister, Marlene, calls the office to see how the siblings are doing. Sheyna answers, "We are doing good. We're busy. Clark is really very busy, scary stressed. Sometimes he gets right worked up. I think his lips turn purple."

"Is he taking his blood pressure pills?"

"I will ask. Remember Jake, the guy I was telling you about? He doesn't want me."

"What's the matter with him?"

Sheyna laughs to herself. 'That's her. Sticking up for me. What's the matter with me? Chasing after a man who doesn't care about me.'

Out loud she says, "Yeah. What is the matter with him and what is the matter with me?"

"Maybe you don't really want another man in your life yet? So, you pick guys who can't be yours."

"Never thought of that. We are supposed to be done here next year, anyway. Clark predicts more like February. Sister, I have to get out more and find friends around here."

Desasǫdrẹh watches and wonders. She does not see the attraction to these two men, Ben and Jake. One has a girlfriend and this one is insulting and grumpy most of the time. Plus, he is mean to her, and at times disrespectful to her brother. Sheyna does not want anyone permanent. She wants someone to help her get over Damon.

To herself, Sheyna thinks, 'I wish I would dream more, or, at least, remember them clearly. I remember most of them, but the details do not make sense. I wish I knew how to decipher them correctly.'

Desah checks in on Sheyna to see if she is still

progressing without mishap. She seems to be getting over the mean man. Maybe Ben will be better for her.

A cute, handsome young man walks into the office. He invites Sheyna to the Cove to hear the song he wrote and recorded. He leaves the office when she says she would go over there one of these days and he should let her know when the guys are there.

Then Ben bounces into the office to see if Sheyna wants to go to the show or supper.

"No. That's okay. I don't need a date. Besides, I know you have a girlfriend, and I don't want to mess with that."

"She won't mind. She's cool."

Sheyna gives him the evil eye. "She must be. She won't go to dinner and show with you?"

"She's got a date with her sisters; a family dinner, or something."

"Oh, I better not. I'm no fun, anyway. Ask my ex."

"Well, I am not your ex. You don't have to entertain me. Let me know if you change your mind. It's going to get lonely around here if you don't start hanging out with people."

"That's true. I was just saying that to my sister. I'll think about it. I'll call if I change my mind."

As if nothing has happened, Damon calls the office. "Good day, beautiful. Do you want to go to dinner at Foxwood on Saturday? We can go to the museum and to dinner some place."

Sheyna covers the telephone; pointing to it, she mouths, "Speak of the devil. I will see you around."

She waves goodbye to Ben as he slips out of her office.

To Damon, she says, "The idea appeals to me, but then a million hurtful thoughts come to mind, especially the picture of you and Moushee. Yuck!"

"I am sorry. I realise what I lost now."

He begins dumping his garbage on her. "She didn't love me, she never wanted me, she only wanted to see what she could get out of me, she knows I still love you, etc., etc."

As he talks, his words become background noise.

When he takes a breath, she says, "So, the woman of your dreams turned out to be a nightmare? I will not be second best to no one, especially her."

"No. You're not second best to—"

She cuts him off and says, "Listen, if I go out with you, you might think there is a chance for us to get back together, and I don't want that."

There is silence on both ends of the telephone, then he says softly, "I understand."

"Damon, she's not twenty-eight and you aren't twenty-five any more."

"That's not the reason. I thought I should be with her because we are grandparents now."

Sharply, she says, "Listen to yourself, Damon! You have five children by five different women. Are you going to leave every time one of them has your grandchild? Face it. You care for this woman! Get a new girlfriend. Don't keep going back to the same ones: me, Moushee and who else, uh, Nancy."

"I don't want a girlfriend. I want my wife back."

"No. You don't. We signed papers. You want your freedom. Now that I have a taste of it, I want to keep it."

After a moment, a little indignantly, Damon says, "Okay, sorry to bother you."

Sheyna and Damon's conversation is over, but not in her mind. She constantly replays the situation. I should have told him off and told him I always hated being second best and the least important person in his life. As usual, I stop the truth in my throat when I am sober.

Observing Sheyna in the situations around her, Desah is relieved to hear her say to her sister, "The reason I am into me, me, me, is because I am self-evaluating. I have to experience bigger and better things, or different things at least, and learn something from my mistakes. I can't keep going back to the same type of man. Maybe that's it. I like Jake because he's familiar. Oh, no, are Damon and Jake basically the same type of man, emotionally abusive?"

The next day she writes in her journal: 'Jake is going away for a whole week! He's going to see his mum in Massachusetts. He said I can call him if I need him. That is a loaded statement. I need him, all right.

I will miss flirting with him. It's my birthday and he's not here, although he got me flowers, which shocked me. I am going to thank him when he gets back. The Decking Crew got me a funny but naughty birthday card with a Victoria's Secret gift certificate in it. That said, the only thing that goes down on you is your computer. Ha, ha, ha. Who would want that done to them anyway? Lindy and her daughters called to sing happy birthday to me. They are so sweet!'

Clark is working late tonight or he's out with the guys. Sheyna's outside her bedroom having a smoke and reading her journal to herself. 'Since everyone I talk to is sick of hearing about Jake, I've decided to honestly compare and write down his qualities and his faults. Qualities are that he is generally good-hearted, analytical, smart, working, travels, has strong ethics, likes his family, handsome, huge shoulders, and chest, and can be tender when he wants to be. That's such a turn-on when a big guy like that can be gentle. His faults are that he can be foolish in some ways, defensive most of the time, cannot tell when someone is kidding, won't take chances with people (me), mean, unsupportive, negative, controlling, and critical, and accuses me of being dozy when he can easily make mistakes like anyone else. Besides, I am only dozy in front of him because I get so nervous around him. Despite all that, Jake always makes my day. I will miss him.'

The week of Jake's return, work resumes. Desah

notices Jake, the guy that Sheyna thinks about all the time. He is back from wherever he was and is at the trailer. He looks like he is waiting for her to express her happiness at seeing him. As Sheyna rushes into the trailer, she notices his big smile. She is about to say good morning when her sleeve catches on the door handle, yanking her back and splashing coffee in the air.

Jake pinches his eyes closed and crossly says, "Shees sus!"

Sheyna smiles at her brother, who wrinkles his nose, trying not to laugh. She knows he is thinking, 'Sheyna sure knows how to ruin a moment.'

Embarrassed, Sheyna hands Clark his breakfast sandwich and what's left of his coffee.

She looks at Jake and says, "Glad you're back." Blushing, she scurries into her side of the trailer to hide in front of her computer. The moment is over.

Desah sees that Sheyna does not realise that Jake was genuinely missing her.

In her journal, she writes, 'Today is an absolutely gorgeous day! Jake has been back a week and I am in love! He gave me a look I'll never forget. Louis says Jake does not know I love him. I'm crazy. Jake has never given me any sign of potential love until today. There were other things that made my day, too. People were nice. They came into the office to tell me their concerns, and for a change, Louis stuck up for me in front of my brother. Dane, a huge, serious, handsome guy from Montreal who has been here before, has officially introduced himself. He seems nice and might have done it for me if it wasn't for his blond hair. Today and every day, it's Jake that makes my day.'

Journal note: 'Another dollar, another awful day today! I hate that man! I am glad I didn't sleep with him. He is a jerk and an a-hole. I'm leaving this job! I hate them all so much! They can have all the redheaded women they want! You'll have to make more money to keep that woman happy, buddy. Play me like a sucker. Lead me up and down heaven knows where. I've had enough of the mood swings of this place!'

'Sorry, guys, for the rant. It's not your fault I choose misery. Like you guys, it's not my fault you are miserable. Although you probably think differently, and blame me as usual.'

Journal note: 'Today, is heck-of-a-lot better at work than yesterday. Louis was pleasant to me. Clark was late getting to work. Jake was friendly and nice. He seems nicer now that I quit chasing him. I caught him checking to see if I was watching him be cute, and I was. He spends more time in the office these days. I love Jake's greenish brown eyes that water up when he smiles. I've got to quit thinking of him for my own good. Today, our bland conversation was about me talking to myself because no one listens to me anyway. He said he wasn't surprised. Louis said the reason Jake won't go out with me is because he doesn't like Clark. Can this be true? I don't think it is a very good reason.'

'According to "choice theory," I am the one that fills my album with pictures. Mine are good pictures, and maybe sometimes they are not realistic ones. I am going to make myself sick, thinking, wanting, and not having real love. Look what I was going after, a big green-eyed monster or another person who I heard is noted for taking cocaine.'

'Is there a faithful, considerate, and loving man out there? One who will rub my back when I want. That's my picture of a real man: tender, caring and loving. Tomorrow I will go to work, and Jake will treat me nasty, again. I'm going to ask him what he gets out of it, then that's it for him. What should I do, get another job? Go home? No. It is too early to leave this beautiful state.'

Journal note: 'Another day, another $120 dollars. What a crappy day today turned out to be! Jake quit! He is not a happy man most days, but I never thought he would quit! I don't think it's work-related. Maybe all the Libras are having a hard time right now. My heart aches, and my mind is numb. Now I will never see him again.'

Sheyna calls Lindy, and sadly says, "Hello, my heart throb quit today."

Lindy said, "Bummer."

Sheyna laughs. "And Jake said I was laid back.

He should have met you and Murray."

"What about that other guy you like?"

"Ben? Yeah, I'm leery of him. He does coke and has a sweety. She seems nice, but she called me Judy the other day when she called to tell Ben to call her. Ben said maybe she said 'beauty'. Yes, he's a charmer, but I am afraid he's like any other guy, too charming at first, then he goes blabbing to the guys on the job. I agree with Clark, it might be a mistake to hook up with someone from the job site."

"Does it matter who you go with? You'll be home in January, anyway."

"I suppose you're right. Last night, Ben made the most effort, so I let him drive me home. We talked, but like he said, he has a cool girlfriend. Not many of the girls on the Rez would be so cool about their guy hanging out with another woman. Anyone who drinks and does coke is certainly a man I can leave in January."

Lindy says, "Yeah, forget those guys."

Sheyna writes in her journal, 'Now I know what the kiss dream meant. It was Jake kissing me goodbye.'

CHAPTER EIGHT – CRUSHES – GUY THREE

Friday morning, Sheyna asks her brother, "Are you working this weekend?"

"No. I gotta go home. I'm leaving around three p.m. What are you going to do? Are you going home?"

Sheyna quickly says, "I think I will stay here. It is the last Saturday of August. If the job ends in January, I'm checking out both local Pow Wows. There's one here in Uncasville and one at the Foxwood."

"Who's going with you?"

Hoping he would stay and go with her, she says, "No one. I haven't made very many friends with the people at work, so I am going by myself."

Offering his brotherly advice, he says, "Well, have fun and don't get too carried away."

"Yeah, with who? Ben's girlfriend is not into pow wows."

On her way home from work, Sheyna checks on the bar the guys go to sometimes. No one in there she knows. She grabs a beer anyway and sits at a table by herself.

A native guy, an older gent, says, "Shé:kon [pronounced saygo]."

So, he knows she is Cayuga. She says, "Sgé:nǫ̂."

"Do you want to sit with me? I am having supper and would like to talk to a woman for a change."

She laughs, knowing what he means because she gets lonesome for women. Who would ever think she would get lonesome for women? She moves her beer over to his table.

She asks, "Where you from?"

"Akwesasne. What about you?"

"Six Nations. I'm working with my brother in the office on the Mohegan Sun."

He nods. "I will miss ironworking. This will probably be my last job. I want to retire soon. Too bad my wife couldn't stick it out. We could be sitting by the river fishing near my cabin."

They continue through the afternoon, drinking too much of the sour springs; then she calls a taxi to take him back to his hotel.

He asks, "Are you okay to drive?"

"Yes, as long as I drive straight home. We were lucky to get an apartment down the road from the site."

"You can always go to my hotel," he says, teasing her.

"You behave now. If I go home with you, you'll retire tomorrow."

He laughs. She drinks the last of her beer, gets up and thanks him for the evening.

Staggering to her car, she thinks, 'Too bad that guy was an older fellow. He's still handsome and witty. Hmmm. Let's see if I can get home without getting stopped.'

It is the next day, and she has a slight headache. She gets dressed for the gym. 'Yuck, I think I need a coffee first.'

While she is having a coffee at Dunkin' Donuts, she writes in her journal. 'It is gym day today. I love going to the gym on Thursday nights and Saturday mornings. There is a spunky black guy that mixes dancing and aerobics for his class. I forget I am exercising when I am having fun. After his class, I stretch in the weight room and then to the sauna. That is another great feature.'

After the class, she skips the weight room and showers.

Sheyna checks out the small Uncasville Pow Wow down the road from their apartment. She could have stayed in her car in the parking lot and looked around, but she decides to try some Mohegan corn soup. She thinks, 'Funny how the soup is unique to each of the Indigenous territories both sides of the border.'

Being up late last night after the bar with the handsome old guy, then watching movies until she fell asleep, the gym this morning, or the corn soup are all very good reasons for being sleepy and wanting to take a nap. It is another thirty-minute drive to the Pequot's Schemitzun Pow Wow or drive all the way back to the apartment to have a nap. If she goes there, she will stay there.

'Maybe the loud drums will energise me.'

She arrives at the Schemitzun Pow Wow. She is wrong: the drums don't do a thing for her, so she lies down in the back seat of her car.

After an hour or so, the sound of drums and the MC's voice in the distance wake her up. She wipes the drool off her cheek and looks around the parking lot. There are more cars than when she first arrived. She spruces up her hair, wipes any mascara residue from her eyes, and looks down at her wrinkled blouse. 'Oh, well, who knows me here?'

She gets out. Her nose and appetite lead her towards the smell of the enticing flour and grease and other fattening Pow Wow carbs. Walking towards her, she recognises two guys from Kahnawake that she registered for work a couple of weeks ago. They reintroduce themselves as Ken and Norman. She remembers Ken as the guy with the handsome face and someone who is way too happy to be at work. Norman is his loud comical sidekick who seems to be a little off.

Norman asks, "Shé:kon. Are you Christina's sister from Snye?"

Before she can answer, he looks at Ken to

confirm, "She's Christina's sister, right?"

Without waiting for Ken's answer, he muses, "What is Christina's sister's name, again?"

Sheyna looks at Norman, crunching her eyebrows together while he talks to himself.

Smiling, Ken continues to watch Sheyna's expression, then says, "She does look familiar."

Sheyna butts in on their conversation. "I get that a lot. People from other Rez's always think they know me, or that I am related to someone from their community."

"Now, what is her name?"

Since Norman can't think of Christina's sister's name, she changes the subject. "I came here to eat some Rez food. Are you guys leaving?"

Norman answers, "Yeah. We're going to the casino, right, Ken?"

Ken, still smiling, quickly answers with, "Or, do you want us to join you?"

Pretending to be scared, she looks over her shoulder and says, "Can't hurt, unless you boys have some Rez girls waiting in the wings. I don't feel like getting my hair pulled today."

Loudly, Norman says, "No. We are both single."

She walks towards the drums, music, and the dancers searching for some frybread and soup. The guys turn around to follow her. The park is alive with people from all over the world. The Hodinǫhsyǫ́:niˀ and other Indigenous peoples have tents and tables set up to sell souvenirs, jewellery, baskets, and other unique items for sale or trade.

They stop at a wagon selling some deliciously greasy carbs, and Ken teasingly asks, "Sheyna? Do you want one or two orders of soup and frybread?"

Sheyna smiles, catching his insulting but cute humour, then says seriously, "Yes, my name is Sheyna, and no. I'll buy my own if you have kids to feed."

Ken pays and answers, "Nah, they'll be all right. They ate yesterday."

Norman orders a large thin frybread sprinkled with icing sugar.

Focussed on his dish, he says, "I had soup already. I'm having dessert."

Ken, taking care of his child-like buddy, says, "Norman, you have that powder all over your face and shirt. Get it off. People will think you are serious about drugs."

To Sheyna, he says, "Where to now?"

Sheyna, carefully balancing her soup and biscuit, walks towards the huge white tent, with them following.

Glancing at Ken, she says, "Hopefully, we will find a seat on the bleachers where we can finish our food and watch the dancers."

They sit on the lowest row of bleachers. Around each huge drum, pounding in sync with her heartbeat, are six to eight handsome, brown-skinned men with long braids. One of the guys sings out loudly, and the others chime in. About the third round of chants, colourful dancers file out and dance to the centre and around the ring, forming a spiral of the people; the males are dressed splashier and dance livelier than the women. The women move gracefully in time with the music, their hair and shawls swaying behind them. Their shiny dark hair is adorned with leather and colourful beadwork or a single feather.

"I just love the feeling of the drum," Sheyna says with her eyes closed.

Watching her, Ken asks out of the blue, "Are you going with Ben?"

Norman asks, "Ben who?"

Sheyna laughs and says, "Heavens no. He has a girlfriend in Niantic. I'm not into threesomes. He just took me to one boxing match because she wouldn't go. Oh, no. Do the guys think I go with him?"

"I don't know about the guys. Ben mentioned he took you to the boxing match at the casino and I wondered if it was a regular thing."

"Hhmmh, I accepted his invitation because I thought he was being a nice guy. Plus, free tickets to a live boxing match, and dinner, who would say no?"

She added, "We work until six or eight p.m. sometimes, except when I go to the gym, or to dinner with my brother. I never go anywhere outside of work."

"Yes, I see now. What do you do? Stay in the

apartment all the time? That must get lonely."

"Sometimes, but not real lonely, yet. Everything is so new. Saturday and Sunday, I shop, go to the casinos, or venture out and tour the countryside."

"By yourself?"

"Yes. I don't eat at restaurants by myself, though. Today, I'm brave. This is a welcome change," she says, pointing to Ken and the dancers.

"Thank you. It is a welcome change for me, too."

In her mind: 'If I were to tell Lindy about this in one sentence, I sense a flirtation happening or feel a small connection with this handsome man. She would be so frustrated with me.' They watch a few rounds of dancers.

She is trying to think of something clever to say to him when Ken notices his buddy fidgeting. "I better get Norman back to his apartment. He can't sit still. Let's see if we can change your loneliness. See you at work Monday."

Sheyna says, "Sure. You work on the hill, and I work in the trailer all day until supper."

Ken repeats his statement firmly this time. "I will see you Monday."

To her disappointment, they leave. She walks around the Pow Wow, noticing how many of the people remind her of someone from home. All of a sudden, lonesomeness comes over her like a big thick heavy wave. Just as she gets up to leave, a lady who looks an awful lot like Norma from the Rez walks by her.

Thoughtfully, she says, "Hello."

The lady turns towards her, startled.

"Sgé:nǫʔ."

"It is you! I was just thinking, boy, that lady looks like Norma."

She laughs and teases, "Yes, it is me and it is you, Sheyna."

The two women update each other since they had last seen each other.

Desah understands why she is drawn to Sheyna on this day. She is about to witness another changing event in her life. Hopefully, for the better this time.

Monday, Ken calls the office to invite her out with the guys. "My crew doesn't know the area very well. Do you have any suggestions where we can go to dinner?"

"Yes, I always wanted to try Mexican food in New London. Do they like that?"

"They won't care. Do you want us to pick you up?"

"That's okay. I will meet you guys there. I am getting groceries while I'm out that way."

She feels so privileged to be the only woman with a bunch of handsome guys from other Indigenous communities. Although they treat her as one of the guys, they are very protective of her, too.

After a few months, it is a regular thing for Sheyna to go out with the guys to supper or to the bar.

She hangs out with the guys and works with men all day, every day. She is getting lonesome for female company. Who would think that would happen?

She calls her fun friend Collette, and excitedly says, "Collette, did you ask John if you can visit? I love the bar life around here, live bands, dancing, dinners, and lots of laughs with my friends Craig, Pierce, Ken, Tony, Dwayne, Tim and, sometimes, Norman. Ben is the only 'white-guy' that hangs out with us. Sometimes, he brings his girlfriend, Lainey, who has a great sense of humour. You will like her and the guys. They know dancing is my thing, so we always go where there's music. It turns out that it is their thing, too. I feel like I am one of the guys, or at least a sister of the guys."

"Oh, good. So, you don't miss Damon and his stunts. I am happy for you."

"Damon who? Just kidding. But, really, that's why I like them. They don't remind me of Damon at all. Most of them are committed to their marriages or relationships, and the ones that are single don't push themselves on me. They are a pretty cool bunch of guys."

Collette doesn't work, so their plan entirely relies on the goodness of John's heart and wallet.

"I will ask John again. He might let me go for the weekend when he goes back to Calgary to see his kids."

"Great! Let me know the time, and which train

station to pick you up."

Journal note: 'Another busy Friday on the construction site. In the middle of the chaos, Ben calls the office. "Hey, Lainey says there is a great band playing in Niantic. Do you want to go?"

"Oh, yeah. Let me know what time to meet you. I don't want to walk in by myself."

"We will pick you up at seven thirty p.m."'

About eight, Sheyna, Lainey, and Ben walk into a musty ancient bar. They sit on stools next to Tim, who is already sitting at the bar. Pierce, Ken, Tony, and the other guys are in the other room near the band and dance floor.

After Sheyna and Tim finish swapping Rez stories, she gets around to telling him about her husband leaving, shattering her heart into a million bloody pieces.

Tim, who is almost asleep, says, "That's too bad. Maybe I can help you out. It might take you a while to get me going, but yeah, let's see what we can do."

Once Sheyna realises what he is talking about, she laughs at his crude invitation. Playfully patting his hand, she says, "No, Tim. That's okay. I'm not hinting. Thanks for your very charming offer, though. It's too soon after my break-up to think about being with anyone that way right now."

Tim does not seem offended by her rejection. She quits talking about Damon.

Feeling a little lightweight, she goes into the

room by the bar and dances onto the crowded dance floor by herself. Ken turns away from his partner and dances in front of her. The guys inherently love dancing, too, so they dance with any obliging women in the room. It's all for fun. Lainey is dancing, too, because Ben doesn't like to dance.

Somehow, she falls backwards on the floor, knocking over a chair, and lands under a table. Her legs fly up in the air before she catches her bearings. A couple of the guys stagger over and pick her up. They work on straightening her blouse and skirt, dusting her off. They pick up the beat again, dancing around in front of her as if nothing happened. She continues dancing, too, forgetting she fell. A couple more songs and Lainey breaks away from the group to get her drink from the bar. Ben pulls her between his legs and looks like he's telling her it is time to leave, because she smiles at him and nods yes. Sheyna goes out to see if they are leaving. On her way by, Ken pinches her sleeve, attempting to get her attention.

She stops and turns towards him. "I should go with them. Didn't we have fun tonight?"

The small gesture plants a thought in her mind. Ken follows her to the bar.

"Ben, where are the guys going to party? Let's go there," Sheyna giggles.

Lainey leans against Ben while she puts on her shoes. In her Bronx accent, she says, "Yeah, sweetie, let's find the pawdy."

"Oh, they won't be partying tonight. They are done in and are going back to their rooms. I think Clark asked them to put in a couple of hours tomorrow. That's why they stayed in town this weekend."

Ken smiles as he watches Ben trying to keep track of his girlfriend and friend.

"Do you need any help, buddy?"

"No that's okay. I told Clark I would make sure his little sister is safe. See you tomorrow, guys."

Ben loads two wobbly women into the vehicle.

"I will take you home first, Sheyna."

Arriving safely at the apartment, she thanks him for the ride and tells Lainey goodbye.

"I will see you folks again. It was a fun night. Thank you."

Sheyna stumbles in alone, with her last thought being, 'Well, isn't this a typical night on the weekend lately, twisted up and alone.'

She hears her brother in his room, clearing his throat. 'Well, not really alone.'

The next morning, the trailer is alive with the arrival of the big boss and his assistant. They are in Clark's office, discussing schedules and the status of the construction.

Sheyna is photocopying info for the meeting as a frantic voice is heard over the radio, "Heads up. The crane is going over. The crane is going over. Heads up."

Sheyna immediately looks at the clock on her way to the radio. She calls her brother in from the other office. "Hey, Clark, listen." She logs the frantic message at 10.09 a.m.

Evan and Clark are already rushing into her office.

Evan grabs the radio, and smooth as silk says, "Is everybody okay?"

With Sheyna's dispatching skills, logging radio communications are on point. The office becomes a flurry of radios, phones and cell phones communicating at the same time. Clark and Louis rush out of the trailer, taking the gator to investigate the damage.

Evan and Sheyna wait for their report. Clark says, "Evan. Office, come in."

Evan says, "This is Evan. Go ahead. What is the status?"

"The crane boom is bent and pointing towards the hotel's west wall. As a safety measure, we will secure the crane so that it doesn't move any further and hit the hotel. Tonight, we need to get another crane for safety measures while we cut it apart."

"Okay, good job," Evan says. "I'm heading to the meeting. As soon as you and Louis can, join us to give a brief report on the structural status of the hotel, and the next steps. We can get another crane and operator for tonight. Out."

Clark responds, "Out."

Sheyna listens; wow, business as usual. The strange thing about this incident is that it will hardly interrupt the schedule of the project. Hardly anything sets back their schedule by much.

When Clark and Louis get back, Sheyna overhears their speculation of what has happened, and the overtime plans to cut the bent boom of a one-hundred-and-seventy-ton crane crawler into smaller pieces so that it can be transported off the site before work resumes tomorrow. There is no damage to the hotel or anything else around it. They prepare their report.

She gives Evan a typed copy of the radio communications for his meeting. He verbally pats her on the back, smiling proudly. "This log is going to be useful to the insurance company."

After office hours, Sheyna knows Clark will not be back for supper. On her way to the apartment, she stops at the only drive-through in town. She sees Ken sitting inside, waving her in to eat with him. She parks and takes her bag in. Trying not to look too eager, she slides into the seat across from him.

They talk about the crane incident and how it happened. He leans forward and says sneakily, "What are you doing tonight?"

Her body reacts but her mind stays cool. So, she says, "Nothing really. What's on your mind?"

"Do you want to go to the casino? I want to show

you something."

"Sure," she says, feeling excited about a sneaky adventure. "Can we leave my car at the apartment?"

He obliges her and she gets in with him. They are both quiet on the drive to the casino. He parks his car on the ground floor of the parking lot. She waits to walk towards the entrance, but he is walking towards the side of the parking lot. She looks at him as if to say, where are you going?

He motions for her to follow. "Here, I'll give you a boost."

He helps her over the cement barrier, then he nimbly climbs over. They walk close to the wall of the casino, looking around to make sure no one else is on site.

She whispers, "Where are you taking me?"

Ken makes a shushing motion and waves her to follow him. They are in front of a long ladder.

"Can you make it?" he whispers.

She looks up at the two-storey ladder and reluctantly nods her head, yes. He leads with ease up the ladder and waits to help her off at the top. She pretends her legs are not shaky and that they don't feel like lead as she follows him across the roof.

"Hey, you're in good shape for your age."

She's only six years older. She rolls her eyes and motions for him to keep walking. They run across the roof, up another ladder and across the rest of the casino roof. By this time, it's getting a bit dark. They can't see the men working, but they can hear the radio conversation between the ground and the lift basket. Sparks splash out from the burner into the dark sky.

Ken whispers, "I thought we would be able to see more."

Disappointed, they turn to leave the building, climbing down all the ladders.

On their way to his vehicle, he whispers, "Don't tell anyone, or your brother. He will be in huge trouble if the company finds out we got up here without permission."

"Don't worry. I don't feel like hearing his disappointment."

Ken drops her off. Before she gets out, he says, "The guys will probably celebrate, if you want to hang with us tomorrow."

The next day, she invites Lainey to have lunch at the casino. They park on the top lot. Lainey says, "The site looks huge from up here."

Sheyna nods, but her mind is on her and Ken's secret.

Leaning over the edge, Lainey says, "I should see if Ben is walking around down there."

"You mean working around there, right? Hey, speaking of Ben, the guys want to celebrate the job. I don't want to be the only woman there, again. Come with us."

"Who is going to be there?"

"You know the guys; you met Pierce, Ken, Tony,

and Tim a couple of weeks ago. Maybe even Craig will go."

"Oh, no. I am too embarrassed after the last time. I can't go."

"Oh, geez, they don't care, Lainey. They picked you up, dusted you off and continued dancing. Besides, who should judge anyone when a good time and alcohol is involved?"

"Oh, gawd." Lainey looks to the sky and moans in embarrassment.

"If Ben doesn't ask you, drive to my apartment; you can come with me."

"Can you pick me up instead?"

That night the girls walk into a room full of tables, mostly occupied by guys. Pierce, Ben, Dwayne, and Craig are at the pool table. Lainey saunters towards Ben. Sheyna sits in the chair Ken pulls out for her. Clark comes back with a tray full of drinks and hands her water. The guys laugh and Tony pushes a beer in front of her.

Tim leans towards Clark and asks, "What's her name?" pointing his chin towards the 'seen better days' barmaid.

Sheyna giggles. "That's Honey. Call her over."

"I'm not calling her that."

She laughs to show him she's kidding, then says, "No. Really, that's her name."

There is always something with these guys. She remembers one time she caught Tim purposely moving a chair out so his hand could bump a waitress' bum. He knew Sheyna was watching him.

Craig moves into Ken's seat while he plays pool. He asks how she likes her job.

She raises her glass and says, "Stressful, but amazing. Sometimes, I go outside to get away from the hectic atmosphere in the trailer. I don't know how Clark can stand doing 'this' type of job again and again."

Craig says, "He must get used to it, or it's the challenge. I wish Missi would quit bugging me about working here."

The guys always tell Sheyna about their girlfriends and wives. They must get lonesome for them while they are away from home.

Her young friend is asking girlfriend advice, and she bites. "Why, what's going on there?"

"She wants me to work closer to home. I'm making good money here. I want to save so I can build a house for her and the kids. I never seem to make her happy."

Sheyna gives him her $2 advice. "Here's a secret, Craig. The only person that can make Missi happy is Missi. It's a person's perception of their world that distorts their feelings. She should be glad she has a man like you."

Ken breaks up the counselling session and says, "I'm tired of playing pool. Let's find a bar where we can dance."

Sheyna's face lights up. That is exactly what she wants to do. Four guys follow Ken out to the parking lot. Leaving Lainey in Ben's company, she waves at them and heads out of the bar with the guys.

They arrive at a bar she has never seen before, and says, "Do I hear Latin music?"

They must look out of place among the many well-dressed people and attractive young women sitting around the room.

Being a little intimidated by their youth and beauty, Sheyna distracts Ken by whispering in his ear, "Do you slow dance? I need to feel a hard body against mine for a little while."

He freezes and looks like he didn't expect to hear that information come from her.

Collecting himself, Ken says, "Yes, of course."

He quickly stands up and offers his hand. Sheyna melts into Ken's arms as soon as they get on the dance floor. The rest of the night is a beautiful blur: dancing, laughing and telling stories about their communities.

The next day, at the end of a long-wooded driveway, a slightly worn B&B is seen nestled next to a high, rocky hill. The hill could pass for an old worn mountain. Huge old oak trees surround and shade the motel. Rays of sunshine find their way through the leaves to the grassy rocks nearby.

Two people are seen talking on the second-floor deck. A woman sits with her back against the wall, glancing up at her host. A handsome bronzed man hands her a coffee and crouches in front of her about two feet away. They are unaware of the beauty that surrounds them or that it's almost noon. Here they are protected from the intensity of the summer heat and the spying-eyes from the guys at work. The woman is unaware of the sporadic warm breeze caressing their skin and gently blowing her long hair across her face. She gently curls it around her ear as she nods in agreement to his opinions on the world.

They are dressed comfortably in the same clothes they had on last night. He in a golf shirt and khakis, and her in blue jeans and a white blouse that shows just enough of her breast to distract his eyes from her ear.

While he talks about investments, she watches his lashes, his lips and then the slight dent in his chin. This gentle, handsome man is exactly what she needs right now. Deciding she likes him, his deep voice, and wonderful accent, her thoughts roam. Piecing together the night's events in her mind, she realises that she boldly told him she was going home with him. She looks down, embarrassed now, and says to herself, 'What does he think of me? What will the other ironworkers think of me? Worse yet, what would my brother think if he hears?'

First impressions are supposed to be important. I don't think I have seen such dark eyes on a person before. They certainly enhance the charm of his smile. His lips are even and as perfect as the shape of his nose. His hair is dark brown, almost black.

'*Mmmmm*,' she says in her mind; at least she hopes the murmur is not aloud. He finally sits down next to her on the deck. She feels the heat from his muscled body through his shirt and pants that are so very close to her now.

"You are a Decker, right?" she says, glad she remembers something about him other than his body.

He tells her about the job and demonstrates how he flips the sheet of deck in the air and jimmies it just right for it to fall into place. She inches closer so that their shoulders touch lightly. She can smell every intoxicating cell in his body, see every muscle in his chest, and feel every pulse of his heart. He is unaware of what is going on in her body.

'He's so sweet trying to impress me. He already impressed me twice; once last night and again this morning.'

Her head tilted slightly, she looks up at him and smiles softly, remembering the night before. As if he is reading her mind, he becomes silent, feeling her presence. She smiles at him and asks, "Can I have a shower?"

"Yes." His deep voice causes a vibration in her chest.

He stands and takes her coffee with his left hand and offers his right to help her stand.

With her hand still in his on her back, pulling her weak body into his, he whispers so close to her ear she feels the wet warmth of his lips, "You can have anything you want, Sheyna."

She whispers back, pressing closer to him, almost begging, "Please?"

They disappear into his apartment. He hurriedly goes into the bathroom and finds them towels. She enters and begins taking off her clothes. Ken is naked, turning on the water, taking her breath away at the sight of his body, and she says to herself, 'Oh my gosh, there is not an ounce of fat on this boy.'

Although they were together last night, she didn't see the superbly shaped muscles of his back, buttocks, and legs. She remembers how they felt in her hands.

She gets in and says, "I can wash your back. Ken, this sounds corny, but, oh my gosh, your body is the kind of body that people write books about."

He tosses the soap over his shoulder with a smile. "Oh, take it easy."

Before she can lather the washcloth, Ken turns around, pulling her slender body against his, slightly squeezing the air out of her.

Sheyna moans, "Don't now, you'll break me in two. Now wash my back. Fair is fair."

"You didn't finish mine."

"Oh, I finished once last night and again this morning," she says slyly.

"You sure have an unladylike mind," he says huskily, washing and kissing the back of her neck and between her shoulders.

Holding her waist, he begins to delightfully kiss too low on her back, when she moves away from him, she says, "Hold that thought. I have to get out of this shower and into dry sheets, I mean clothes."

Wrapped in huge towels, they move into their favourite room. Ken picks her up easily and lays her gently on the bed. Without removing her towel, he aligns her body under his with one arm pulling her hips up to his. The rest of the story is history, delicious history.

Back at the hotel where she left her car, Sheyna thanks him for an adventurous evening.

"Your brother won't fire me, will he?"

"Over what? He is my brother. Not my husband," she grumbles.

"Over the unwritten code that men don't hit on a friend's sister," Ken says seriously.

"Well, you don't have to worry. You're not his friend," she says, smiling. "No. I'm kidding. He won't say anything to you. You know how brothers are. He will give me a speech, though. Sheesh, I'm almost fifty and he treats me as if I'm still twelve. Even his wife had to say something to him. I don't think you will get fired; just don't go around the site saying you had sex with the boss's sister. He'll be fine."

He puts one arm around her and grabs her hand with the other. "I will not say anything. I don't think that's cool when someone does that, anyway. I will be in touch."

He gives her a final peck on the cheek before they part.

Sheyna calls Lindy as soon as she gets back in the apartment. Excitedly, she says, "Guess what!"

Lindy says, "What? Did stingy Jake come across, or did you meet someone special?"

"Oh my gosh! Yes, I met someone special, very special. Remember Ken at the Pow Wow? We hooked up last night. He's very, very special, if you know what I mean."

"That's good news if he's not married. He will be good for your spirit."

"He's single right now and good for my physical self."

Lindy cuts her off. "Never mind, I don't wanna hear about your physical self. What do you mean, right now?"

Sheyna giggles.

Turning serious, she says, "Ken mentioned his wife wants to try it again."

"Did he tell you that before you two hooked up?"

"Yes, but he didn't seem too enthused about it. He told me when I was just one of the guys."

"Well, you're not helping him stay in his marriage. I am going to start calling you Moushee."

"Hey, hey, hey. I am not like her."

"Would he have told you if they were back together?"

Sheyna says, "I wonder. Oh my gosh. My dream I had a few weeks back. See if it fits my Ken scenario." Flipping through her dream journal, she finds it and reads:

"'I am walking in a muddy ploughed field. I can hardly walk in the mud when I meet a man sitting on a stump; smiling at him, I turn left and walk past. The ground turns from mud to dirt and then to snow and ice. I am walking along the left side of a river. In front of me is a hill covered with sheets of ice. I attempt to walk up the hill that slopes down to the right towards the river. When I walk on the hill, the sheets of ice break up like panes of glass. I slide on the ice into the water. The ice pulls me into the current of the river. There is no ice in the river. I am aware that I don't go under. I still have my coat on; it's dry and I don't sink. Then I wake up.'"

"Hmmm, okay. The muddy field could mean something is holding you back or down. I can't think of anything for the stump, but maybe the guy on it is not making moves on you. Who is the man? Do you know him?"

"No. I didn't see a face, only that the person was a male and he smiled. It must be Jake. He could be a real stick-in-the-mud at times."

Lindy agrees, "True. He's a male that you don't really know, even when he was around you every day. You passed by him. Climbing a hill is a good sign that you are changing for the better. It's just the sheets of ice when water means emotions. You are carried down a river of emotions. That's the best I can do."

Sheyna takes a deep breath. "Yes, the cold emotions is certainly true."

"Ken broke up your icy emotions last night. I think the coat you wore in the river means that although you are getting carried away with your emotions, you are not losing yourself like you usually do in your relationships. This time, you are protecting yourself against them."

"Yes, I tend to be so gullible. Nyá:węh, sister. Sounds good to me. Tonight, I am going to thank the Creator for the stars in the sky and the stars in my family."

"Yep, that's me."

As time goes by, Desasǫdręh checks in on Sheyna to see if her potential mate will stay.

Sheyna is in her office smiling while she turns a little bumpy shiny thing in her hand. She is talking to her sister, Lindy, through the black object she has to her ear.

"Ken gave me a key to his apartment."

Lindy says, "Wow, that's progress. What are you going to do with that, sneak into his bedroom one night?"

"Hey, that's a great idea. I would love to wake him up with some kisses on that muscular back of his."

"Never mind. I was kidding! How have you guys

been?"

"Excellent. I smile just thinking of him. I feel so safe with him."

"What do you do, besides go to his apartment?"

"We do stuff. We still go out with the guys, but we steal time to ourselves as well. The other day we went to the casino on Valentine's Day. With $10, I won $75, so I bought our dinner. He said something to me in Mohawk. I swear my heart fluttered. I asked him what he said. He said, 'I thank you from the bottom of my heart.'"

"You are such a romantic."

"Oh, yes, that was a beautiful moment I will never forget."

Desah is happy for her and tells her grandmother her thinking: 'Maybe he will stay.'

"That could be. You know her well enough to see her signals to run away. Keep watching."

"What do you mean?"

"From the stories you have told me, instead of facing her fears of pain, she runs away before she has anything to run away from. Look. The love she had felt for anyone left her somehow: death, sour springs, or they abandon her. Instead of feeling good about the love she feels, without realising it she runs or sabotages the relationship."

"How can I keep her from doing that?"

"I am not sure you can. Keep watching."

Sheyna comes back to the apartment with coffee.

Ken has food cooking on the stove. She puts the coffee down and stands beside him, looking at his pan full of sauce.

"Where's your apron?"

"These are my work clothes."

He bends to kiss her. Liking what he tastes, he turns towards her and wraps his arms around her, making the kiss last longer. The boiling sauce splashes her arm. She jumps away from him.

"Ouch."

He turns the stove down. She takes her coffee to the coffee table in the living room. He follows.

"So that you don't burn me out before lunch, let's go for a walk up the old mountain. We can follow the huge path of hydro towers."

"Yes, I would love to. Can I finish my coffee first?"

She sits on the couch, and he sits in the chair opposite her.

"Why are you sitting there? I won't bite," she says, glancing to the empty space beside her on the couch.

"No, but I might."

She watches him as he throws his coffee cup in the garbage. He turns the sauce on low. He gets his coat on and grabs hers. She stands. He helps her into her coat and crouches in front of her to zip it up. As she watches him, she cannot believe the electricity between them. He presses his mouth against her. She cannot get enough of this feeling.

He smiles up at her. "Let's go."

"You tease."

She suddenly feels sad because she has a feeling it is going to end soon.

They go out and begin to climb the mountain. Their breaths create frosty steam in the air. She is surprised that the altitude leaves her breathless. She didn't think the mountain was this high when she said she would walk it.

Sensing her needs, he says, "Let's sit here."

She sits on the cold rock beside him, leaning on him. His arm is around her back and they enjoy the peaceful solitude of their surroundings. Neither says a word until she complains the cold rock is too much for her. He laughs and sticks out his hand to help her stand.

"Let's carry on up the mountain."

"I could have sat there forever, but I am glad to get moving. I was sweating before we sat down. The sweat makes up for the gym this morning."

"Sorry for changing your routine."

"No. Are you kidding? I love this, Ken. I will never forget it."

They are quiet again, saving their breath for the climb. They are above the trees when he turns to see how far they have climbed.

"Let's check on the sauce when we get back. If everything is still good, we will get another coffee and warm up."

They get back with the coffee from the local coffee shop. Inside, he grabs her coffee and then her hand and walks into the bedroom with their coats still on.

"I didn't think this is what you meant by warm up. What about our supper?"

He does not say anything. He proceeds to unzip her jacket. Crouching in front of her, he presses his face on her body. His hot breath is felt before he touches her.

He stands up, kissing her face and her neck. He gently leads her to lie down. He slowly unzips her blue jeans and gently pulls them off. She rubs the back of his head and wants to pull his head closer, but she quits. He kisses her inner thighs. She arches her back and pulls his face up and away from her thighs. He takes off his jeans. Before he makes gentle love to her, he makes sure she's ready for him. He's a big guy.

After their feast of spaghetti, they are too tired to do anything but sit on the couch, taking turns rubbing each other's back. After they have played a couple of games of chess, they lie on the couch like two lazy cats. Their luscious mood is interrupted with the phone ringing in Ken's bedroom. He leaves to answer it. Sheyna can't hear what is being said, but Ken is not in the same contented mood when he returns.

"What's up?"

"I am not going to bore you with the details. Basically, she wants me to go back to the Rez next weekend to split up our stuff or work it out."

Desah waits for Sheyna to ask what the man of passion is going to do. The question does not come. Only silence. She looks like she is holding her breath, waiting for him to tell her his decision.

Desasǫdręh enters the longhouse and waits for her eyes to adjust before she seeks out her grandmother. She is sitting with the other grandmothers having tea.

She sits beside her, and, leaning towards her, she whispers, "I have a question."

Desasǫdręh's questions are always interesting. They are usually about her check-ins with her little girl on the raft. They go into grandmother's sleeping space, where Desah tells her the changes that are due to Sheyna.

"All that we know about Sheyna, why does she hold herself back from this recent man in her life? She did not ask him to stay with her."

"Desasǫdręh, we can only see her side of the story. This man has brought her everything she probably asked for. Do you remember her conversation with her sister about wanting a temporary relationship to last her until her brother's work was done?"

"True. They get along so well. They are good for each other. She is very happy with him. I assumed it to be in their nature to finish their lives together."

"We do not know his side of his story. Waiting to see what she wants next is the only control she has in her life."

Desah knows deep down her grandmother is right about Sheyna.

CHAPTER NINE – AWAKENING

Desah finds her mother and grandmother together under a tree by the water, watching her little sister play with the other children. She asks if they have time to discuss how she will make sure she is correct in her connection with Sheyna. Her mother pats the ground between them.

Grandmother says, "What is it?"

She starts in, "I was watching Sheyna's history. At the time, I thought I was watching her current life until she had grown from a little girl to a teen in one winter. I was told to learn everything about her history to guide her in future."

"I understand. You became involved with her life with your commitment to help her."

"Yes. I found out why the little girl in her was sad. I do not know why the woman in her is sad. I know she ached for children of her own. I think she is lonely."

"She had her mate's children to love."

"Yes, they had moved away from her home to experience life without her. They did not need her any more."

"Where was her mate?"

"He was getting ready to leave her. He did not need her now the children were not coming around as much.

"She told her sister the images of her dream: 'I am upstairs in a wheelchair. My hips are fractured trying to give birth to a baby. I am in our old house on First Line. There are big holes in the floorboards and tattered and wrinkly curtains hanging on the windows. I open them to look out at the back yard, but they are smokey or dirty. The images I saw were blurry.'"

"What is a wheelchair?"

"It is a seat for someone that cannot walk; someone must push it to move her. I think the ancestors used her hips cracking to warn her that her security would soon be separated. To show her it relates to vows to her mate, she was in their first family home after their marriage vows. She looked out and she could not see outside their home. She was warned that she would be unable to see her world clearly. I think they meant that in her mind she would not see things clearly and not that she would be blind. To tell her when her relationship with her mate would end is when she is trying to give birth to a baby. She was taking medicine to help her conceive when her husband left."

Her mother says, "The message is clear to you. Was it clear to her?"

Desah says, "No. The dream was not clear to her

and her sister. I learned later that her sister is close to spirits and her personal dreams."

Grandmother says, "Yes, her sister and her friend are close. They understand and are able to trust the messages."

Mother says, "Her dream messages will mean something when she starts to connect the dreams to her life. As you have learned from the ancestors, show her images that she will recognise, people who are in her circle at the time of the event, and events that relates to her life."

Grandmother asks, "Did you make the connection?"

Desah reports, "The spirits showed her that her memories of her mate and the shared family, and the relationships, are holding her back from finding someone new."

Grandmother says, "Explain."

She dreams, "There is a man holding her. It is a man that takes her places, visiting places while they are together. The guy is full of ideas, athletic, confident, and talks too much about everything except his feelings. She knows him. The other guy in her dream, she does not know. He wants to be with her, follows her. He seems to wait for his chance. He is quiet and follows her around."

"Who are these men in her dream?"

"She feels the energy of her mate. She does not see his face. I think that her memories of her life with her mate are holding her back. She is aware of her actions and that she is being observed. I want her to know there are men around her following her actions and her loneliness. There is one man that is coming when she is ready. There will be a moment when the man can approach her."

Grandmother says, "Yes, I remember you telling me about that message. You were very upset because she did not heed the warning from the ancestors. I am not sure it would have made a difference. That was her path."

"How does she tell you she understands the messages?"

"She tries to interpret them. She does not fully trust or realise that she is close to the meanings of the messages until she compares them to her life situations. Sometimes she talks to me and does not realise that I hear what she says. At times, I understand her discussions with her sister about her dreams. Together they try to figure them out. In the dream of the two men, the spirits try to let her know her past is holding her back. She tells her sister the images in her dream, the energetic, sure, full of ideas, athletic guy she knows is her past mate, Damon. This is Damon's energy. In her dream she felt she knew him. She does not realise the man's energy is her past mate. The other quiet guy in her dream that she does not know follows her spirit through his spirit for the right timing. She needs to know that the man she does not know is the man that is coming. Through her and her sister's attempts at explaining her dreams means she is in the process of trusting the messages are meant for her.

"As you suggested, I put trust in the spirits around us to help us understand each other. I attempted to show her images in her dreams. In the mornings, I watch as she scratches them down in something she calls a 'journal', along with the events that happen in her life before sunset. She tells her sister a dream and together they interpret the images close to the meaning. The only mistake they made about the interpretation is they try to put a name to the man she does not recognise. The man represents any man that she lets into her life when she releases the emotions she holds for Damon. The man represents she will want to love again."

"She is a woman now?"

"Yes. She has been a woman for a long time. I am worried there is something else coming that will change her life. I do not fully understand what it is I see. I do not understand what it means to Sheyna or how it will change her life. It involves the country where she lives."

"The country?"

"Yes. Country is what the seventh generation calls land between borders."

"Will she survive?"

"Yes; her strength within her spirit survives on all

the other elements of her being. She seems to understand her future is up to her. I can have a restful sleep, or will I?"

Sheyna wakes up the next day and writes her strange dream in her journal: 'Last night I had a foggy dream. It seems like me and my friends were crawling around searching for trenches or bunkers to hide in. When we crawled out, there were flags everywhere. The flags were from different countries.'

Almost as if she is talking to Desasǫdręh, she says, 'What is this dream about?'

She finds Clark in the kitchen, making an egg sandwich for his breakfast. "I had a weird dream last night."

"Oh, yeah?"

She tells him the dream. "I know the flags are from different countries, but there is not one that stands out. None of them is Canada's flag. I have never seen a trench or a bunker before, let alone try to hide in one. Now, was it a trench at night or a dark bunker? Anyway, it was dark inside, wherever I was crawling around. I don't know who my friends were in the dream, only that they were with me, crawling around and looking for some place to hide, too."

"What does it mean?"

"I am not sure. I wish I knew how to decipher them."

Clark says, "Well, don't ask me."

Sheyna smiles. "Lindy tries to help me. She

dreams all the time. Sometimes she doesn't have to be asleep to be dreaming."

He nods in agreement on his way out the door.

In Desasǫ́dręh's dream, she watches an eagle gracefully flying above the surface of the river to snatch a fish in its talons. The eagle is quite a distance above the water when it begins to descend on its prey. She is amazed at the keen eyesight of the eagle.

Sheyna reflects on the strange dream she had last night. 'I am going to call Lindy at lunchtime to see what she thinks. Let me see, now how does it go? *We are driving down a dirt road through the beautiful countryside of green trees and green grassy hills. I am a passenger. We turn right into a lane. I notice a dead cow lying on the grass in front of a big, new, well-kept barn. We park in front of a white farmhouse on the right. No one is home. Everything is well-kept, clean, and green. The driver pulls into the lane framed with a white picket fence bordering the land and the yard. I notice another dead cow. We turn around in the lane. I think we are leaving. Then I notice little pigs or little horses on my left. I feel sad for them because the wolf has got after them. They are running around with their bums bitten and bleeding. There is another big cow, bloated, and lying on its side, its tits swollen. The animals are either piggies or skinned calves, and even the wolf is skinned. The man pulls up to a white fence as if to park. I can't believe it. I ask him without talking, "Are we staying?" When he turns to face me, it is Damon with wild eyes waiting for my response. I am scared. We leave the farm and drive down the lane. I am driving.*

'The only good part of the dream is that Damon may have been in the driver's seat in the beginning of the dream, but I am driving in the end. I am in control of my own life.'

Standing beside the river, Sheyna wonders at the eyesight of the eagle and its skill to pick a fish out of the water. A man exits the office trailer next door, interrupting her thoughts. He stands next to her to watch the eagle. He notices she is staring at the river.

Sensing her reason for being there, he says in a deep voice, "The water is very calming."

She recognises his thick accent to be indigenous of Africa.

"Yes. It is." After some moments, Sheyna, being a bit philosophical, says, "Maybe it reminds us of our mother's womb."

With a common Indigenous connection to mother and earth, he nods his head in agreement. They stand in silence for a bit, then he takes a deep breath and says, "Back to the site meeting."

He walks away without another word, leaving her with her best friend, her cigarette.

Louis walks swiftly out of the meeting in the main trailer, which is unusual for him. He looks distraught or disgruntled. He watches her smoke.

Out of the blue, he snidely asks, "Do you think

you will ever quit smoking?"

"Yeah, probably," she says as she deeply inhales the smoke and slowly blows it out, "just not today."

He laughs and is in the middle of excusing himself to return to the meeting when Richard calls her from the office trailer, "Sheyna, you have a call."

It is odd for her to get a call during work hours because everyone she knows is on site. Quickly, she goes into the office and nervously takes the phone from Richard.

Slowly, she says the greeting in a questioning tone, "Sgé:nǫ?"

The caller says, "Hello, beautiful."

Sheyna's heart thuds so hard that she is sure Richard can hear it from the other office while he eavesdrops on her conversation. The caller is Damon, her ex-husband, bothering her in the middle of a workday. There's silence on her end of the line. She's a bit unnerved because his voice still affects her spirit. She is not sure if she should respond angrily or without any expression of feelings.

Swallowing her emotions, she says, "Hello, Damon. Why are you calling me? Where's Moushee?"

Pushing past her questions and the sting, he says, "Me and your nephew, Chad, are visiting my brother, John, and Collette in New Jersey. I was wondering if I could take you out to dinner tonight. We could visit them in New Jersey and have supper in New York

City after."

"Is Chad with you now, or are you alone?" she asks cautiously.

She figures Damon brought her nephew along to smooth the way because although they are aunt and nephew, they were raised more like siblings. Chad and Damon's friendship goes back to teenagers, way before Sheyna knew Damon. They used to steal cars together, strip them of their parts and sell them to prospective buyers or garages.

"Yeah, I told him I was coming out and he wanted to come along for a ride. We're staying at the Best Western near the casino."

"Okay. I'd like to see him. I can go with you guys as long as we go wherever and do whatever I want."

She wanted to add, 'for a change', but she decided she had already stung him with her thoughts on the Moushee relationship.

She added, "No to the long trip to New Jersey. I'll show you guys my favourite hangouts around here because I want to be available to work this weekend. We can go to the casino first. It has a great steak dinner, or we can eat at the buffet before we head to the bars."

She is not leaving any decisions up to him ever again. Unlike when they were married and most of the decisions went his way because he was 'the man', which is one of the reasons for their separation.

"Sure. Steak dinner at the casino and then to your

favourite bars," he says, glad and surprised she agreed. "I'll pick you up at four thirty."

She is not letting her pushy ex-husband know where she lives in Connecticut. Firmly, Sheyna says, "No. I will meet you at your hotel around six p.m."

The guys must be back from the meeting and listening to her phone call. She can hear nosey Louis asking Clark what is going on. Sheyna can't see, but she knows her brother is rolling his eyes or shaking his head when he says, "Her ex."

Clark is standing in the doorway to her office when she turns around. "You're not going out with that guy, are you?"

She can hear the disdain in his voice and see it loud and clear on his crunched-up face.

"Don't worry. I'm not going to make it fun for him. Chad is with him. I miss him. I am meeting them at their hotel so he will not know where we are staying."

Before she leaves the trailer, Sheyna calls Ken playfully, "I'm going out with my ex and my nephew tonight. Do you want to meet us somewhere?"

Ken laughs. "You are cruel. No. I'm not doing that. I have to work tomorrow, remember? Besides, it sounds like the man has feelings for you. I won't do it."

There's honour in Ken's words, no surprise. She knew he would decline her invitation. There is some unwritten man's code which he always goes by that she finds attractive.

She giggles. "No. I'm kidding. I didn't think you would do that for me. I just want you to know that if you have plans for tonight, I can't be in them. See you again?"

"You sure will."

Sheyna arrives at the hotel at six p.m. as promised. They are waiting beside Damon's black Shelby Z. Glad to see her nephew, she gives him a big hug.

"Sgę́:nǫ², Chad. Glad you made it out. How did that happen?"

They are almost caught up on the Rez news by the time they park on the top floor of the casino parking lot. Even the parking lot brings back memories that make her smile. Recently, catching a glimpse of Ken in his coveralls working on the site made her day. Sometimes he senses her near, looks up and waves. She is not looking forward to the end of this job. She knows she will miss him.

At dinner, Damon talks off their ears. Chad and Damon are not gamblers, so their time at the casino ends quickly. They leave.

She directs them to the Cove near the job site.

"We can have a drink here first."

There are few people in the bar tonight. None of the guys from work are out, probably because they have work tomorrow.

Sheyna is not surprised that Damon asks, "Is this

where you go out all the time?"

"Not all the time. Sometimes. There are more dead-end bars in the boroughs, but let's go to Niantic, where we can dance."

They arrive at the noisy, crowded East Lyme Tavern. She doesn't know anyone, but there are familiar faces at the bar and serving the tables. She comes here sometimes with the guys and is sure that Ben introduced her to this place because Sheyna loves dancing.

She looks around and she sees Ben and Lainey talking to some friends that leave as Sheyna's group approaches their table.

"Hello, you two. Let me introduce you. This is my nephew, Chad, and this is Damon. Meet Lainey and Ben, who are very good friends of mine."

Shaking Ben's hand and looking at Lainey, Damon says, "Hello. I'm sure you've heard about me."

Lainey says, "Yes, glad to meet you, Elvis."

Everyone laughs because it is not the first time people have referred to him as an Elvis look-alike because of his black sideburns and yes, his handsome face.

Ben offers to share their space. "There's room here if you want to sit with us."

Sheyna sits next to Lainey and Chad quickly takes the seat next to her, leaving a seat for Damon next to Ben.

Sheyna says, "It's funny you should call him Elvis. He gets that quite a bit. We were driving around in a convertible in Hawaii, taking pictures and trying to find a good one of the mountains that did not include telephone lines to spoil it. A woman pushing a buggy on the streets saw us and screamed, 'Elvis!' She sounded as though she really thought she had an Elvis sighting."

Damon says, "She had to be kidding. I was surprised by her reaction. We went to have dinner in a bar that night. There was a man with dyed black hair and long sideburns also having dinner. I felt ridiculous. I went back to the room and shaved my sideburns."

The evening seems calmer than Sheyna had anticipated. Damon mentions that he heard Ben is working on iron for the casino. His question leads to the two of them talking about ironworking and their jobs. He and Ben hit it off. Sheyna has a few laughs talking to Chad and Lainey. The band begins to play. Damon asks her to dance. She likes to dance in front of the stage near the band, so she pushes her way through the crowd. She turns around and Damon is not with her. Finally, he makes his way through to the band.

He says, "It seems like the crowd parted to let you go through and closed behind you. It was strange. Do they know you?"

She laughs, "I don't think so. I come here

sometimes when I don't go home on the weekend, but not enough for people to recognise me. This place is close to where Lainey lives, so we like hanging out here sometimes to eat, drink or dance."

Sitting back at the table and out of breath, Damon, who likes dancing to Rock'n'Roll as much as Sheyna, says, "I didn't think I would miss dancing, but I do."

Lainey asks, "Are you having a good time, sweetie?"

Chad says, "Yes, I am, sweetie."

The girls laugh.

Sheyna says, "Yes, catching up with Chad about the family and Rez news and dancing is always a good night."

The band begins to play a slow song. Sheyna gets up to go to the bathroom, and Damon stops her to ask her to dance. After a short pause, she agrees and walks to the dance floor. Damon's familiar body presses against hers. He nervously talks about the children, her beautiful stepchildren he separated from her.

Then the dreaded question comes out of that handsome mouth, "Can I see you again?"

Sheyna doesn't say anything immediately until she can figure out how to say no.

Sensing her reluctance, Damon adds, "It will be different this time. I have a good job in New York City. I will come home every weekend. You can make all the decisions from now on."

She wrinkles her nose. "Okay, then my decision is no, sorry. The last decision you will ever make for me was the decision to leave the marriage and to leave me."

Damon's arms loosen. Looking down, he says, "I thought you would say no. You took me back once; I didn't think you would take me back a second time. I understand."

Sheyna's instant anger is mixed with the right amount of booze, and she asks, "What do you understand, Damon? Do you understand how broken my heart was when you left the first time? Do you understand that I didn't want to live without you? Do you understand that my security and family were destroyed? Do you understand what it is like to be left with house payments, a bank loan, and the household and credit card bills, thousands of dollars to pay back by myself? No, Damon, I *really* don't believe you understand."

Damon hugs her as if to hold her there forever.

"I am sorry. I don't know what was wrong with me," he says solemnly.

She could have consoled him and tell him, 'Well, you just lost your father, and you didn't know how to deal with what you were feeling.' She doesn't give him the satisfaction that she is still trying to survive the ordeal of their separation. That him leaving her forced her to face all her past issues of abandonment. Had he not left, she would never have started the counselling she needed. She did not tell him that he was meant to be in her life to bring out all those hurtful things from her past, issues that she thought she had buried for many years. She did not tell him that he was her best teacher, learning various depths of trust and strengths that she never knew she possessed. She isn't going to give him the satisfaction of knowing she's stronger now for loving him. She learned to do things on her own and some day she'll be strong enough to be alone or confidently seek another relationship. She would rather return the ten years of guilt he had inflicted on her low self-esteem, leaving her to cling desperately to her toxic marriage.

Instead, she says, "We should go. I have to work tomorrow."

"Okay. Sure."

Lainey winks at her because they are leaving earlier than usual. Sheyna knows what she thinks and laughs. "I will call you later."

At their hotel, Damon and Chad get out for their goodbye hugs. Sheyna lets them go and feels a freedom she has not felt in a long, long time. She leaves them waving from the parking lot.

Instead of driving straight to the apartment, a little high and needing company, she drives up the hill with the lane lined with huge oak trees. She is a little nervous about dropping in on Ken unannounced at this time of night. She has never visited him without an invitation. What if he's with another woman, or worse, his wife? What if he's grumpy and he doesn't want to see her? She has only been with him a few times and is not always sober. Although there is a dim light on, she knocks cautiously. A sleepy Ken with his cute bedhead answers the door.

She walks in and hugs him. "Sorry for waking you, handsome. I am not staying long. I just had to see you before I drove home. Plus, if Damon is following me, I didn't want him to know where I live."

Sheyna kisses lips that are trying to say, 'Oh, thanks for showing him where I live and possibly setting me up to get my ass kicked.'

She laughs and peeks out the curtains to see if anyone has followed her. "No. See? No one is following me. Okay? Gotta go."

Before they part, he gives her back a rub, sending the familiar electricity through her body to her fingertips. "See you tomorrow."

She moves back into his arms and places her cheek on his, saying, "Have a good night. Tomorrow, I will bring some supper after work."

Sheyna drives the few minutes to the apartment. She turns the TV on to distract her mind from the events of the night.

To Desah, Sheyna says, 'The gym in the morning will be good for me.'

Sheyna calls Lindy. "Clark said that the job would be ending soon. I told him, I'm not ready to go home to Canada yet. I love it here. Ben mentioned that he knows of a place where I can live in Niantic if I stay. My roomies would be his girlfriend, Lainey, and her sister, Dawn. Maybe I can apply for work in a nearby town, or at the casino."

"What did he say?"

"Clark said" – imitating her brother's voice – 'That's what I would do if I was single.' How would he know what he would do if he was single? He has been married to Shanana since they were kids, init?"

Sheyna and Lindy giggle.

"The other morning it came up again after I told him the dream I had the other night."

"What did he say?"

"What do you have at home to return to?"

"Straight and to the point. Ummm, what dream?"

Sheyna tells Lindy her strange dream about the flags. "Usually, my dreams are about normal things: men, hugs, kisses. This dream sounds scary."

"We will have to watch what happens to see if it is a warning of something."

Desah approaches Ken's place among the trees. There is no light on there and she cannot feel Ken or Sheyna's energy. She visits where Sheyna and Clark work. Most of the trailers are gone. They are not there. She checks the place where they sleep. Her and her brother have packed their things and are putting them in the truck, when Ken drives up behind them.

He gets out and comes up to them.

"Sheyna, can I talk to you?"

Before she can answer, Ken looks at her brother and says, "Clark, can you excuse us?"

Surprised, Clark says, "Oh. Yes. I'll get our other suitcases."

Ken stands in front of her with his head down. He looks like he is trying to think of the right words; obviously he is emotional.

"Remember the night we refused to be sad because we knew that some day this job would end, and our time together would end?"

Smiling, she says, "Yes. It was like a dam burst of loving energy."

"That's right. I had a great time. As you know, I have to go back to Kahnawake this weekend to sort things out. I've put it off long enough. After that, I have a job on a bridge in New York. You have my contact information. I don't have yours. Can you let me know how to contact you so I can tell you what happens?"

Sheyna puts her arms around him, and her chin shakes, feeling this could be the end of this beautiful part of her life. She does not tell him she wants to hold him forever, that she cannot imagine Connecticut without him, without that boyish smile, without that knowing glance when they are thinking the same thing. She wants to say, 'I have fallen for you, handsome Mohawk man. Please come back to me.'

With a sad smile, she nods and says, "Yes. I will."

Desasǫ́dręh is sad for Sheyna and tells grandmother.

"You cannot help her with this issue. He showed her what kind of man she wants for herself. He is matched with someone else right now."

"I will hope for him to return to her."

Desasǫ́dręh continues to tell her grandmother and mother Sheyna's experiences of her energy, a story of what she sees and hears in Sheyna's life as if she walks beside her.

Sheyna is living near the magnificent waters in the southeast with two women, Dawn and Lainey. They do not live where she and her brother lived. Clark moved away to work somewhere else in New York state. She stays behind to work for another company. Dawn welcomed her into her home and her life. She is an older woman who tells Sheyna she is worried about her future security because of her age. She has many skills and experience, yet she worries that the people will not ask her to work, that she has seen too many winters.

Sheyna and her friend, Lainey, are having a coffee in the sunny kitchen of her new residence. She tells her the dreams that stand out for her. "*I am looking up at a clear blue sky outside Dawn's house. Dawn drives into the lane. I run to her all excited, pointing up at the sky, saying, 'Look up, Dawn. Look up. Where are they coming from?' Dawn's crystal blue eyes turn from me to look up at the sky full of mesmerising butterflies. Three swarms of them come over the trees. They cover the whole sky above our heads. As we are marvelling at how many butterflies there are, Mary drives up and parks on the lawn in front of the house. She gets out and walks towards us. Of course, her blue eyes sparkle when she sees her mum. Pointing to the sky, me and Dawn say, 'Mary, look up! Look up!' Mary looks up and she sees three batches of butterflies fill the sky. Then the butterflies turn into flying dollar bills and are released from cages. The huge dollar bills fly towards us."*

Lainey looks suspiciously at Sheyna and says, "There was something about people releasing butterflies on TV. Maybe you dreamed about that."

"Why? Did someone do that? I didn't see anything about butterflies on TV and no one told me that it happened. What a coincidence, though! I doubt if their swarms of butterflies turned into money in cages, then released."

"No. They probably didn't. Now that would be a story for the TV."

"The dream is strange. I didn't dream the butterflies were put in cages, only that they were released into the sky, then turned into money and released from cages. Oh, you know how dreams are. It must mean something good, right?"

"I'm not sure dreams mean anything. I hardly remember mine, let alone think they mean anything except electricity moving through my brain while I sleep causes images in my mind. Usually, if I eat spicy food, I dream. I don't think I dream all the time."

"I have been tracking my dreams consistently since I've been in Connecticut, and over the years there have been a few significant ones. The first one I remember, and most important, was telling my mum she would survive an operation. She had a mastectomy. I often wonder why I was not warned that she would die."

"Maybe some things are not meant to be known ahead of time. Funny, but I never paid any particular attention to my dreams before."

Sheyna and Lainey drive a few minutes to Niantic. They walk along a harbour street uptown. If you can call it 'uptown'. The highlights are a beat-up old theatre, a doughnut shop, and an old hotel where they partied with the guys. There are a couple of old shops or two, a restaurant, laundromat, and a bank lining the main street. Lainey waves for Sheyna to follow her and she ducks into The Book Barn. Soon, Sheyna gets tired of looking at books and stares out the window at the only other two people in town enjoying the sunshine and fresh air. Lainey shoves a little blue book in front of her face, and proudly says, "Look what I found, cookie."

Sheyna reads the cover. "*Dreams and what they mean to you*. Omigosh! Now I can see what the butterfly dream means. Thank you, Lainey!"

Together, they read the interpretation for 'butterflies': '… indicates prosperity and good fortune. If you see them flying, it denotes pleasant news from distant friends or relatives. To a woman, it foretells a faithful lover who will make her a fine husband. 55, 75.'

In her deep, husky voice and Bronx accent, Lainey says, "Well, it can't mean you, 'Miss Fifteen-dollars-an-hour-and-no-man,' or my niece or sista, who are both unemployed."

Disregarding her joke, Sheyna is delighted with the treasure, and buys the book.

On their way back to Oakwood Street, she tells Lainey about a commercial she had seen on TV. "An Indigenous person looked straight at me through the camera lens and said, 'How will I be able to talk to you through your dreams, if you don't know your language?' That line always stuck with me."

As they drive up to the house, they see Mary's car in the laneway.

Sheyna is excited. "I'm going to tell Mary and Dawn about my dream and the interpretation, since they are both in it."

The girls walk into the kitchen, where Dawn is in front of the stove, cooking up something that smells Italian-like, and Mary is next to her, excitedly telling her some news.

Mary turns towards them, grinning from ear to ear, and says to her Aunt Lainey, "We have great news! Mum passed her interview and is now employed at the casino hotel! And I got a job in a hair salon in New London!"

Sheyna and Lainey exchange surprised and knowing expressions.

Lainey teasingly swats Sheyna's arm. "You couldn't dream about me and the butterflies."

Letting the swat go, Sheyna laughingly says, "I really don't think it works that way. I am not magical. I just dream and wonder about the meanings of them."

Dawn says, "What are you girls talking about now?"

Sitting down with her book, Sheyna tells Dawn and Mary about the butterfly dream. "That dream was so clear, except for the blip where the swarm of butterflies turned to cages of butterflies made out of money. There were three batches of butterflies that filled the sky. We know the 'butterflies' mean prosperity and good fortune, which directly relates to your good news, Dawn and Mary. Let's see what 'three' means. Three means 'an expansion and humour'. That's true," Sheyna says, pointing at the two sisters from the Bronx.

She adds, "Good fortune to come. Warns of confusion and doing too much all at once. Happy reunions and new contacts."

Lainey says, "I have to admit that dream could be a message about you two getting jobs. What was the part about the faithful lover?"

"It says to a woman it can mean a faithful lover that would make a fine husband."

Dawn says, "Yes. It is true. We have lovers knocking down the doors every day. I usually don't know who to pick."

"Yes, make fun. The fine husband probably means Mary and Steve. You know he is going to ask her to marry him. And you have to believe that the other parts are true, too."

"I looked up a dream I had about an old house, and an image of my hips breaking that foretold my marriage would break up; 'marital or love difficulties, sickness, and disappointments'. It makes sense since hips are the location of our first chakra, our grounding and security. Dirty windows mean 'fruitless enterprises and wasted hopes are in store'. The fact that I was ready to have children and Damon wasn't, marked the time in the future when we would break up. In the dream, my hips broke trying to give birth to a child. Did he really leave because I wanted children of my own?"

Desasǫdręh realises, "Sheyna has found a method to understand my messages. I know she is beginning to trust them. There was a time after Damon left, Sheyna was telling her issues to a woman who can help her sort out her jumbled mind. It hurt for Sheyna to bring forth those memories and the feelings that are associated with them. She wanted to quit going to talk to the woman. I wished I could tell her to continue the

281

meetings with this good woman that could help her move past that time so that she can live again. When Sheyna told the woman the message she received in her dream, I knew the spirits were there helping her in her dreams. When she tells the new people women the meanings, I know that now we can connect through the instrument she found."

Grandmother says, "What did she dream?"

"She told the woman who was helping her, 'I drive my car up to a building. You come out and put a big basket of red apples in the trunk of my car. Then you get in the driver's seat.'"

"What does that dream mean?"

"Looking at the instrument we are going to use to communicate, Sheyna tells the women she lives with in Connecticut, 'According to this book, receiving apples mean "your hopes will be realised". This is an excellent omen signifying peace, prosperity, and good fortune. Basket means if you see or carry a basket, you will meet with much success, as long as the basket is full.'"

Desah's mother asks, "Did she keep talking to the woman?"

"Yes, for three winters. Talking to the woman helped her do the job she was meant to do for her community. She told the woman about the dream she had about a job that helped her survive. At the time, she was doing work that did not match her skills and teachings. She was happy to work with her friends from her territory."

"What were the images?"

"She was shown that she was walking down her stairs in her house in the dark, carrying a dried bush. As she descends, she can see light at the bottom of the stairs; it shines on both sides of the wall in front of her. The light comes from the dining room and the kitchen. The woman helps her interpret the meaning. The dried bush represents the tobacco she works with at a company in her community. The light shining around the corner means she will have a job that matches her skills and it is just around the corner."

Grandmother says proudly, "Good. Now you are able to enter her dreams. She has the instrument to help interpret your messages. Continue doing what you are doing. She will eventually trust the direct connection from your message to her or to the spirits around her that transfer your messages to her. Now that the connection is secure, you will know when she needs you. The spirits around her will tell you as well."

As images of Sheyna's new life comes into view, Desah sees her leaning over a workstation that has a light under it or in it. She hears her new leader say he is sending her to New London to brush up on her computer skills. The place is a charming little town on the harbour of Block Sound and the Thames River.

Desah does not understand why Sheyna seems hopeful and contented with where she is when she has been warned her life is about to change.

That night, Sheyna dreams that she is watching herself look through the window of the shop where she works now. She sees herself working at her light table. It catches on fire under the table. Her hands keep working without getting burned.

The next day, she notes the dream and writes the interpretations in her journal: 'Window means fruitless enterprises and wasted hopes are in store for you. Work, you will succeed in life through determination and energy if you see yourself working. Fire is a favourable omen predicting prosperity and a good family life so long as you don't get burned.'

'Geez, I hope that dream doesn't come true. I thought I would stay in Connecticut for ten years.'

Desah tells her grandmother, "She understands she can decipher the messages. She does not listen to them."

"As long as we can prepare her, it might be enough of an understanding for her to accept what is going to happen without the event crushing her or surprising her when it happens. She can keep balanced enough to make rational decisions and not emotional ones. Stay with her through the event."

It's Tuesday and the instructor is taking forever to get to the eight thirty a.m. class. Sheyna waits for a few minutes.

She says to the other sleepy students in the class,

"Tell the instructor I'll be outside having a smoke."

On her way to the front door, Sheyna passes Reception. The young person at the computer who usually has a professional smile and friendly wave has a shocked or worried look on her face as she stares at her computer.

Not being able to imagine what would be so shocking at eight fifty a.m., Sheyna asks, "What's the matter?"

The Receptionist says very slowly, "A plane... has crashed... into the Trade Towers in New York City."

Then they both have the same look on their faces.

She goes over to the Receptionist's computer to see for herself. "What the heck! The pilot must have had a heart attack."

She finishes her smoke, wondering why they haven't called her in to class. Surely, the instructors aren't stalling class to watch the Tower burn.

When she goes back inside, the Receptionist says, "Another plane hit the other Tower!"

Immediately, she asks, "Where is a phone I can use?"

The Receptionist, still in shock, slowly points to the phone across the hall from her desk. Sheyna calls her brother, who is working in New York.

"Oh, rats! There is no answer."

Sheyna tries to think of what to do or who to call next. She calls her roomies. No answer. Either they are out shopping or still sleeping. She calls her sisters in Canada and there is no one home there.

"Where the heck is everybody?"

She goes back to her desk. Over and over, she watches the video of the smoke billowing out of the towers on her classroom computer. The instructor returns to inform them to leave the building immediately. "Go straight home to wait for emergency instructions." That was simple and very methodical. No expression, opinion, emotion, or discussion among these strangers. Arriving at her place in Niantic, she finds the sisters, her room-mates, watching the black smoke billow from the Pentagon on TV.

Gasping, Sheyna asks, "Now what has happened there?"

Without looking at her, they both shush her at the same time. Slowly comprehending that the US is under attack, she sits down on the stairs to the upper level. As an observer, she's thinking this is a well-planned and sort of a unique strategy to invade the US security. She decides not to say that aloud to the very devout Americans who keep flipping the news stations back and forth from the Pentagon in Washington to the Towers in New York City.

"Did anybody from home call me?"

No answer.

"No? Okay. I'm going to try call home," she says a little louder.

Finally, someone is answering her sister's phone.

Lindy says without saying hello, "When are you coming home?"

"Not until the weekend. Why?"

Astonished, she says, "Geez, Sheyna. There's something awful going on over there. Why don't you come home?"

If Lindy is excited and says it like that, the attack on the US is finally sinking in.

"Oh, no. What will I do? Maybe I'll see if my boss will let me go home this weekend. The borders should be clear now."

"Good. I will see you Friday night. I'll wait up," she says, sounding relieved with Sheyna's answer.

The weirdest feeling is coming over Sheyna, who prides herself on being a strong Ǫgwehǫ:weh woman; yet it seems natural for her to wonder, 'Where are all the men? What man is going to protect me here? My brothers are in Canada.' She begins to call the only two male friends she knows in the area, ironworkers that she met through the Mohegan Sun job, of course.

Jake answers and says, "I got my gear packed and waiting for a call to go to New York City."

"No. Stay here and keep us safe."

He quickly says, "You'll be all right. The unions are taking names of ironworkers willing to clean up the rubble and iron in New York and Washington. I'm on the waiting list."

"What about Ben?"

"He's going with me."

"Hmmm. Talk later," she says as she hangs up.

Because the roomies are so engrossed in the news reports, she says to herself, 'Oh, for heaven sakes. They are waiting to go to New York.'

Her brother finally calls her back, answering the frantic message she left on his voicemail.

He says, "I am heading out as soon as I can. Our job rolled up and is shut down for a week, maybe longer."

She begins to cry and takes a deep breath. "Why? Are you in New York City now?"

"Nooooo," he drones. "We are about an hour from there, but we are working in New York state. Deliveries and transportation are stalled indefinitely. What are you going to do? How come you didn't go home?"

"I have to work this weekend. I'm going to see if my boss will let me go home when the borders open up."

Sounding frustrated with her, Clark says, "They are open for the Ǫgwehǫ:weh who live in Canada. You can get across the border. What's going on in Niantic?"

Glad that he's asking, she says, "The incident happened this morning and FEMA, or the Federal Emergency Management Agency, had evacuation directions in our mailboxes, and website links and phone numbers are being announced on the radio stations and TV. I am impressed that they are on the ball around here, as if this type of thing happens every day. Dawn says that the instructions are in the mailboxes all along the shores. They suggest we carry overnight bags in our cars and have a place to stay outside a ten-mile radius of the harbours and airports in case we receive an order to stay outside the restricted area. We're within the radius of Niantic and the New London harbours and marinas. I won't have just one bag packed, I will have my suitcases packed and will go home if the protected radius is in effect."

Clark says, "Yeah? That's good. The TV and radio stations are continually announcing telephone numbers for counselling and crisis calls. The News is focussed on the emergency services being affected by the response, and all trades are requested for clean-up. What a mess in New York City. Well, miss-miss, I'll talk to you later. I'd better get some sleep so I can leave first thing in the morning. The streets are already bare, which is freaky. If I left today, the border will be crazy by the time I get there."

"Oh my gosh, Clark. Remember when I told you that dream about me crawling around looking for a hiding place in trenches or bunkers and the flags from different countries? Lainey found me a dream book."

She grabs her journal. "It says, 'Flags mean a foreign flag indicates broken alliances between nations. 72, 14.' There are no meanings for trenches, bunker, hiding or searching. I wasn't scared in the dream. I was more worried or anxious that I couldn't find somewhere to hide. I suppose bunker and trench could represent war, which means 'difficult conditions in business and in your affairs in general'. 92, 57."

"Yeah, I remember it. What do the numbers mean?"

"Not sure. Our niece is into numerology; I'll see what she says."

"What the heck? Well, I'd better get some food before the restaurants close on me; I'll have to grab something at the variety store down the street. Be careful."

"You, too. Love you, bro."

After she gets off the phone, Sheyna tells her roomies, "I am glad my brother isn't thinking about being a hero like my Connecticut ironworker friends, Jake and Ben. He is leaving for home tomorrow."

Sheyna's spirit is low and sending an energy of being lonesome for her family and home. Her friends feel it and try to cheer her up. She fights the urge to run as she always did in the past. She is drinking more, which is like running and a repeat of her past life. Also, she had a disturbing dream and wanted to find out what it meant. Although it was a dream, it felt very real. It was more of a connection of energies rather than a dream. She felt she was half awake and half sleep. She calls a friend she has relied on in the past to do Readings for her.

"Good day, Sheyna. I am glad you contacted me. Is there something specific that you want to ask, or just a general reading?"

"Hello. I want to learn about a dream I had and then a general reading if you see something else."

"Good. Go ahead with your question."

"I have been sad lately, repeating old behaviours like going out more and drinking. What happened might be a connection to the effects of drinking. It was the afternoon, and I was sleeping in my bedroom. *I could feel someone coming towards me while I was lying in my room. I thought it was one of my roomies. I opened my eyes. The sun was shining in the window behind her so I couldn't see her face, but I could see she was thin and had long dark hair with grey in it.* I got scared. I know she wasn't a physical being. Just as she got close, I said 'don't' and turned my back to her. Scared, I forced myself to go back to sleep."

The reader's voice turned gentle and soothing. "That energy you felt is one of your spirit guides. The fact that you see her means your connection is very strong. She was there to comfort you. You said you had been very sad. She felt it and came to you. She is a very loving energy."

"Wow. That was a different experience for me. My sisters were here visiting a couple of weeks ago. They said they saw someone float past the upstairs window while they were sitting in the back yard. It couldn't have been someone walking past the windows because the stairs descend below the windows."

The Friday following the towers incident, Sheyna is at work at the print shop/Western Union. Ella bustles over to her light table with her usual cheerful personality, and says, "Some native guy is at the front and asking for you. He describes you as the Mohawk woman that works here."

Sheyna goes to the front and finds Will from Akwesasne standing there with a slightly shy smile. He usually comes into the shop to send money home to 'the Mrs', but not today.

Surprised to see him, she says, "Oh, you're still working around here?"

"No. We dragged-up our job in New Jersey as soon as the towers happened. We are on our way home now. I wanted to see if you were still here."

Because he drove all this way from New York City to tell her something, she asks, "What did you think about those planes running into the towers?"

"That was something else!" he says, looking at the floor and shaking his head.

He looks up at her with raised eyebrows. "We were working on a high-rise on the other side of the Hudson River. Work stopped after the first plane hit. We were having a smoke when the second one hit. That's when we heard over the radios, 'Everyone off the building.'

"We left everything and got off the steel. One of

our guys froze watching the smoke and fire. We thought he didn't hear the message. He just stared straight ahead, looking at the towers, and wouldn't move. It took three guys to get him over to the ladder and off the building. We had to lower him down the ladder with his harness and a cable. It was as if his brain shut off. He was shaking when we got him to the ground. It was weird."

Concerned, she asks, "What has happened to him recently?"

Will tilts his head and looks at her with an expression that asks, what do you mean?

She repeats her question, "What tragedy has happened in his life in the last year or so?"

"Oh. He lost his son in a house fire last spring."

She covers her mouth with her hands, understanding what had caused this man's brain to freeze. Sheyna stares past him out the window and Will looks at the floor.

To avoid crying, she chokes back the lump that is beginning to form and changes the subject. "What now? When will your job resume? Do you think you will come back?"

Snapping out of wherever he was, he says, "We're on our way back to Akwesasne. The job shuts down for a month until things settle down around New York City and New Jersey. The Mrs wanted to leave as soon as it happened, but we had to wait for our cash and find out what the job was going to be doing first."

Sheyna looks around to see if anyone is eavesdropping before she says, "Oh, yeah. I know how she feels. I am a bit nervous about living here now."

He nods, understanding. "I'd better get her home; she's grabbing a Sub for us."

"Yeah, thanks for stopping in. Have a safe trip and hope we run into each other again. Maybe you will bring your wife to meet me one day, if you work around here again," she says in a questioning tone and with a chin nod.

He starts to make his way to the door, stopping to say, "Yeah. I should have introduced you two sooner. Maybe next time? Later, then."

She nods yes in response.

That night, Sheyna goes back to her place in Niantic and tells her roomies about the ironworker friend that came to visit her. The landlady does not like ironworkers because of her baby sister's experience dating one from here.

Dawn, her landlady, says, "Oh, no. Not another ironworker."

"No. He's a native ironworker with his wife in the car. He is one of the good guys."

She didn't see the need to tell her the longer version with a bit of gossip. Sheyna goes up to her room to write in her journal.

In her room, she says to Desasǫ́dręh, 'She's a

funny gal, judging all ironworkers from Connecticut by the one guy she knows. I know the guy she is referring to and he isn't all bad. He is good to me. The thing is, I don't know if he is good to me because Lainey's my friend, or that I am the sister of an ironworker, Clark, a man he respects. The memories of Connecticut will forever be close to my heart because of my renewed friendship with my brother, the women I live with and the people I've met on the job, and especially Ken, my very passionate ironworker friend.'

Desah looks at her mum and grandmother after telling them Sheyna's story. She says, "No matter what is going on around her, I feel there is a bit more peace surrounding the little girl on the raft now. She has made new friends who have welcomed her into their home and their lives. She seems to laugh whenever she is with them. She is handling her world incident as best she can. I still hope she decides to return to her territory for good."

CHAPTER TEN – GOING HOME

Desasǫdręh senses another major life-changing event coming in Sheyna's world and sees she is learning about it with every update and conversation she has with her brother.

Desasǫdręh consults her grandmother. "How should I warn Sheyna about the change coming to her life? Her brother is going to pass on to the next step of his life path. How will I warn her?"

"You can tell her there's a life change coming, but you cannot tell her that her brother is passing on. Has she been in contact with him? She may already feel the thinning of the spiritual connections."

"It sounds like she is not going to handle it well."

"How she feels cannot be helped. Only she can sort it out, and it is her choice how she acts on those feelings."

"Yes, she has had many changes: her separation from her mate, moving to another country, new jobs, new friends and people, Ken leaving, and now the attack on those tall structures. None of it compares to this next change. She is scared to lose her brother. She is drinking more of the sour springs to mask her fears. She's more sensitive and the leader where she works has mental health issues and is abusive to her and the other people that work there. She needs to go back to her territory with her people, her own culture, and familiar energies, and mainly to be around her brother in his last days. She is not in a good space mentally, emotionally, and spiritually. I do not know why she is staying. She seems to be waiting for Ken to return, but I sense that he is with his wife after the attack on that country."

Grandmother says, "Show her. Show her that life will be better if she leaves. Do not tell her about her brother. She will be in a good place in time. She will adjust to a new life in her home territory. Everything that happens will point her in the right direction."

Sheyna is in Connecticut, New Year's Day, talking to her brother, Murray, on the telephone. He is telling her about the party at Chad's place last night, and who was at the bar.

She asks with a chuckle in her voice, "Who ended up with who?"

"I don't know. None of our business, meatball."

"Come on," she whines. "Well, who went home with who? I can probably figure out the story."

"I said I don't know. I woke up here at Whalehead's and partied with him and Sez. I couldn't get drunk anyway."

"What did you do, drink yourself sober again?"

"No. I'm having trouble swallowing. I contacted my doctor's office for an appointment before

Christmas to get a check-up. I couldn't get one. The on-call doctor gave me a pill for a sore throat. Some good that was, I couldn't swallow it."

Sheyna's anger spikes. "What an idiot! You can't get fluids down your throat, for Pete's sake! Go to another doctor. Your wife's doctor is a quack!"

"Geez, what if I have cancer?"

"Nooooo. Don't say that! Think positive."

A few days go by, and Lindy calls Sheyna. "Hello. I talked to Murray yesterday. His scope for his throat isn't happening until next week. His consultations are the following week."

"Okay. Thanks for telling me. We've been in touch. He doesn't sound worried, but he keeps coming back to the topic. He'll be okay. His operation has to happen before he can eat and get his strength back. He cannot believe the kindness of people these days, and how nice everyone is treating him. His wife says he can stay with her after the operation."

"That's who he means, probably."

"That's good of her after all their stuff. He says he lost a lot of weight. He said he wished he could be skinny his whole life, now he is. He can't be giving up if he's going for the operation."

"Yeah, tomorrow."

"Yuck, tomorrow. I have to work. I love graphics work; it's that toxic workplace, it is so depressing and stressful. I'm constantly braced for abuse. I don't know if it is because we don't know what's going on with Murray, or because my employer is off his bean. Today, he ranted and raved over nothing. I started laughing because he looked like a banty rooster ruffling his feathers, his bald head turning red, squawking, and prancing back and forth. He really got mad this time, and hollered as big as his mouth could stretch, 'WHAT ARE YOU LAUGHING AT?'

"I told him he looks funny when he's mad. After that, everyone within earshot disappeared into their corners; probably didn't want to laugh out loud and get in trouble. He forgets he made a million in the first month I worked there, and the month after 9-11 when everyone thought the economy would get worse. I tried everything with him: reasoning, explaining, hollering right back, arguing, and ignoring him. Finally, I looked at it from a more positive way and laughed."

Changing that sorry tune, Lindy says, "I know I shouldn't have asked. I had a dream about you last night. I dreamt you came home early. You woke me up. You were standing in my bedroom with two suitcases."

Sheyna says, "That dream might come true. I can't stand my boss's bullying methods of management. Ella said not to worry because he always treats them like that. All I could think of is, he can pay you a pittance and treat you guys like cows, but he's not treating me like that. I told Murray I am going home for Jenny's birthday party."

"Good. I don't know why you stay, either. So, you're coming home, February 3rd. Where are you staying?"

"I asked Waynie if I could stay there. He laughed and said. 'Of course, auntie, it's your house.'"

"I'd better get off the phone. See you February. Let me know how the consultations turn out. Talk to you later."

A week later, another update comes from Lindy. "Hello. It is confirmed Murray has cancer. Friday, they put a scope down his throat. They had to get past the six c.m.-size tumour to see if the cancer was attached to his stomach. They will check his bones and blood to see if he has cancer in other parts of his body."

"Murray told me he wants to stay with his son because it's too noisy at his ex's house. Nothing ever seems to go his way. He probably hasn't felt good physically for a long time. I love our bro."

Lindy's voice is strained. "Me, too. I wish he didn't have to put up with so much in his life."

Together they cry silently over the phone.

"He was always my hero growing up. Always took my side. Teased me to tears sometimes when we were kids. I can pick out the spot where he built a lean-to in the bush. We were so proud of our hard work that day. Teasing me, after all the work we did, he said it was only big enough for him. I wanted to put more branches on it, but he said he didn't want to waste more fresh branches. We took turns sitting in it, even you for a little while until you crawled out. Then we had to walk home in that high snow. He picked you up and I dragged the shovel. We walked out of the bush and through the weeds. We tried to follow the same path he shovelled into the bush, but we could hardly see it. The snow drifted over while we were in the bush, leaving a shallow dent to mark the path to the road. We finally made it out. He turned the shovel over to make a toboggan. He sat you on it and told you to hang on and try to keep your feet up."

"I think I can barely remember that."

Sheyna changes the subject. "I had a long dream a few months ago."

"What is it about? Me, being a cute baby?"

"Omigosh. You were a cute baby, but no. My dream, of course, was about me, and it is a long one, so stay on the phone."

"Oh, okay. Go on."

"Well, let me think a minute. Okay, I'm driving a car along a long bare highway and at first I think it looks like a desert. There are hardly any trees around. It seems like I'm being directed by a little old woman, sitting in the passenger's seat. Without words, she is telling me where to drive. I keep sneaking peeks at her out of the corner of my eye. Everything around her is golden: the landscape, and in the distance the trees, the sky, the mountains. Maybe it is the golden light that surrounds us that makes it look like we are in a desert. It is so bright it reflects on her skin and clothing. She is wearing a white dress with little blue flowers. Her grey and brown hair is tied in a bun on the top of her head. Her hands are clasped in her lap. She stares straight ahead, never looking at me. I turn back towards the road and see that the sky in front of us is golden, too. In the distance I can see a huge golden house, a mansion. As we approach the door, the woman disappears through the wooden door. I open the door and follow. Once inside, the woman disappears through a big oak door at the top of the stairs. I stay at the entrance, looking at the glass ramp that looks like a kaleidoscope. I can hardly make it up the slippery floor, scared that I will break through the glass ramp. Hanging on the railing, I slowly make my way up to the steps that are at the top of the ramp. I walk the steps and sit on the top one, waiting for someone to let me in the oak door.

"Finally, a very handsome man opens the door. He lets me into the room; it's pink. Everything is pink: the walls, the floor, the fireplace on my right, and, on my left, a bed with a canopy. Even the women who are in the room are wearing pink chiffon clothing. I wait on the bed, naked. Then Bethy floats by on my right. She doesn't seem to notice or recognise me. I ask her how Jenny is doing. She says she's okay as she floats by me. I get off the bed and walk into another room on the right side of the fireplace. It is like a mudroom; smaller than the room

I had entered. I look out of an old-fashioned glass door that has six panes. I see a corral in the back yard that has a dry tree in the middle of it. The corral is made of old dry tree trunk rungs. The ground is worn and the animals in the corral are black and fat. A little bull is on its back, trying to squeeze out under the fence, but his belly is too fat.

Through the window I am watching the animals when a snarling dog jumps at me. He scares me away from the door. I go back into the weird room and search for my shoes. I put them on and leave the building."

To Lindy, she says, "I looked up some of the meanings, like bed, which means I will be faced with a change of residence soon. If it is fresh and clean, I will solve my most pressing problems. That will be true if I get away from my nasty boss. There is something wrong with him. He's so greedy, stupid, angry, and miserable all the time. Lainey said he must have the Napoleon syndrome. Bedroom means I will travel to distant lands and enjoy the company of pleasant friends. The room was pink: the walls, the fireplace, and the chiffon on the bed and the clothing the women were wearing. I was the only one naked and sitting on the bed. Even Bethy had pink chiffon on."

"What does pink mean?"

"The emotions; love; joy; illusion. I know you're thinking I am walking in an illusion all the time. I know I romanticise everything, driving people crazy, but I can't help it."

"Are you talking about your butterfly dream you had last year?"

"No, this dream was about the old lady directing me to the mansion. I am not sure what the kaleidoscope hallway floor means or the slope up to the steps. Kaleidoscope means swift changes with little betterment of improvement. I wonder how swift it is, because in my dream I had a hard time trying to walk up the slippery kaleidoscope ramp. The meaning for naked doesn't sound better. I will face scandals and unwise engagements. Sheesh! What is going to happen next?"

"Maybe it means Murray's situation. Were you the only one naked in the bedroom?"

"Yes. When I left that place, I put my shoes on."

"Why did you put on only your shoes? How come you didn't get dressed?"

"I don't know, Lindy, it's a dream. I assume I had clothes on when I put my shoes on."

"Oh," she says, giggling. "Sometimes your dreams are a bit fairy tale-like, different to my dreams and visions. I can usually decipher mine."

"You and your kids don't even have to be asleep to receive your messages. They are more like visions, init? Anyway, I am coming home for Jenny's birthday. Murray will probably be there."

After they hang up and she's alone, Sheyna cries,

thinking about their childhood and the love she has for her brother. To Desasǫ́dręh, she says, 'I cannot see life without my brother.'

Lainey pokes her head round her bedroom door. "Are you okay, sweetie?"

"Yes, I'm okay. It's my brother. I got more bad news. Me and Lindy were talking about the good times. I don't understand why he has to go through this. He is so sweet, funny, and tenderhearted. We were so close growing up, even after we were adults. He could always make me laugh. I could tell what he was thinking with any of his expressions. He didn't care who he teased, either. His poor wife was the brunt of most of his jokes. Sometimes I think she said something in a certain way because she knew he'd say something comical in response to it. It is a wonder she didn't kill him after his wedding speech. He said Jay has four beautiful daughters and he gets the ugly one. People laughed, but they knew he would not have married her if he didn't love her and adore the kids."

"How many kids does he have?"

"One boy and one girl when he got married. He didn't say it, but I knew he didn't want anyone else to raise them. Now he has four girls. You know, he could have been a great artist. The same teacher that talked me into the art course tried to talk him into taking that course. Instead, he took a two-year welding course in college. One time I asked him why he took welding when he was such a good artist. He said the course was only two years and he could start making money sooner. Welding was his career for thirty years. Now, that's what could be killing him," she cried.

Lainey held her friend. "I know sweetie, we don't know how things are supposed to work."

"Heck, everybody loves him. Why does this have to happen to him?"

Later in the week, Lindy calls with another update. "Murray has been tired and sore lately. He only weighs 180lbs because he can't eat. His cancer might be everywhere. They want to put a balloon down his throat so he can eat."

"Did sister visit him? I hope she's not mean to him. She doesn't do well with pity. You know her, she thinks the old way, that tough love helps. As long as Murray doesn't give up, he'll be all right. Deed quit drinking after he got hurt; maybe Murray will quit drinking and smoking."

"There's something else. He is having an operation after the bone test. They will give him radiation on the tumour in his oesophagus near his stomach."

Sheyna is crying by this time. "I can't think of Murray having cancer anywhere else but in that tiny tumour. I have an upset stomach. Sorry, but I have to go."

The next day at the printshop, on lunch break with the pressmen, she tells them about her brother's sickness and their adventures together.

"Being his sister has been a lot of fun. So many memories of my adventures with my brother flood back. He never cares who he teases. A trait he inherited from my dad. Our oldest brother fell at work, hitting his head on an I-beam. After he healed, one of his eyelids drooped down, almost covering his eye. Murray called him 'Eyelid'."

The guys laugh and shake their heads.

She continues, "He nicknamed my girlfriend 'Pickle Legs'. Her husband got jealous of their friendship because he thought she slept with him. She told him how she got the name when we were teenagers. We had been out partying and she missed her curfew. She was locked out of her parents' house, so she stayed the night at Dad's house. She accidentally touched my legs with her legs. I told her to get her pickle legs off me. Murray could hear us from his bedroom and has called her Pickle Legs ever since. Another time, at a family reunion, our great-nephew, who had been a preemie baby when he was born, weighing only 1.5lbs, the size of a pound of butter. At four years, he was skinny and still small for his age. There he was, a shirtless, skinny boy climbing all over his mother's truck, and Murray looks at him and says, 'Sheesh, boy, stay away from those mosquitoes. One sip and you'll be drained.'

Sheyna and the guys laugh. Tears come to her eyes.

Jeff, the pressman, says, "Your brother sounds like he'd be fun to party with. Did they nickname your nephew 'One Sip'?"

"No to the nickname. And oh yes, he sure was fun to party with. He was comical all through our childhood. I laugh every time I think of something he did or said growing up."

That night, Sheyna calls Murray to reminisce about the good old times. "Murray, remember when you said Paula's legs were so skinny, a wood tick wraps its legs around it to stick on?"

Murray laughs and says, "Yeah, I think we were at Lindy's place. Remember when we shared an apartment with your friends in Brantford?"

"We didn't share it, you were there all the time, especially on the weekends, because you were going with Cindy. You were so crazy. When she was having a bubble bath, you said she looked like a fly in milk. I loved that place. There were a lot of laughs with the girls that lived with me."

"Yeah, so many people woke up there the next day after the parties. Oh, yeah, you had a crib mattress on the floor to be one of the couches."

"Oh, yeah. Callen stayed over one night, init? He said you broke your heels getting out of that bed. That was a fun place, so many people coming and going all the time. At one time there were five girls living together. After one of the lacrosse game tournament parties, I woke up the next day and we collected eleven cases of empties to take back to the breweries."

Murray says, "I remember meeting June's boyfriend. I wonder if he could see that I was a gentleman and a scholar?"

"Oh, yeah, I told June what you said. She sure got a kick out of that line. She said gentleman and a scholar; you didn't even get up off the couch. You had on a welding t-shirt full of holes and a cooler of beer sitting on the floor next to the couch. In those days, we didn't have a care in the world, just work and party."

"I'd better get going. I'll see you next month."

After the laughs that night, Sheyna forgets how sick Murray is and goes to sleep.

For a regular update, Lindy calls to tell her about Murray's operation. "They are poking a hole into his stomach to feed him and give him his morphine."

"Why are they doing that? Oxygen makes cancer spread faster. Look what happened to Mum. If they hadn't opened her up a couple of times, she might have lived longer."

"Sheyna, does it matter now? He can't fight this cancer. It has spread to too many spots in his body. All they can do now is make him comfortable."

Dealing with her brother's cancer and putting up with her abusive boss is too much for Sheyna. She is working at the light table trying to make the printing plates match when her boss calls her to the meeting room. All she can think of is if this guy hollers at me one more time, I am walking out.

They get to the meeting room, and he starts saying something about the wrong font on a business card. A job that costs $75. She looks at the order sheet and points out that the incorrect information is his wife's fault.

"I already called to apologise to that customer when I noticed I used the wrong font. The customer said she did not complain about the font, she complained about the colour. We looked at the order. The pressman used the right colour according to the order sheet. Listen. I can put up with your criticism when I make a mistake, but I will not take your abuse when it is your wife's fault! That's it! I am out of here."

Sheyna gets up and walks down the stairs with her short, miserable boss still hollering at her to get back to the meeting room. At the bottom of the stairs, she turns quickly and says, "Steve, I quit! Are you still abusing me?"

He steps back quickly when she turns, almost as if he expects her to strike him. She feels like it, but the tone in her voice tells him she means what she says.

She grabs her things and walks out the door, leaving another toxic relationship.

Desah gives her mother an update on Sheyna's changes. "She is not dealing with her brother's illness very well. She left her job. She knows he is going to pass on and tries to be positive on the surface, refusing to believe the reports of decline. She is finally moving back to her Ǫgwehǫ́:weh territory."

Weighing only 119lbs, Sheyna returns to her home territory for good.

Awę́hę? says, "Good."

Desah says, "It is good she is with her family to deal with her brother's illness. She seems to go through the motions of living. She is at her neighbour's birthday party, then she carries on at another friend's party with her sister and brother and their friend.

"She gives them a ride home. She lets her brother out at his place, and Lindy, who drank as much sour springs as everyone else, gets out and starts walking to her house, which is half a mile down the road. It is a cold February night. Sheyna tries to get her back in the car, but she refuses. She drives her friend home to the village and rolls her car over near the corner gas pumps. Sheyna is hanging upside down in her car. Her friend, who is lying on the roof of the car, is screaming at the top of her lungs. Sheyna tells her to quit screaming. Pointing down at her friend, she tells her she better not sue her. Her friend quits screaming and looks up to see Sheyna dangling from her seatbelt above her, and starts laughing. They both laugh. Sheyna quits laughing when the police arrive. The emergency services cut her out of her seatbelt."

"Did everyone survive?"

"Yes, physically. Sheyna looks for some security, but she has no job now and none in sight. Her nephew and his family live in her house, so she moves in with them. She needs them to provide the netting for her security."

One night in her room, Sheyna's brother Douglas knocks on her bedroom door. Desasǫ́dręh recognises him to be the brother that she saw consoling her after their mother died.

His chin shaking, he says, "I talked to Murray today. He told me the doctors said he has less than six months to live."

Sheyna looks at him, angry. Douglas waits for her to understand what he is saying.

"No," she says. "That can't be true. If we believe them, he will die. No. He's not going to die! They can take that tumour out and he can get his strength back and fight this thing."

Douglas is crying now, and he tries to hold her. "I know. I know. I don't want him to die, either."

Sheyna's body gives up fighting him and she cries into his chest.

"Oh, no. He's so young. Why him? There are so many nasty people in this world. Why him?"

Douglas doesn't say anything until she quits crying. "He wanted me to tell you because he said he couldn't do it himself."

Through a clenched jaw, she asks, "You mean he believes it? So, the wicked witch got her wish."

Douglas softly says, "It's no one's fault. It must be his time."

After a few moments, Sheyna is calmed down. "Thanks, bro. Sorry I got so mad. I don't know what to do with this awful feeling I have had these past months since I heard. Whenever I try to picture life without him, a heavy sadness comes over me. I'm angry at everyone, and self-pity. What about his kids? He was always scared for their lives if he wasn't there. Sometimes I feel pity for him."

"Yeah. I wonder how his kids are going to handle it. We cried together when he told me. I love my baby bro. I told him his kids will be all right. I love them, too."

"I love them, too. Geez, what are they going through? Yeah, they are probably safe now because they're big enough to get away."

They smile while picturing the scenario.

After her brother leaves her room, she knows the protective energy between the brothers. She remembers when Douglas was a boxer and dad was taking him to his match. Murray was standing there waiting to be invited, and dad told him he could not go.

Douglas said, "I'm not going if Murray can't go."

Dad looked at Murray and said, "Get your coat, then."

Desasǫdręh says to her mother, "She seems to know I am available to her. She tracks all her dreams and tries to interpret my messages. I see that she is going to a Seer in her territory."

"Who or what is a Seer?"

"It is a person that connects to the spirits for her."

"She goes to them about a dream she had about three snakes. To relieve her worry, they give her medicine to protect herself and some to clean her womb. She has had her moon since she's been home, and it scares her. They tell her she is going through 'the change' and is on the spiritual side of her life. The woman said the medicine would help to clean out the womb and lessen her sweats, depression, and mood swings. Her moon will give one last push and quit. It will quit around the time her brother passes. I told the Seers to tell her she is going to work for a big woman who is like a queen of the castle. She is strict but very gentle and caring on the inside. She will be good for Sheyna, until her mental and emotional health returns."

Sheyna calls Lindy. "Listen to these dreams. See if you can tell what they mean. I am at a community event. Many of our people from work are there. A baby eagle, an eaglet, is sitting above the doorway of a building. I try to catch it, but it flies away. It seems I am taking care of it for someone, but the little fluffy thing flies away on me. As I am following it around the event, I come upon a feast table with big greasy roasts of meat in trays. The meat is so rich I can see the grease at the bottom of the pan. Paula is standing in line to eat. She smiles and points at the eaglet as it flies past us. I chase it."

"My daughter, Paula, was in it? Maybe you two will be working together."

"Maybe. This is the second one. I am in my bedroom in Connecticut again, wrapping three books together. Mary, Dawn, Lainey and I are bickering over the colour ribbon I should put on the gift. I end up wrapping them together with a pink ribbon. I thought it was weird to be dreaming about the gals from Niantic. I wonder what is going on there."

"Call them and find out. Like I said, your dreams are different to mine."

Desasódręh tells her mother, "Sheyna will return to her culture. She is in the Longhouse where she received her name. She stirs ashes and says, 'I am ready for another change.' She did the same ritual after her car accident, saying she never wants to drink again. She means she does not want to drink the sour springs again."

"I am glad for her. She is finding her way."

"Yes. She learned that two brave women who are gifts from the Creator start an energy business to help people. They will teach her it is positive to love herself, and to forgive her husband. She goes to them again to quit smoking. When she tells people how she quit, she says, 'I quit during my sister-in-law's ten days. To quit, spiritually, I stirred ashes at Longhouse and told the Creator I was ready for another change.

Mentally, I took counselling to learn why I was subconsciously killing myself. Physically, I was taught how to breathe whenever I craved a cigarette. I went out to the car and slapped the patch on my arm, and vowed I will never smoke again. I wish I had done something about my emotions and tears. I pity myself more than usual after I quit. It felt like I was grieving my best friend."

"She still carries something dark in her body and spirit. I know what it is, but she needs to know, or she will get sick. She's scared to be in a relationship. She feels she doesn't deserve to have someone. It is almost as if she is matched with Damon for life."

"Are they together?"

"No. He is matched with someone else and tries to talk her into taking him back, but she does not trust him. She caught him in lies. He told her he went to his room for the night and that he would see her tomorrow. To see if he had changed his habit of telling lies, she called his room, and there was no answer. He keeps breaking every promise he has been saying since he has been around."

"What do you think she needs?"

"Her trust and emotions are mixed up since childhood. There is a gloomy space that must be closed so that she can truly be happy again. As an adult, she knows where it starts, but she cannot rationalise why or if it happened. She feels sick inside. She has been counselled through various methods and has taken different types of training to help other people. There is one more way. It is a method of self-counselling that will help her get her power back and see her world differently."

"Can you direct her to her helpers if she cannot do it on her own?"

Sheyna writes in her journal: 'Another strange dream: I was showing Damon, his brother and a man who looks like a Chinese man, a lawyer, around a house. To get to the upper level, there was a ladder. Under the rungs there were cocoons. Seemed to me there was someone trapped in one of the cocoons. I went up a ladder or stairs to my room. Damon had arranged for a good-looking man to flirt with me. Damon was watching and was leering at me. He didn't care. Damon was very spiteful in the dream. I was afraid. He seemed like he loved looking at my icky fear, and he drove off in a taxi. There was some issue with the keys to the house; either I lost them, or Damon had them. His brother led me to believe Damon took them.' She writes without looking up the interpretations. 'My dream is telling me that Damon is planning on deceiving me and warning me to see he does not care about me. Almost as if he is setting me up to fail. As for the ladder and cocoons, that might mean me hiding away. Maybe I should get more counselling. The book says, to see a cocoon in your dream signifies a place of safety and solitude. It may also represent transformation or healing. Ladder is about hopes being realised only if I climb them. I must have climbed them because that's where the man was that Damon set up for me. The lawyer either means Damon will use one, or the book says, the image can point to the shadow, the stranger within. Rejected or unknown characteristics in yourself that you don't want to see. For keys, to lose a key portends disagreeable adventures and experiences. Yes, I have been romanticising the past too much. My niece and friends keep trying to push me out of my past and to get on with it. I will see what happens.'

Desasǫdręh sees Sheyna with a group of tormented women. They have come together through shared experiences. Someone hurt them when they were little and powerless. She hears and feels Sheyna's torment of anguish, anger, and frustration.

To do the work, she recalls the time that the little girl's life had changed. "He snuck into the house when everyone was outside drinking. He snuck into the room where I was making clothes for my dolls. He picked me up and carried me upstairs. I struggled to get away from him. He stank of alcohol and cigarettes. I don't know what he is trying to do. I cried when that old man touched me, and Dad hollered at me. My brother, Murray, held me and stuck up for me. When this man is on me, I feel like it is no use getting away from him if no one will listen to me. I scream, but no one can hear. I am too little, and he is too heavy. No one can hear me scream or cry. I can't breathe. Where is everyone? Why am I alone? I don't know what happened because he was gone when I woke up. I feel like puking. This man is a friend of my brothers. He stays at our house sometimes because his grampa gets mad when he is drinking and won't let him go home. This is not the first time that he has done this. I don't remember what happened at that time, either. I just know I am sick to my stomach every time I see him talk to my brothers. I hide."

As part of the training, the helper walks Sheyna through a process of accessing the gifts that she was born with from the spirit world. Recalling those times she was powerless, Sheyna is red, and her eyes are swollen. She feels like screaming; instead, she says, "I need power and strength to get that stinky, ugly man off of me."

"Okay. Count. What else do you need?"

"I am small, but I have my voice and words to stick up for myself and to protect myself."

After the training, she tells the woman, "When I think back to that time, I heard him come into the house and it was going to be the last time he will sneak to my room. I used my voice to stop him for the last time. I was big enough to grab the hair and pull it as hard as I could. I told him to leave me alone or I would tell my brothers. He left without hurting me and never bothered me again. I never let my little sister be alone whenever he was around. All these years this is the first time I remembered the moment it stopped. I did have a voice. I was so tormented by what had happened, I forgot it stopped when I hollered at him."

Desasǫ́dręh tells her mother, "Sheyna has taken the last steps of her recovery. She has returned to her core beliefs, learning about a good mind and the gifts of the higher power. Now she needs to learn how to love and trust again."

Sheyna returns to Longhouse, slowly learning generations of wisdom. She hears the songs in Gayogohó:nǫ꞊ and watches the women tell the stories through the graceful movements of their dance. She learns a few words in her language.

It is fall-time and visitors, Chiefs, Clan Mothers and Faithkeepers from all over Hodinǫhsyǫ́:ni꞊ territory have travelled to her territory for Gaihwí:yo (the good message), which runs all week. Her Longhouse is hosting, which means the women are cooking, and many, many dishes need to be washed. Sheyna is in the cookhouse washing dishes. It has been a gruelling morning, even if the atmosphere is lighthearted. Feeling a bit sweaty and tired, she leaves to go into the Longhouse. She enters the Longhouse and climbs onto the first empty spot on the top bench next to her friend. Danah has travelled from the United States and is staying for the week with her mother. As Sheyna looks around the sunny Longhouse, she notices it is full of people of all ages, some serious, nervous, happy, or tired.

Anticipation hangs in the air while the visitors from the northern States and across Ontario wait for the speakers to begin. There are small groups of men and women catching up on their news and laughing. Young siblings are seen entertaining or carrying around the young ones, so that their mums can hear the week-long stories of the Peacemaker.

As Sheyna continues to scan the room for familiar faces, she stops at a strikingly handsome man sitting across the room from her. His long dark hair frames his handsome dark features and light brown eyes. Immediately, an electric shock radiates across the room as their eyes lock for a minute. Puzzled by this weird sensation of electric energy between her and the stranger, she quickly looks down at her lap to twirl the important loose thread she found on the hem of her blouse. She had heard about 'the bolt' before, but she never believed it existed until now. 'What an odd feeling.' Did the mature stranger strike her, or did she strike him?

She leans towards her friend on her left and whispers, "Who is that guy?"

Danah smiles and looks suspiciously at Sheyna. "What guy?"

"I didn't get a good look, but the big guy dressed in a tan colour ribbon shirt. You know. The guy with broad shoulders, long hair, who is so very handsome with all that brown skin."

Danah pretends she does not know who she

means and looks around the room except at him. "Where? Who?"

Gritting her teeth, Sheyna continues, "Sitting with the other speakers across the room from us, Danah. He's looking at us."

Danah says, "Oh, that guy. I was wondering when you would notice Treyton. He is from Onondaga."

Danah laughs, nods, and gives Treyton her brightest smile. He acknowledges her with a smile that turns up more on his left than on the right side of his mouth. Sheyna melts away in her seat, afraid to look at him for fear he can read her mind and see her blushing foolishly. To herself she thinks, 'Oh, take it easy and calm down. You will get to see more of him in the dining hall or maybe at one of the Socials this week. Hmmm, I hope.'

Desasǫ́dręh looks on the scene, knowing that the ancestors are pleased that Sheyna is finally on the path she is meant to walk. She is no longer the sad little girl on the raft, carrying the world on her back. She is the rabbit that stands on its hind legs, watching and waiting for the little girl to become aware of herself before she disappears through a secret path among the plants that closes behind her.

CAYUGA (Gayogǫhó:nǫ²)
DICTIONARY*

Names and words	Meaning
Akenhnhà:ke (Mohawk) / Gęnhéhneh (Cayuga)	Summer (Desah's Mohawk friend)
Awę́hę² (awenheyh)	Flower (mother's name)
Desasǫ́dręh (daysasonh drenh)	You join two things (Desah)
Deyawę́dǫh (dyawendonh)	It shakes (oldest sister, has children)
Ekwawayéhǫ́h (aycwa wa yenhonh)	She is a good cook (Desah's grandmother's name)
Gaihwí:yo (Giweehyo)	The good message
Gajihsdǫdáha (gadjees donh daha)	Star or Venus (baby sister's name)
Gayogǫhó:nǫ² (gi yokonhno)	Cayuga
Gotsahniht (gutsah neeht)	She is a good worker (Desah's aunt, mother's sister)
Hadáhnyo² (hadanh nyo)	He's a fisherman (Hasegá:dǫ:'s friend)
Haihǫnyánih (hi honh yawnee)	He is a teacher (older brother's name)
Hao² (howh)	All right (agree to a request)

323

Names and words	Meaning
Hasegá:dǫ: (hay say gah donh)	He tells a story (youngest brother's name)
Hodinǫhsyǫ́:niˀ (hodinh seeownee)	People of the Longhouse
Jiˀnhǫwę́:se: (dze honh wenh say)	Hummingbird (Desah's friend)
Nyá:węh (nya wenh)	Thank you
ohwíhsdaˀ (o whis dah)	Money
Ǫgwehǫ́:weh (ongway honh way)	The people
Oná̇ˀno (o nat no)	Cold to touch (Hasegá:dǫ: name for Desah's friend, Akenhnhà:ke)
Onráhdagǫ: (on rah dahgonh)	In the leaves (Older sister's name, no children)
Sgę́:nǫˀ (skanonh)	Peace, wellness
Shé:kon (Saygo)	Peace, wellness

REFERENCES

Froman, F., Keye, A., Keye, L., and Dyck, C. (2014). *English-Cayuga/Cayuga-English Dictionary.* Toronto: University of Toronto.

Gonzalez-Wippler, M. (2000). *Dreams and what they mean to you.* St Paul, MN: Llewellyn Worldwide.